Leave this first page blank

Alicia's Sin

The Alicia Trilogy – Book Two

by
Nick Iuppa & John Pesqueira

This book is a work of fiction. Names, characters, places and incidents are either the product of the author's imagination or are used fictitiously. Any resemblance to actual persons, living or dead, or to actual events or locales is entirely coincidental.

ALICIA'S SIN

This eBook is licensed for your personal enjoyment only. This eBook may not be re-sold or given away to other people. If you're reading this eBook and did not purchase it, or it was not purchased for your use only, then you should return it and purchase your own copy. Thank you for respecting the hard work of the author.

Cover designed by Nick Iuppa
Cover Photo: Persians iStock # 524725678

Published by Dos Milagros Press
Visit the author website: http://www.nickiuppa.com

ISBN: 978-1-940745-07-7 (eBook)
ISBN: 978-0-9989806-4-5 (Paperback)

10 9 8 7 6 5 4 3 2 1

Praise for Alicia's Ghost

"Irresistible characters in a wicked tale of suspense"

— Suzanna B. Stinnett. Author of *Starship Interlude*

"Who could have guessed that ghost sex would be so hot?!?! This page-turner had so many twists and turns that my head was spinning."

— Janey Baker, Actress

"Ghostly crime drama at its best!"　　— Mark Wade, Screenwriter

"Funny & fun to read! Kept me wondering what would happen next."

— Eric Dueker, Filmmaker

"Incredibly imaginative!"　　　　　— Chuck Reedy, Author

"The storytelling is excellent. Can't wait for the sequel."

— Elke Hitto, Writer/Journalist

"I love the characters, and Alicia... these guys have the Latina in her down to a science."

— Becky Escamilla, Constant Reader

"So intriguing... demands attention."

— Rick Emond, Graphic Novelist

"These guys certainly spin a great tale. Hope they keep cranking out stories for readers to enjoy."

— Dave Couzins. Author of *Domers*

"If you think you'd like a world where ghosts whip up dim sum and enjoy making love with the living, then this book is for you."

— Terry Borst, Screenwriter

Dedication

For our wives, Ginny and Marika, who showed such great patience, understanding, and faith during the many days it took to make this book a reality.

Acknowledgments

We'd like to thank the friends who offered valuable advice during the creation of this book, especially: Norma Cervantes-Broussard, Lauren Ayer, Bram Druckman, Kimberly Behl, Bobbi Milke, and Bill Habeeb. We appreciate the fast, professional, and very competent services we received from our graphic designer Laurie Douglas. And, again, we want to express special appreciation to Janet Grady, for her honest, dependable, and courageous story advice and editorial work.

Sometimes magic is just plain magic.

— The ghost of Dr. Sigmund Freud

The Living and the Dead

THE LIVING

<u>Mexico</u>

Dr. Carlos (Mancowski) Mann – Leland University logic professor

Fernando de Cervantes (Señor Popcorn) – Mexican drug lord

Raquel Sandoval – Famous Latina model

Enrique Córdoba – Director of Anti-Narcotics Operations for the Mexican Government

Yolanda Córdoba – His wife

Eva Córdoba – His daughter

Lilia Garcia – Eva's best friend

Miguel Carillo – Señor Popcorn's right-hand man

Victor Estephan – Señor Popcorn's lieutenant

Doña Cuca – A curandera

La Bruja – A witch of the Yucatan

Maclovio Renta – A rival drug lord

Marty Marinara – An FBI agent

<u>Los Altos, California</u>

Dr. Oliver Q. Applebee – Newly appointed Dean of the Leland Philosophy Department

Dr. Charlotte Burke – Professor of Philosophy

Lupe Bravo – Wife of deceased Mexican poet

Pedro Bravo, Leland University benefactor

Dr. Andrew August – Head of Research for August Technologies, the living brother of Carlyle August the ghost

Thom Johnson – Carlos's teaching assistant

Assad Madani – Part owner of the Torquemada Record Store, Carlos's friend

Veronica Joy Madani – Assad's wife and the adopted sister of Tiger and Amy Joy

Chinatown

Amy Joy – One of Carlos's Logic students

Helen (Tiger) Joy – A dominatrix, Amy's adopted sister

Abigail Joy – Leland Medical Center nurse, also Amy's adopted sister

Albert and the Joy Boys – Enforcers for the Clan

Vienna Austria

Miriah Septova – Owner of Madam Miriah's Gypsy Carnival

THE DEAD

Mexico

Alicia Maria Mejias Mancowski Mann – Ghost wife of Dr. Carlos Mann

Sylvia Morales – Professional model and friend of Alicia

Chula Contrerras – Another model and friend of Alicia

Norma de Cervantes – Señor Popcorn's deceased wife

Teresita de Cervantes – Señor Popcorn's deceased daughter

Padre Hidalgo – A priest and revolutionary

Austria

Rudolph Hapsburg (Rudy) – Crown Prince of Austria, heir to the throne

Clarissa and Sebastian – Rudy's drinking buddies

Maximilian the First – Emperor of Mexico, a Hapsburg and Rudy's uncle

Elizabeth Hapsburg (Sissi) – Rudy's mother; Empress of Austria

Sigmund Freud – The Father of Psychoanalysis

Anna Maria Pessler – Dr. Freud's former patient and aid

Johann Strauss – The Waltz King

Wolfgang Amadeus Mozart, Fredrick Chopin, Franz Liszt – Classical Composers

Chinatown

Mr. Lum – Founder of the Joy Lum slave trade

Mother Joy – Slave trader

Mr. Fu – Ancient worker from the days of the railroad

Los Altos, California

Carlyle August – A wealthy entrepreneur and proprietor of the Purgatory Bookstore

Mr. Friedman – An elderly gentleman and safecracker

Jenny Beck – A teen Goth skateboarder

Royce Clayton – A gay biker

Pedro Bravo – A famous Mexican poet

Alicia's Sin

The Alicia Trilogy – Book Two

Prologue

The room is midnight dark. Cold. Smelling of incense and agony.

Amy Joy sits cross-legged in the corner, working her iPad.

Far across the floor, her sister Helen, also known as Tiger, slides into a high-backed mahogany chair engraved with dozens of wicked dragons. The mythical creatures snake over the back of the chair, down its legs, across the seat, and then extend out to form two heavy arms.

Tiger toys with the gaping mouths and dragon teeth at the ends of each arm. She turns sideways and slides her hands up over the sensuous outlines of the dragons on the chair back. She can almost feel their ancient powers flowing into her.

Tiger smiles, but it's a cruel smile. The girl is twenty-two at most, dressed in black martial arts gear. Her feet, usually pumped up on five-inch high heels, are bare, her toenails painted celadon green.

Amy watches her sister from the shadowy corner. Then a harsh rumble startles her. It sounds like the roar of a huge Harley motorcycle just outside the door, but it's not.

Sid Vicious, a full size Bengal tiger, pads into the room, across the well-oiled mahogany floor, and up to the girl on the throne.

Tiger Joy smiles.

"Are we hungry today, Sid?" she coos. The animal purrs and seems to nod.

"Well, sorry about that," Tiger says with a sneer as she gets to her feet, "you'll just have to wait."

Tiger's long black hair extends over her shoulder almost to her waist. She wrangles it behind her with both hands, and then swings one leg up and over the back of the big cat. She lowers her full weight onto Sid Vicious and slowly, languidly, begins riding him around the room. The beast seems to be moving in slow motion. His mistress has her eyes closed. Her arms have fallen to her sides. Her smile is erotic, as though she is drawing enormous energy from the big cat.

Amy watches all this, knowing that it's some kind of evil sacrament that she has no right to witness. Her eyes search desperately for a means of escape. But there is none. The realization scares her so much that she drops her iPad.

Sid Vicious jerks his head toward Amy. Tiger's eyes pop open. Her lips pull into a hard smile; she dismounts.

"Enjoying the show?" Tiger asks as she glides up to her sister. The 500-pound cat follows. Amy shakes her head nervously. "I wasn't watching."

"Your sister's riding a tiger, and you're not watching?"

"No. Honest."

"I'm disappointed."

Tiger cocks her hip. "I thought you'd already finished the notes from this morning's meetings."

"Just now," Amy answers.

Suddenly, Sid Vicious launches a full-fledged roar that shakes the whole building. "Aw, pet," Tiger pouts. "You really are hungry, aren't you?"

Sid snarls.

Tiger grabs Amy by the wrist, drags her directly in front of the huge animal, and pushes her arm right up to the tiger's mouth.

"Have a little taste, Sid." Tiger says, with a crazy gleam in her eyes.

Amy's too terrified to try and wrestle her arm away, afraid that any sudden movement will encourage the hungry cat.

Sid studies the young woman being offered to him. Amy holds her breath. Finally, Sid shakes his head and steps away.

Amy almost faints with relief.

"Gotta go," she manages to whisper. "Logic 101 at Leland."

"Still trying to pass?"

"I have to."

"No, you don't. You're out of the program, Amy. No one's going to marry you. In fact, I plan to sell you off to the first guy willing to pay your debts."

"Don't," Amy says. "I can handle them."

"Yeah, right."

"I can pay them back. Really. But right now I have to get to class."

"Who's your prof, that prick Carlos Mann?"

"He's not a ... *you know.*"

"Sure he is, sis. Wake up and smell the oolong."

Tiger slouches. Suddenly she's bored with the whole conversation. "Okay. Just get the hell outta here."

Tiger walks back to Sid Vicious and strokes the monster's side. As the big cat begins to purr, she turns back to Amy.

"But give Carlos a message for me, will you?"

Amy carefully retrieves her iPad and moves toward the door. "What message?"

"Tell him I hold him responsible for the deaths of our Mother and Father. And I plan to make him pay for them ... *with his life.*"

"I can't tell him that."

"My pet's still hungry, Amy."

"I'll tell him."

Amy hurries from the room.

"That was fun, wasn't it?" Tiger purrs to her pet. Then she climbs back onto the huge cat, closes her eyes, and begins restoring her animal energy with another slow, sensuous ride around the dark, deadly room.

4

#

Carlos Mann here.

It's later that same day, just before class. Amy enters my office totally freaked out. She tells me everything that just happened.

"You're in terrible danger, Dr. Mann," she says. "Tiger won't stop until she's killed you. I don't even think your ghost-friends can help."

"Not even the ghost of Attila the Hun?"

"You know him?"

"No," I laugh. "But I always thought he was the one guy who could handle your sister."

That at least gets a smile from Amy. It also stops me from running into the storage area and compulsively rearranging the all the psychology department supplies just to escape from this conversation.

"Go wash those tears out of your eyes before we start class," I say.

Amy gives me another frightened smile, gets to her feet, and heads out the door.

After she leaves I shake my head and wonder how long it will be before Tiger starts putting her murderous plans into motion.

Like everything else Tiger does ... the only thing for certain is that—sooner or later—she *will*.

I
Alicia

Chapter 1

A ray of sunlight glances off an otherwise well-hidden rifle, but it's enough to tip off Señor Popcorn. He's been sitting in his black Mercedes looking out at the Mexican bazaar where his beautiful wife and daughter are visiting shops, chatting happily like two little birds, unaware that they are about to become murder victims.

It's 1995. Señor Popcorn is 45 years old, madly in love with his girls as he calls them. His wife Norma is 40; his daughter Teresita is 20. They're all the best of friends at this point in their lives.

And now the popcorn man spots other rifles moving through the crowd, carried by thugs he knows are part of the Machado Cartel. They are his rivals, his enemies, killers who practice the cruelest acts of violence to defend their turf. And they consider Señor Popcorn an invader.

"Get moving!" the popcorn man shouts as he begins pounding his driver's shoulder frantically. The Mercedes lurches into the bazaar, shattering booths, making women and children dive out of the way as it rushes toward the little store where Norma and Teresita are shopping.

It's already too late.

Gunmen have circled the place. They launch a lightning-storm of bullets that rip apart the shop and everyone in it. They blast a firebomb through the doorway, and it sets off an inferno.

Señor Popcorn drives right into the flames and jumps from the car into the mess of bloody victims. He grabs his wife and daughter, pulls them into his limo, and tells his driver to plow right through the back wall of the shop as flames consume the salespeople, customers, the colorful clothing, and everything else.

#

The popcorn man sobs as he tells this story to Carlitos and me. We are on our way to Cancun, flying in his private jet. He is taking us on a trip during summer vacation from Leland University. He tells us this is a good time because he wants a special favor from us. We ask him what it is, and we get this story of death and tragedy.

There is a bedroom on the plane, and Señor Popcorn has made it into a welcoming romantic suite, complete with champagne, bouquets of orchids, lilies, plates of candies and fruits. The bathroom offers a bubbly Jacuzzi and lots of soaps and rinses. As a ghost, I must take on a physical form to enjoy all this, but I do not mind. It's another way to make love to my Carlitos.

This is well before we hear the story. That comes later in the flight, after much lovemaking and ghost champagne. Afterwards, we join Señor Popcorn in the main cabin and ask him about the favor he wants.

Even then the popcorn man is excited. His hands shake as he tells us that he is in love again, something he thought could never happen.

"But there are complications," he says as he gives a great sigh.

"I thought you were celibate," Carlitos says.

The old man laughs, and then he begins to cry … right there in front of us. I go to him at once, pull him to his feet, and hug him to me.

"What brings on such sadness?" I ask.

9

Señor Popcorn pulls an orange silk handkerchief from his pocket. He wipes his eyes, and tries to smile. He fails badly.

"I'd better tell you the *whole* story," he says. "If you don't understand the first part, then you'll never understand the rest."

Carlitos and I nod. We all sit down in comfortable airplane seats that face each other. Señor Popcorn is by the window facing backwards. I am next to him, still petting his shoulder to make him feel better. Carlitos faces us.

"I was married, you know, Niña," he tells me. And so he tells us his story that ends so tragically. Here is more of what he says ... in his own words.

#

Like all Mexican men in love, I feel that I am married to the most beautiful woman in the world. But I have some proof. She is Miss Maravillosa ... a spectacular beauty pageant that features young Latinas of amazing grace and elegance.

Norma Consuela Ramirez is her name, and she travels all over Latin America, attending functions and doing other jobs that come with her title. I follow her everywhere, admiring her, and finally meeting her, dating her, getting to know her very well, becoming her friend, and later someone who loves her ... and whom she loves in return.

"Take me away from all this," Norma says to me the night she completes her year of public appearances. So, I marry her immediately, and even though I am *one mean hombre* in my business, with her I am a *little boy* whose eyes are wide with wonder.

We are very young. She is nineteen; I am only twenty-four, and we have a little niña of our own so quickly that it feels like an instant miracle.

It is. Waking up next to this goddess every morning is a miracle. Holding my little daughter in my arms is a miracle. And the miracles go on for twenty more years.

It's such fun having my girls with me all the time. They share a secret smile that I love. It's like there is a hidden, very playful idea in the back of their minds that only they understand ... that they will share with me if I am lucky. And believe me, in those days, I am a very lucky man.

My Norma is a strict mother, but as Teresita grows, my daughter quickly learns what is expected of her, and she is always obedient.

When Teresita begins bringing young men home to meet me, I make sure that they know that they'd better be good, or they won't be around very long. Only brave boys go out with my daughter ... brave, smart boys who are too intelligent to misbehave.

There's one young man named Juan. I remember him so well: small but strong, with big curious eyes, which grow even bigger as I escort him into my study and question him about his intentions.

"Where do you plan to take Teresita this evening?"

"To the high school dance, Señor."

"And afterwards?"

"For a stroll down by the river and then to my parents' house for a small party."

"No strolls by the river," I say as I pound my fist on my desk.

"No, Señor."

"No kissing down by the bridge where her mother and I used to kiss."

"Of course not, Señor."

I reach into my desk drawer and take out a pair of heavy scissors that my veterinarians use to castrate bulls on my ranch. I brought them to my office for just such an occasion, and now I lay them on top of my desk. Juan's eyes grow wider still.

"When you take Teresita to your house after the dance, there will be no petting, understand?"

"Understood, Señor."

"You will keep your hands to yourself."

"Sí, Señor."

"No copping of feels."

"NO!"

"Because if you get fresh with Teresita, even if she begs you to, I will use *these*!"

"And then I pick up the bull scissors and snap them three times right in Juan's face, and then I roar with laughter as he scrambles from the room."

My wife and daughter fill my home with music. They're always babbling, always giggling, always singing, and always having those secret smiles … hidden mysteries that they share. When I ask either one of them what it is they are smiling about, they always respond with the same answer, "Wouldn't you like to know, Papá?" Even Norma calls me Papá.

Yes, I would.

I strengthen my business, become stricter with my friends and enemies, so that I can make even more money and provide my girls with everything they want: the finest clothing, the best cars, trips to Europe and around the world. If any other drug lord tries to take from me, I take back from him in most unforgiving ways.

Norma and Teresita do not know anything of this, of course. They do not know my business.

They think I am a rich exporter, which I am. They simply don't know my products.

Doing the devil's work, however, demands the devil's payment, I believe And, in the end, the devil makes me pay.

#

Carlitos and I listen intently to this romance from Señor Popcorn who now gives us a great sigh as tears form in his eyes.

"Victoria!" he calls, "tequila!" and one of the flight attendants brings him two bottles and four shot glasses. The popcorn man passes the glasses around, pours a shot for himself and Carlitos from the regular tequila, and then a shot for me from ghost tequila. Then he pours another shot for Victoria and he raises his glass.

"To love," he calls, and he downs the shot before the rest of us can do the same. He has a second shot before we even lower our glasses.

"My enemies kill them both," he says. "And they kill my soul in the process."

And at this point he tells the story that you heard earlier, about the death of his wife and daughter.

"My wife and daughter are massacred," he says. "Their sweet faces are turned to unrecognizable masks of blood. We fight off the flames so we can save their bodies and bring them back to our home ... never to be a happy home again, I think. And for many years I believe this to be so.

"But God forgives," he says. "God is good. God gives us chances, eh?"

"Is that why you had so many young models living with you?" Carlitos asks the old man, who now swallows his fifth shot of tequila.

He nods. "Just to have that happy chirping in my home," he says. "Just to have the feeling I had when my wife and daughter were with me.

"Alicia, you beautiful girls were never quite as beautiful as my Norma and Teresita. I'm sorry to tell you this, but at least you came close."

At this point I am sobbing along with him, and I nod over and over again.

"God damn any man who tries to take advantage of the girls I bring to my home," he shouts. "These beautiful young women are there to give it the sweetness it knew when my wife and daughter were alive."

Señor Popcorn throws his fist into the air as though he's reaching for someone to strangle. "I *use* my bull sheers on some of my workers. I kill a few. You are my girls, Alicia; I am your protector, and I swear to be a better protector than I was to Norma and Teresita."

Carlitos and I are shaken by Señor Popcorn's words. He sees this and lets out an embarrassed laugh.

"Relax, amigos," he says. "Remember God is good, God is kind, and that is why I need this favor."

"God has given you another love?" I ask.

Señor Popcorn grins so brightly that happiness is suddenly restored to the airplane, even though our stewardess at least is now quite drunk.

"But God also is a tricky bastard," he adds. "Apparently, Jesus likes a good joke as well as any man."

"Hows shooooo?" Victoria slurs.

"Because He makes me fall in love with a woman who looks very much like my Norma with all the playfulness of Teresita. She is a woman who shows the same secret smile that I so adored in them."

"That's wonderful," I say.

"Yes," he sighs, "but her name is Eva Córdoba."

Carlitos almost jumps from his seat. "She isn't related to Enrique Córdoba ... the Director of Anti-Narcotics Operations for the Mexican Government?"

Señor Popcorn blushes. "She's his daughter."

There's silence in the cabin ... except for the engines (and the snoring of flight attendant Victoria who has fallen into a deep slumber).

The popcorn man sits there shaking his head. "Maybe it isn't God, Niña," he says to me. "Maybe it's the devil's doing after all. Maybe he is seeking revenge. But I don't think so. Eva is too wonderful."

I suddenly think of a question. "Why are not your wife and daughter ghosts like me?"

"Not everyone who dies becomes a ghost, Alicia," Señor Popcorn says. "Some people are good enough to go straight to heaven."

Carlitos nods. The flight attendant makes whistling sounds as she breathes. They're almost musical.

"How did you meet Eva Córdoba?" I ask. And once again the popcorn man resumes his story.

#

I first see Eva Córdoba in church with her family. Even though she is kneeling and praying, even though she is older, perhaps as old as maybe twenty-five, there is something playful about her.

Sitting in that pew she has that same secret smile that my wife and daughter had. What mystery is she keeping? I wanted to know. Her eyes are dark and beautiful as were those of my wife and daughter, and every now and then I think I catch Eva glancing at me, and once, as the mass is ending, she *smiles* at me. I'm sure of it. ¡Dios mío! It is like blinding sunlight exploding through the clouds. That's what it is for me, the sunlight of the chance to find happiness again.

Trying to figure out how to date her is very difficult; believe me. After thinking about it for almost a week I decide to have one of my best men, Hector Flores, get to know *her* best friend … a sweet young woman named Lilia Garcia. When he gains Lilia's trust, and I might as well admit, her affection and her favors, he arranges for a double date.

I am not confident enough to ask Eva on the date myself. After all, I am over sixty and she is so much younger. Plus, I believe she spent her childhood in convent schools, so her knowledge of the world must be quite limited.

Instead, I set her up with Victor Estephan, one of my handsomest lieutenants. At the time I hope that she will fall in love with Victor, they will marry, and I can at least have her near me. That has to be enough, I think. It's a recipe for sadness, I know. But don't worry, my friends.

Eva turns out to be a very surprising young woman.

#

"We should go salsa dancing at the Wicked Rabbit Cantina," Victor says to me. He's such a proud and macho guy.

But the Wicked Rabbit is a wild place. Lots of lowlifes hang out there. I don't want to take Eva anywhere near a place like that. But Victor argues with me.

"You could buy out the Cantina for the evening, boss. Fill it up with *our* people: models who live in your mansion, my fellow hombres. You can guarantee that everyone there will give you their best behavior."

The Cantina may be a good idea, I think. But then God grants me an even better one: The Cancun Opera Festival is performing *La Bohème*. It is perhaps the most tragic love story of all time, perfectly designed to make women weep.

I've seen women melt during the final scene of that opera; they're so shaken that all they want to do is fall into the arms of their lovers and be loved.

"Not a pinchi opera, boss," Hector says. "I hate those things, and besides, they're always in Italian."

"But you will be in the company of two beautiful Latinas," I say to him and to Victor. "What difference does it make where you are or what you have to sit though. Just looking at these women will make you excited."

16

"Yeah, excited to get into their pants," Victor whispers to Hector. I hear him, and I walk right up to him and slap him across the face. Victor has the strength to kill me, but he does not. He wants to keep his job and maybe his life.

"Sorry, boss," he says as he holds his aching jaw. "You're el jefe."

I just growl at him and wonder if my plan is ever going to work. But I have to try. So, Hector arranges the date for Sunday afternoon: a matinee at the opera.

We drive to the Córdoba Estate in my new white Mercedes limo. We are dressed in brand new Italian suits, which I have purchased just for this occasion.

We pull into the great circular driveway of the Córdoba mansion. If this man is a government worker, he has some other sources of income, I know, like lands and riches from his Spanish ancestors.

We hike from the driveway to the front door, up a flight of stairs and across the wide porch.

But before we can even knock, an English butler greets us.

"Gentlemen, right this way," he says, and he shows us into the entryway of the great hacienda.

Señora Yolanda Córdoba, Eva's mother, rushes up to greet us. The woman is very attractive, a more mature version of Eva, but she is still very slim and athletic looking ... tall, dressed in tan slacks and a pink polo shirt. She wears just a bit of make up on those dark eyes and full lips.

Mmmmm.

My men are excited by this beauty, but I step forward immediately. "Señora Córdoba," I say. "It is an honor to meet such a youthful and angelic woman who exemplifies the excellent lineage of her family and her daughter. I am Fernando de Cervantes, your daughter's chaperone for the evening."

Señora Córdoba likes all these flowery words. She flashes those dark eyes proudly at me, and she smiles.

"An honor, Señor. You must be a fan of the opera … as am I." She lowers her eyes and looks up at me through long lashes. She's flirting with me.

"You are all such handsome men!" she sighs.

"But where's Papá?" I ask.

"Enrique is in Guadalajara on business."

I shuffle my feet nervously. Yolanda Córdoba has designs on me.

And then stupid Hector speaks up: "Señora, perhaps you would consider coming with us …" he begins, and I give him a swift kick right in the back of his ankle (in a way that the Señora cannot see, of course). He hides a cry of pain while I finish his sentence.

"… would you consider coming with us when we go to Mozart's *Don Giovanni,* which is being performed *next* month?"

I want no one limiting my ability to drink in the beauty of Eva Córdoba this night, not even her magnificent mother, who now smiles and continues to give me all her attention.

"My husband will be out of town next month as well," she grins. "So, perhaps, Señor de Cervantes, I could be *your* date, and we could all go together. The truth is, I love the opera, and my husband hates it."

"It's a date then," I manage to say nervously. I don't want any part of this lovely woman who is married to my enemy. But I've been backed into a corner. "It's a date," I continue, "that is, if …" I'm frantically searching for excuses, when suddenly I am saved, because, at that very moment, Eva and Lilia come down the great staircase at the back of the hall.

I'm overwhelmed, as are all the others: Victor, Hector, Señora Córdoba, and even the English butler.

Eva's hair is auburn, falling over her shoulders like a fiery waterfall. It matches her olive skin perfectly. Her eyes are deep brown, her lips are full, and she wears as little make-up as her mother. Her dress is very formal, gorgeous, and expensive.

Eva smiles at Victor who cocks an eyebrow and gives her his handsomest look. She is amused, and then she bites her lip. My heart sinks. Teresita used to do that whenever she really wanted something. Eva wants Victor. Dios mio.

Eva turns to me, and, though her smile is polite, there is nothing in her eyes but respect.

Where is that welcoming smile I saw in church? I wonder. And now, as she moves up to Victor, electricity crackles between them.

I am instantly jealous; my grand plan a disaster. There is no way on this earth that I will let Victor have this woman as a bride just so that I can be near her. Eva has to be *mine*. Completely!

Lilia now descends the staircase and approaches Hector. She is lovely too, but I cannot say anything more about her. Eva outshines her in every way.

"Señor de Cervantes, please keep me in your plans for *Don Giovanni*," Yolanda says to me as we leave. "I would love to go on a triple-date with you."

I see Eva rolling her eyes. She feels about this triple-date as I do. Still, I do my best to smile and nod.

"I look forward to it," I say. Yolanda likes me very much. I wonder for a moment how her husband would feel about that.

"You might also consider visiting us some evening," she adds. "I'm sure you and Enrique would have a lot to talk about."

If she only knew. I have been hiding from her husband for nearly fifteen years. The last thing I want is to have to talk to him about *anything*.

#

Soon, we are in my private box at the Cancun Opera Festival. It's the last act of *La Bohème*.

19

The music soars. Hector stares at the stage in confusion. "What the hell's going on?" he whispers back to me. "Who can understand all this Italian bullshit?"

Eva too seems confused. But it is the confusion of a romantic. She does not want to face the fact that Mimi (the heroine) is dying. Absolute despair is sung in the most beautiful music ever heard.

Suddenly, the music tells us that Mimi is dead. Eva bursts into tears, turns to Victor, and he's there for her. He gathers her into his arms as she sobs.

The heartbreaking music builds. Eva peeks at me out of the corner of her eye. She sees the tears streaming down my face. She smiles sadly at me and then ... she bites her lip, and winks.

My God! I can't believe it. With that little bite, that wink, my hope returns.

The music ends. There is silence, then applause. The curtain calls come. The audience rises to its feet cheering more loudly. Eva and Victor stand beside each other clapping frantically. She does not look at me again. But I am left to wonder what she meant by that look.

As the crowd begins to leave, I suggest we go to my favorite restaurant for dessert and coffee. Victor looks at Eva, and Hector looks at Lilia. There's nervous silence.

"There's a place I've always wanted to go," Eva says. "It's called the Wicked Rabbit Cantina. Maybe we can go there this evening."

Victor laughs out loud. My heart sinks further. Can there be such distance between the desires of a woman of twenty-five and a slightly older man?

"Shall we, Señor de Cervantes?" Victor teases. Eva turns to me with a pleading look. She bites her lip. I shrug. Why not? At least I have taken Victor's advice. I bought out the place for the night and invited my handsomest young men and women to party there.

"'Lets go," I say.

#

The Wicked Rabbit Cantina is full of partying. A band plays salsa music and margaritas flow. The models who live in my hacienda have come in a group and I am allowing them, just this once, to be with my men. I know that there will be a lot of ugly sorting-out to do in the morning, but I don't care. Tonight, I am with Eva and I will do everything to make her happy.

There is cheering as we enter the doors. Raquel Sandoval, one of the hottest models in Mexico, immediately asks me to dance. I can't say no, even though I know that this lets Victor, Hector, and the girls find a table and start their own little party without me. I move onto the dance floor.

The music is sexy, Raquel knows all the moves, and soon there is a group cheering us on. I do not want to make a fool of myself, so I let her get all the attention. She dances so well, and I'm exhausted as the song ends.

"Victor is with the girl you love, isn't she?" Raquel asks as she leads me back to the table where Eva and the others are sitting.

"Who told you?" "Word gets around."

I blush. "Eva cannot know."

"Of course not." She holds her fingers to her lips. "Señor, we all love you. We only want the best for you." And then she stops in her tracks, getting a good close-up look at Eva for the first time.

"Wow! Go, Señor Popcorn!" she cheers. "Let me help you make this work," and she rushes up to Victor and shouts, "Come on, handsome! Let's salsa!" She jerks Victor to his feet, pulls Eva up beside her and escorts us back out onto the dance floor. Hector and Lilia follow.

The music begins. Raquel is dancing wildly with Victor, and I much more slowly with Eva.

Eva is smiling politely, not sure of what to say. She bites her lip again. God!

Then Raquel taps her on the shoulder. They talk briefly and then move away from us. Raquel has challenged Eva to show us her sexiest moves, and my sweetheart does just that.

The girl focuses all her attention on me. She shows her pretty ankles by lifting up the hem of her skirt, and then she stomps out a harsh Latin rhythm.

Again the circle forms. Raquel and Eva are challenging each other to more and more wicked steps. Victor and I are on the outside. The girls are shaking and shimmying and grinding and other moves I can only marvel at. I'm enjoying it, and at least keeping time to the music. That's when I look at Victor's face ... and Eva's. Their eyes are locked on each other.

Now they move back together. Their dancing gets more and more intense, like they are having sex on the dance floor. I'm feeling dizzy. I don't belong here. Raquel sees my sadness, cuts in on Eva, and begins dancing with Victor. Eva watches for a moment, then becomes frustrated, gives up, and slowly makes her way back to our table. I follow.

We slide in together. "Victor's so handsome," she sighs.

"I know."

"Oh, but you are too, Señor ..." she smiles and bites her lip again. What the hell's going on?

Somehow drinks have magically appeared on our table; no doubt my workers are taking care of me. I reach for a cervesas. As I do, Eva sees the bracelet that I wear on my wrist and points to it. It's a simple leather band that Mexican men and women often wear.

"What's that?" she asks.

I pull it off and hand it to her. She bites her lip again and her eyes grow wide. "So cool," she says.

"You like it."

"Very, very much."

Her lips form a secret smile just like Norma and Teresita used to. "What's that smile about, Eva," I ask.

"Wouldn't you like to know?" She smirks as she slips the leather band onto her wrist, twists her arm this way and that admiring it.

"Keep it then, as a gift."

Eva bites her lip. "Oh, no, Señor. I could never do that." "Please."

She hands the band back to me nervously. "Thank you, no." But now she is studying me intently. That secret smile re-emerges. She bites her lip again.

I am so damn confused.

That night, as I drive the girls home, Victor and Eva are kissing in the back seat of my car. Tongues are involved and it's clear that my innocent Eva knows her way around a pair of lips.

I'm so caught up in the lovemaking back there, that I readjust the rear view mirror and stop watching the road. I only glance back to it at the very last minute when I hear a bell clanging.

A huge bull is waddling down the center of the highway!

I have to slam on the brakes to avoid hitting him. The car lurches so hard that the couples jerk forward and separate.

"A warning from God, muchachos," I scold as the four of them straighten themselves and relieve the strangling grip of their seatbelts.

We drive on silently for another mile or so, and I finally glance back in the rear view mirror again. Eva is staring at me. Her eyes are locked on mine. And then that secret smile forms on her lips.

It's a very quiet ride back to my estate after the young ladies are delivered. Victor and Hector are excited but concerned about my feelings. I see them glancing at me nervously through the rear view mirror. Finally I speak up.

"Victor!"

"Yeah, boss?"

"I have a special assignment for you and Raquel."

"Together?"

"If you are up for it."

"I've always wanted to work with Raquel."

"Good. But you know the rules."

Victor sighs. "Yeah, boss. I know them."

"And you still want the assignment?"

"Where?"

"Paris, for three months."

"Three months in Paris with Raquel?"

"Damn, you've got good ears, Victor."

He laughs. "But what's the assignment?"

"Find the perfect villa for a honeymoon ... somewhere in France ... or maybe in Italy. I guess you'll have to go to Italy to check it out too. Better make it four months."

"With Raquel?"

"That's right."

"Wow! And who's the lucky couple?"

I smile at Victor and then at Hector. "Who do you think?" I ask.

"Me and Eva?" Victor asks.

I slam on the breaks and almost skid the car off the road. "Of course not, you imbécil."

"*You* and Eva?" he asks.

"Not sure you can pull it off, Señor," Hector says. I shake my head and sigh.

"I'm not sure I can pull it off either."

Chapter 2

"Do you know what happens next, Alicia?" Señor Popcorn asks me as we fly on toward Cancun.

I shrug. "You go on a date with Señora Yolanda, I guess."

The popcorn man shakes his head. "Not even that," he says. "There's a call from Amy Joy in San Francisco Chinatown saying that your husband is about to be assassinated by her sister, Tiger. So I put the whole Eva project on hold and come to your rescue."

"I thought we were simply taking us on a little vacation." I say.

"So did I," Carlitos adds quickly.

"I didn't know that a Joy girl was involved. Where is she?" I look at Carlitos. "Did you know about this?"

He squirms in his seat nervously.

"Relax, Niña," Señor Popcorn says. "Your rival is still in San Francisco. She is bound to her evil sister now, in ways that I cannot understand and she will not explain."

I turn to Carlitos to see if he is concerned about this little tramp. But he merely sighs and shakes his head. Then he surprises me.

"What about Victor and Raquel?" he asks.

"I send them abroad," Señor Popcorn answers. "I don't want that pendejo messing around with my girl. I also have Hector deliver two dozen yellow roses to Yolanda along with a nicely worded note telling her that we will be calling on her and her daughter soon … after a short business trip.

"And so, here we are," Señor Popcorn continues, "I've rescued you even though you didn't feel that you needed rescuing. And now I'm just wondering, Alicia, if you … as a ghost … you know … have any magic you can use to make Eva …"

"Fall in love with you?" I ask.

"Sí, Señora."

I smile. This man is so sweet as he sits there fumbling hopefully with his fingers, and I can think of several ways that I can encourage Eva to appreciate him.

"But I can't actually make her fall in love with you, Señor," I say. "I have no love potion number 9 … or even number 8. I am not a witch."

Carlitos laughs. "You've bewitched us all, mi amor. But what can you do with Eva?"

"I think some study must happen first," I answer. "I can enter her dreams; see what is going on. Then maybe I can make things happen there … in her dreams."

"That's good, that's good," Señor Popcorn says with nervous quickness. "Of course, winning her love is only part of the problem."

"I was thinking that," Carlitos says.

"Yes, we still have to deal with her father, Enrique."

"Señor Córdoba won't approve of your profession, since his job is to rid the world of men like you."

"The bastard doesn't really know me," the popcorn man answers. "He doesn't know my heart. To win Eva, I would be willing to change my business entirely."

We look at Señor Popcorn in amazement.

"You would give up your empire?" Carlitos asks. "After you fought so hard to save it?"

"I might be willing to move into more legitimate forms of agriculture," he says, "if it will gain Eva's hand. I just wish that I could think of some other crop that would be as interesting as marijuana."

"And as financially rewarding," Carlitos adds.

"Something good for our Mexican people," I suggest.

"If that's possible. But where can I find such a crop ... one that grows well in Mexico, is very profitable, and would be useful to the people of our country."

Flight attendant Victoria has sobered up and is back with a cart full of goodies: sodas, candy, cookies, coffee, sweet rolls, pretzels, and, of course, Señor Popcorn's favorite food. She gives us each a drink. She hands Carlitos a large, freshly baked chocolate chip cookie, and also places a big silver bowl of popcorn in the center of the table.

"I need an ambassador who can speak intelligently on my behalf to Enrique," Señor Popcorn says as he grabs a handful of his favorite treat. "After I have successfully wooed Eva, of course.

"That's where you come in, my boy," he nods to Carlitos, "in the 'intelligent speaking' not the 'wooing.'"

"I'd be happy to help," my husband answers.

"You must convince Señor Córdoba that I am ready to reform, and that it will make him look good. It will be a peaceful transition from drugs to some other product, whatever it might be."

"Oil," I suggest.

"No fun in that, and cracking those oil cartels is even tougher than staying in the drug business."

"Tequila?" I ask.

Señor Popcorn shakes his head. "Not sure there's enough money in the sale of tequila to match my current business. Not many products can compare. I'm thinking it has to be addictive too, somehow ... legally addictive."

"Tobacco?"

Victoria now shows up with a bowl of *ghost* popcorn and I grab a big handful. Carlitos and Señor Popcorn are already stuffing their mouths. As I watch them I start to giggle. Then I laugh out loud. It's something I have been taught never to do. But this is too funny.

"I think you are eating your new product, gentlemen," I say. "Popcorn?"

"Sí, pero más." I say.

"But more?" Carlitos asks.

"More than popcorn, estupido. Corn! Maíz, tortillas, corn bread, pig food, cattle feed, corn gasoline, corn on the cob … high fructose *corn* syrup!"

Señor Popcorn's eyes grow wide with excitement. "A global player in the corn market," he says. "Alicia, you are a genius.

"Yes, I will become more than Señor Popcorn," he shouts as he gets to his feet. "I will become El Rey del Maíz, THE KING OF CORN!"

Chapter 3

I fight my way through beautiful dresses and stumble over high heel shoes. I climb over drawers filled with jeans, t-shirts, sexy bras, and panties. I get tangled in wraps and shawls, but at last I get out of this terrible closet, and wonder why I could not simply pass right through it.

I am haunting the mansion of Señor Enrique Córdoba. It is two in the morning, and at last I am in Eva's bedroom.

It is beautiful, in the Spanish style with a high ceiling, a great oak dresser, a chair, and a writing desk. In the center of one wall is a full-length mirror and beside it, a painting of a blue woman with the name "Picasso" written there.

Across the room is a great bed with soft white sheets and a coverlet. The pillows are bigger than my whole bed when I was a little girl. And, in the middle of all of this lies Eva.

I go to her and look at her face in the moonlight.

There are creases in her brow, around her mouth, in the corners of her eyes … even when she is sleeping. Eva is older than Señor Popcorn thinks, I see. But she is also more beautiful than I expected.

I wonder if it was her makeup, or his lover's eyes that fooled him. Macho lieutenants like Victor and Hector would be too horny to even notice, I am sure. And then I suddenly understand: the fact that Eva is probably forty rather than twenty-five is a good thing … at least for Señor Popcorn.

I smile and decide to visit her dreams to see what else I can learn. I cross my eyes, focus my thoughts, and throw my spirit into her brain.

I am in an open field at sunset. Mountains stand in the distance. The air is warm, birds still twitter at this hour. A tree digs into the earth near a stream that runs over rocks and right pastme.

I see a horseman and horsewoman riding. The woman is in the lead. The man trails her, chasing her. The woman is standing in her stirrups, looking back and laughing.

They turn at the stream, and ride straight toward me. Their dream-images would destroy me except, of course, they pass right through me, and I get a good look at the two riders. The woman is Eva, but in this dream she is a teenager. She races the man, and she is winning. He is truly handsome, much older, and he looks just like her. It is her father, Enrique, of course.

She leans forward over the horse, and charges ahead ... never letting her Papá catch her, or even come close.

What does all this mean? I wonder.

Eva dreams of being a teenager, of racing her father across the fields of Mexico. Can I use this fact to help Señor Popcorn? I think so.

Now, I'm somewhere else ... in a stable. Eva pulls the saddle from her horse. She's falls backward under the weight and bumps into someone behind her. The two turn and look at each other. It is Señor Popcorn ... as handsome as he can ever be.

She bites her lip and gives him a smile full of secrets. "Señorita Eva, how are you?" he asks.

"Wouldn't you like to know, Señor?" she answers.

I leave the dream and sit in a chair in the corner of Eva's room. I look at her. She still has that smile on her lips, and then she giggles. She likes the popcorn man, I'm sure of it, at least in her dreams.

I decide that now is the time for action. But what to wear? It is a question for all women living or dead. And so I ask myself what is the one outfit that would never scare a girl even if she woke to find a ghost standing beside her bed wearing it. The answer is obvious, is it not? Or do you just not know anything about girls?

I spin around and am wearing the perfect gown (yes, gown). I have selected a special shape for myself. It's a living shape, but one that has soft edges, so that when I move, trails of starlight are left behind. All of this will tell Eva that I am a ghost, but she will not be scared because of what I am wearing.

And now I glide over to the desk and pick up an old, worn Bible from the corner. Does this girl read the Bible? Interesting. I approach the side of the bed, stand right beside her, reach out and drop the Bible at the foot of the bed with a heavy noise. Fortunately, I miss her feet. But the noise is enough to wake her.

Eva turns to me, looks up, and smiles.

"Am I still dreaming?" she asks. "Are you really Cenicienta?"

Cinderella!

Yes, I have infringed on copyrights and am wearing the very dress that Cinderella wore in the Disney movie. What girl of any age can resist her? I move my arm across Eva's bed, trailing stardust that actually tinkles as it floats down toward her. This stardust is better than I though it would be. But Eva is now more awake, and she is becoming excited.

"Your movie thrilled me when I was six," she says, "and I spent the next whole year looking for my fairy godmother."

"And did you find her?" I ask.

Eva's smirks and looks suddenly very grown up. "Of course not."

"How about Prince Charming?"

Eva's smirk goes away. So does her smile. "I don't think so," she sighs.

"Señorita," I say, and now *I* have the secret smile, "I am not really Cinderella, you know ... but I have been sent by Prince Charming."

"Really?" That grown-up look is back.

"Yes, I have been sent by a wonderful man who offers you an invitation that will bring joy to your heart."

Eva sits up in bed. She likes flowery Mexican invitations. She lets the bedding drop away to reveal a lacy nightgown and a beautiful figure, and then she smiles that secret smile.

"Is it someone I've dreamed about?" she asks.

"A dream is a wish your heart makes," I answer. Like all little girls, I know my Disney.

"Who is he? Victor?"

I shake my head. "Pablo?"

"Who the hell is Pablo?" I do not say those words aloud though. I simply reach into a secret pocket in the gown and pull out Señor Popcorn's leather bracelet.

I hand it to Eva. She takes it and then looks back at me in confusion. "The old man?" she asks.

"The *sexy* old man!"

She studies the bracelet, looks inside it and reads an inscription that I did not know was there: "Para mi amor para siempre, Norma" ... to my love, forever.

"Was this given to him by his *wife*?" she asks, a look of shock suddenly taking over her face.

"She died tragically many years ago. You're the first woman he has wanted to date since then."

"He can't give this to me," she says. "It's too personal ... and too important."

"He wants you to have it."

She moves to give the bracelet back to me, but I push my gloved hand toward her. Magical ghost-trails follow the movement with that silly tinkling sound.

"Please," I say.

"He wants to *date* me?"

"Very much."

Eva thinks hard as she continues to study the bracelet. She runs her hand over the leather very slowly, almost lovingly.

"Where would he like to go … on the date?"

I smile. I have some secrets of my own, like the fact that I have visited her dreams. "Horseback riding?"

Eva looks down at the leather band. She raises it to her nose and takes a deep breath. She must like the smell of it because that secret smile returns to her lips. It spreads across her face to her eyes, which are now sparkling.

"Sexy old man," she murmurs as she slides the bracelet onto her wrist. "Tell him that I would love to go horseback riding with him."

"I will," I answer. "He will be contacting you."

"Thank you, Cinderella," she sighs.

See, I told you. What other gown would she trust as much as this one? And then, with the leather bracelet still on her wrist, Eva curls up in her bed and goes back to sleep.

Mission accomplished.

Chapter 4

"Fernando," Señora Yolanda gushes as she opens the door to the Córdoba home three days later. The English butler is nowhere to be found. Her words are welcoming, but her smile is forced.

She thought she could have Señor Popcorn for herself and hates losing him to her daughter, I think. I am invisible as I stand beside the popcorn man when he steps into the grand hacienda.

La Señora's smile warms. She likes what she sees now, I think, and she decides she may be able to claim Señor Popcorn after her daughter loses interest.

I know these are not proper ideas for a wife and mother, but then Señora Yolanda looks like the kind of woman who gets her way whether it is proper or not.

"So, you think that you are more appropriate for our Eva than your silly cowboys?" she asks.

The popcorn man smiles thoughtfully. "Perhaps I am more dedicated to her happiness," he answers.

"Good answer!" I think, though I cannot let them know that I am here.

"Yes, well, we are all dedicated to her happiness," the Señora says.

"Then we share a common goal."

Señora Yolanda moves further into the entryway letting the popcorn man follow. Suddenly Eva comes gliding down the stairway in a riding outfit that would make horses glad to be ridden. Tan slacks, a trim red riding coat, a black silk blouse underneath it, high brown leather boots, and of course she carries a riding crop and a helmet. She brings her secret smile with her, and it thrills Señor Popcorn and unnerves her mother.

The popcorn man clicks his heels. "You look lovely."

"A *lovely* riding outfit ... really?" Eva flirts. "Why, thank you Señor." She bats her eyes with a quickness that I can only envy.

"Well, you two have a wonderful time," Señora Yolanda says as Eva breezes by her and takes Señor Popcorn by the arm.

"Oh, we will, Mama," Eva calls. "Don't wait up."

And just like that she and Señor Popcorn are out the door and on their way to that pure white Mercedes. I trail behind them smiling all the way, praying that this woman will not play with the love of the sweet old man. Or maybe Señor Popcorn would like to have his love played with.

That's more the truth, I think.

#

Is there such a thing as a ghost horse? There must be, because I'm riding one. He is a black monster called Espanto Negro (black ghost) who would normally *not* be ridden by anyone, I think. He must have been broken and trained after his death, because he takes charge of our journey, but also takes care of me.

Eva and Señor Popcorn have saddled up and are racing along the beaches of Cancun. The sea is crashing around them, but their horses are spirited; they pound through the surf, and over the sand. Eva is standing in her saddle as she did in her dream, and she turns and looks back at Señor Popcorn with a smile that says "catch me if you can?" I know that because I am riding very close to her, thanks to the speed and skill of

35

Espanto Negro. For a moment I think she is aware of me. But that would be impossible would it not? I am not sure.

I glance back at the popcorn man who is slapping the reins back and forth across his horse's neck. I'm not sure if he is trying to catch Eva or merely letting her lead for the thrill of it.

She rides around a bend in the shoreline and I'm right there with her, now looking out at the great beaches of the Yucatan. She charges on for another hour during which Señor Popcorn finally catches up to her and rides along beside her for many more miles.

Now, he pulls in front and finds a cave along the shore where the two of them can rest their horses and themselves.

"You ride well, Señor," Eva says.

"As do you."

"Well, I seldom have anyone who can keep up with me."

"I can see that."

Señor Popcorn takes the bridle of Eva's horse, leads both horses over to the edge of the shoreline, and ties them to a great driftwood log. He brings his saddlebag back to the beach where Eva is sitting, staring out at the waves and breathing in the salt air.

"Some refreshments?" he asks.

"Yes, please."

"Wine, cheese, fruit?"

"All good."

Señor Popcorn spreads a blanket and then lays a picnic out on the beach. The shadow of the cave and the salt air give relief from a very hot afternoon.

"Do you dream, Señorita?" the popcorn man asks.

"Please, I am no Señorita," Eva answers.

"No?"

"I am nearly 42 years old, Señor. I have been married and divorced."

The popcorn man looks confused; then he shrugs, sighs and smiles. Like me, he realizes that it may be good news for him.

"You look so young."

"I take care of myself, exercise, eat well, and get lots of sleep."

"But do you *dream*, Señora?"

He pops the cork on a bottle of champagne and pours glasses for both of them. He holds one out to Eva who takes it and gives him that secret smile.

"Of course, I dream," she says.

"Good, and can I ask what your dreams are about, Bella Dama?"

I giggle because I know and have told the popcorn man about Eva's dreams. But still I wait for her answer.

"Lovers and friends, fun, adventure, a home, a ranch, horses, children."

Señor Popcorn raises his glass in a toast. "To dreams," he says. And they drink. I drink too ... of the smiles they are sharing.

"How about *one* lover to dream about," Señor Popcorn asks, "instead of many?"

"I tried that. It didn't work out very well."

"May I ask why not?"

Eva sighs. "He was one of my father's captains: a powerful man, a little too macho for my taste. He beat me ... eventually."

"Why?"

Tears form in Eva's eyes from the memory. "Apparently I wasn't a very obedient wife."

Señor Popcorn takes a tortilla and prepares a tasty taco for his lady. He has brought all the ingredients and has even managed to bring along some carnitas wrapped in aluminum foil so that they are still hot. He adds peppers and salsa and beans. And he hands it to her. She takes it daintily.

37

"In what way were you not obedient?" he asks.

"I didn't appreciate the roughness which he enjoyed, especially when it came to sex," she answers. "So then I denied him."

"Denied him sex?"

"I did."

"And what was his response?"

"More roughness without sex."

She takes a bite of the taco so that her mouth is full and she can't answer any more questions. But Señor Popcorn doesn't seem to want to ask any more questions anyway. Instead he prepares himself a taco and then wolfs it down. He opens a tray full of chips and salsa that somehow he has managed to keep undamaged in his saddlebags. He also offers hot peppers, cheeses, sliced avocado mangos and papayas, and still more tortillas.

He is enjoying himself, and as Eva watches him in his careful, excited, but comical food preparation, she starts to giggle. It is cute the way he makes another taco for her, this one of cooked shrimp, limejuice and guacamole. He presents it to her as though he were the finest chef in the world.

"Why thank you, Señor," she says.

I've never seen anyone eat a taco so delicately.

"Ummm," she murmurs. "So good, Señor." Her white teeth sparkle as she takes each bite.

She licks her lips. Sexy.

The popcorn man is trying to think of another treat that will bring on even more sexy eating from his date, when she suddenly speaks up. "My father had him executed, you know?"

"Your ex-husband?"

"Sí, Señor. After we were divorced, we discovered that he was also an undercover man for the Machado drug cartel. He was gathering information that blocked many of my father's efforts and led to the death of many innocent people. He was tried and executed."

"You were married to Vicente Gomez then," The popcorn man says as he recognizes the situation she is describing.

"I was."

"He was an evil man. How did your papá ever let you marry him to begin with?"

"I'm my own woman, Señor; I marry whom I choose."

"I see."

"But when I marry again ... *if* I marry again, it will be to someone who knows how to care for a woman, respect her independence, and love her tenderly."

As I listen to this conversation I wonder if La Señorita ... I mean La Señora ... understands how perfectly her desires are answered in the person of Señor Fernando de Cervantes, the popcorn man. I'll have to find a way to tell her.

Meanwhile Señor Popcorn produces a big plate of flan and now offers some to Eva. By this point they have consumed all of the champagne but there is still hot coffee in a thermos.

They share the dessert. When they are finished and the popcorn man has packed up all the picnic things and placed the saddlebags over his horse, he turns to her.

"Where would you like to go now, Señorita?" He catches himself and blushes. "May I call you Señorita?"

"It is not accurate, you know."

"You are *my* Señorita. ¿Sí?"

"I would like that," Eva says as she walks up to him and kisses him on the lips. The popcorn man reels. This is something he has dreamed of for so long.

That secret smile forms on Eva's lips, the one so like the smile of Señor Popcorn's wife and daughter, the one that first drew him to her.

"What are you smiling at?" he asks.

"Wouldn't you like to know?" she answers, and then she pulls her horse free, jumps onto it and charges back along the beaches toward Cancun.

Chapter 5

I easily make my way through Eva's closet this time, but I find her room empty.

I'm upset because there is so much I want to say to her.

I stand in the middle of the room wondering where she can be at twelve o'clock midnight. And then I hear it: terrible arguing from down stairs. A deep man's voice, her father's I'm sure, is swearing and cursing almost certainly about the fact that his daughter wants to date Señor Popcorn.

Señora Yolanda is there too, trying to be the voice of reason, I think. But Enrique will not listen to either of them.

"You married a drug lord once," he shouts at Eva so loudly that it's like he's in the bedroom with me. "I'll be damned if I'm going to let you marry another one."

Eva's voice sounds like that of a rattlesnake as she hisses back at him.

"Father, I am a grown woman. I make my own decisions. And besides, you don't know that he is a drug lord."

"Fernando de Cervantes is the king of all drug lords!" Enrique snaps. And then I hear several doors slamming.

I hurry down the stairs past the kitchen where Eva and her mother are huddled together spitting curses back and forth. They are cursing all men especially Enrique.

I make my way into the study where Eva's father is talking on the phone. I listen to him, and what I hear terrifies me.

"Damn right, Sergio!

"The Renta gun battle? That's the best you've got. Okay. It's not really enough, but it'll have to do."

41

It will have to do *what*? I wonder.

"Allow us to arrest him," Señor Enrique answers me without even knowing I asked.

"Yes, that's what I said. Damn it! Arrest him!"

And then he starts to whisper even though no one is in the room but an innocent ghost.

"Try to make it *rough* too, you know, so that he'll resist. And if he even looks at you cross- eyed, kill him. That's right; kill the fucker."

¡Madre de dios! I guess the fucker is Señor Popcorn. And Señor Enrique is planning to kill him. My mind starts racing. What do I do? Who do I tell? How can I save my beloved popcorn man?

Perhaps I should tell Eva. But no, I realize. I do not know the best way to tell things to her right now. I don't know what she will say or do. I need to think about this some more … and maybe tell Carlitos what I have heard.

#

It's early morning at Señor Popcorn's hacienda. Carlitos is nowhere to be found and the ghosts I ask have no idea where he is. I never sleep so I am here, prowling around like a jaguar, wondering who I can chew up with all the hatred I now have for Señor Córdoba.

There's a knock at the front door, and Raquel Sandoval, who was so much fun at the Wicked Rabbit Cantina, puts on a thin little bathrobe and answers it. It must be before 6AM because the sun is only now waking up.

Eva Córdoba is outside the door dressed in a coat and a kerchief. Her eyes grow wide as she sees Raquel in her tiny wrap.

"Eva?" Raquel says with a happy smile. But Eva does not give the smile back.

"Oh, I'm sorry to be dressed like this," Raquel says pulling at the hem of her tiny robe, "I just got up. Won't you please come in?"

Eva steps across the threshold wondering what this beautiful woman is doing in the home of the man she wants to love.

"Do you live here?" Eva asks.

"Yes, with the other girls."

"Girls? There are more of you?"

"You don't know about us then?"

"No. I don't."

Raquel smiles, though it probably does little to end Eva's worries. Is her intended lover living with a large group of women, at least one of whom is drop-dead gorgeous?

"Señor Popcorn allows models to live in his estate," Raquel tells her. "He is a very chaste and good man; believe me. But he does take care of us, feed us, clothe us, let us drive his cars."

Eva's eyes darken. She doesn't like the sound of this.

"I see," she says, and she turns to leave. But she can't, because I am standing right behind her in my ghost form with the soft edges. I'm wearing my Cinderella dress, and my arms are crossed.

Eva jumps backward in surprise, right into the arms of Raquel, who catches her. Eva shakes free and frowns at me.

"Cinderella, what are you doing here?"

"Helping you understand what a good man is Fernando de Cervantes."

I'm getting upset, but I know that Eva Córdoba is too important to be chased away by Señor Popcorn's house full of beautiful women.

"Look Señora," I say, "Fernando lost his wife and daughter to gang leaders fifteen years ago. He swore he would never love another woman until he saw you. He fell so in love with you that he needs to have you by his side, forever. I have

43

to tell you about the danger he is in and how you can help save him."

Eva sighs in confusion. "I know that my father is a very dangerous man."

"More dangerous than you know. He has given orders to have Señor Popcorn murdered."

"My father would never break the law."

"No, he would not. But, if Señor Popcorn were arrested in a way that made him have to defend himself, your father's men would be able to shoot him, would they not?"

"If he resisted arrest, yes."

Raquel takes her by the arm. Eva looks at the model with distrust, but soon gives up and follows her into Señor Popcorn's grand living room.

"Can I ask you one small favor?" I say as soon as Eva is seated in the large sofa that fills half of the room.

She shrugs.

"Can I get out of this god damn gown? It's too pinchy, even for a ghost. Those Disney artists are too cruel to their princesses."

Raquel laughs.

Eva does too, and so I spin around and am now dressed in jeans, high heel boots, and a t-shirt that has the words *Intoxicating Spirits* printed across the front.

I sit down beside Eva. I take her hand and look into her eyes. "We must save him," I say. And Eva nods.

Chapter 6

Señor Popcorn joins us. He is dressed and ready to start a day full of business meetings even though it is only 6:30 AM.

"You have to save yourself, Señor," I plead with him as soon as he enters and greets Eva with a chaste kiss on the lips.

"Really?" he asks with a slight smile. "Why is that, Niña?"

"Because Señor Córdoba has ordered his men to arrest you and to murder you as they do it."

Señor Popcorn thinks the warning is funny.

"They will murder me for *resisting* arrest, of course," he says, still smiling.

"Sí," I say sadly as I downcast my eyes. But then I hear him laughing.

"It's not a problem, ladies. Señor Córdoba has been trying to arrest me for years. And I'm sure that the order has *always* been for his officers to kill me."

"You don't know my father, Señor," Eva says. "He's even more vicious than the drug lords you deal with."

"I doubt that."

The popcorn man gives her a smile that all three of the women in the room find insulting.

"Please," Eva says. "I know a place where we can hide."

"And is it safer than here with my body guards and lookout towers, machine guns and radar? I doubt that."

"Fernando, run away with me."

"Willingly, my love, but not to escape your father."

He spins around and points to the doorway of the dining room. "Now, come. Let's all have some breakfast."

Eva is so angry with him. So am I. He is way too sure of himself. Finally he notices the looks on our faces.

"Okay, Okay, I'll double my guards."

"Hide!"

"Breakfast!"

Eva turns to me, but all I can do is shrug. "Please Señor Popcorn," I plead.

His eyes darken. He is starting to get annoyed. "No! And that's final. Now, are you girls going to have breakfast with me or not?"

Eva rushes up to him and slaps him. She turns and starts to run from the room, then she hurries back to him and kisses him on the lips, and this kiss is anything but chaste. I have to disappear for a moment so I don't have to watch. When I return Raquel is blushing.

"Take care of yourself, Fernando," Eva sighs.

"I'm an old hand at this, relax."

Señor Popcorn dares to pat her on the backside as she leaves.

I scowl at him; I could shoot him for his stubbornness. But I don't have to, because at that very moment, *real* shooting starts. It's out in the courtyard.

I fly through the door to see Señor Córdoba's agents moving toward us across the lawn. Señor Popcorn's defenders have already started shooting back. Men in black suits on both sides are gunning each other down. I count seven government men and ten of Señor Popcorn's. But the government men are winning.

Four of our guys already lie dying on the veranda. I turn, the door opens, and I see Señor Popcorn stepping out to see what's happening. He does it at the worst possible time, and takes a gunshot right in the shoulder. He falls backward against the doorway as other bullets shoot through his body. ¡Mierda!

The government guys are charging across the lawn now, getting shot up just to get to the veranda and finish the job. But just then Raquel decides, gracias a Dios, to play the hero. She opens the door and offers her own body to the bullets so that she can pull Señor Popcorn to safety.

I stand there on the porch hypnotized by the violence. Seeing gun blasts all around me, through me, it doesn't matter. I'm a ghost, after all. But now the last of the agents makes it to the porch and reaches for the door. I don't know what to do except *freak out!*

I jump up in my death face. I scream and reach my claw hands toward his throat The guy turns, fires six shots that pass right through me, and then he turns and runs right into many bullets from the last of Señor Popcorn's bodyguards.

The agent returns the fire, and now both men dance with bullets, death, and almost each other before they fall to the ground covered with their own blood.

I look out through the gunsmoke across the lawn and see that there is one more government agent left in the driveway, near the evil black cop car that they all came in. I fly at him screaming and flailing rotting flesh that hangs from my skeleton's arms. My head is a skull with green slime dripping from it. My fingers grow long as I point at the agent and wail, "Diiiiieeee!"

He dives into the car and peels out away from me. I swoop in front of him, pushing my death face to the front of the windshield, hoping to scare him off the road and into the side of a tree. But he closes his eyes and still holds the wheel. And, though I ride with him for over a mile, he does not give up.

"¡Pendejo!" I finally call as I pull away and flash back to the compound so I can learn if Señor Popcorn has survived.

47

Eva is with him, on her knees. She is doing her best to bandage him with strips of cloth to stop the bleeding.

"I'm going to take him with me now," she calls to Raquel and the others who have come into the house. "Help get him to my car."

No one argues.

Two men lift Señor Popcorn and carry his unconscious body out into the yard. They place him into the back seat of the Jeep Grand Cherokee that Eva is driving.

"Don't you think he needs a doctor?" I ask.

"A curandera," she answers, and I know just what she means, a native healer. It is a profession I've come to know well.

"Come with me, Cinderella," she says, and I do. I glide right into the front passenger seat of the Jeep, knowing that I will have to come back later to explain all this to Carlitos, wherever the hell he is.

But now Eva is already peeling out of the driveway, waving goodbye to the others. We are taking Señor Popcorn somewhere that we hope her evil father will never think to look.

#

An hour later, Eva's jeep is off the highway, plowing through what is left of a narrow dirt road that winds into the jungle. The tangling vines and other growing things hide our way and do everything in their power to slow us. Still we bounce along. Señor Popcorn is groaning. As much as it hurts me to see him this way, one small part of me feels rewarded because he was so stubborn in the face of our warnings.

Eva is superwoman, winning her fight with the steering wheel as we plow on through ruts and across streams that have regained their way across the tiny road.

Another hour later and we are no longer following a road. It isn't even a trail any more, but the vines have fallen back, and we are driving along an open grassy space with great heavy trees hanging like shadows in the distance. Eva turns the wheel suddenly and heads right into the deepest part of the jungle. The vines are thick, and I feel there is no way to get through them. Then I realize we won't have to because there is a strange old building hiding just inside the edge of the jungle.

Eva slams the Jeep forward as far as she can, then jumps from it and runs up onto the porch of the place.

"Doña Cuca! Doña Cuca!" she calls, and she pounds hard on the door. It opens. Eva talks wildly with someone inside, and then she and a short, tough-looking old woman run back to the Jeep.

They jerk open the door, and when they do, the old woman sees me at once. She is a curandera no doubt, because the old healers have spiritual powers, and they are always able to see ghosts.

She smiles at me.

"Bella Dama," she croons.

"Señora." I return her smile.

Eva and Doña Cuca lift the popcorn man from the back of the Jeep and carry him carefully into the old building, which is very oddly shaped for the jungle. There are two thick columns holding up the corners of a front porch that is otherwise completely falling down. The stucco walls are dirty orange, but they are also stained with dozens of other ugly colors. The dirty floor is made of pink and white tile with a pattern that makes me dizzy. The ceiling is of wood beams, and all kinds of creatures are hiding up there, I know. I watch then scurrying away as we enter.

The two women take Señor Popcorn into a side room that has a bed in it. Though the bedding is old, it is clean and well cared for. There are two big windows that open out onto a garden with a rough brick wall framing it.

"Quickly, quickly," Doña Cuca says, and she rushes out into the garden and begins gathering flowers, leaves, herbs and twigs. Then she heads into her kitchen and starts brewing a strong-smelling tea with some of the things that she gathered.

Eva brings a few of the leaves back to the popcorn man. She uses them to dress his wounds, and though he is barely conscious and sweating terribly, he tries to smile.

I watch Eva working so hard on my friend, and I realize that she too is a curandera; she too is a healer.

Doña Cuca brings a big cup of tea for Señor Popcorn, and Eva takes it and holds it as he sips. He makes angry faces at the taste, but still looks gratefully into her eyes.

"I should have listened to you," he says.

She cups the side of his face in her hand and smiles. "It's a lesson you'll need to learn if we are to be together," she sighs as she kisses his lips. "Now, rest yourself. We'll be in the next room."

She turns to me, nods, and then gestures toward the door. Even though I am invisible she sees me. Yes, she *is* a curandera, and, as I thought on our ride, she has been able to see me all along … in the dress I chose to be seen in, yes, but whether I wanted to be seen or not.

We go into the kitchen where Doña Cuca is still brewing up potions.

"You're in love with him," she says to Eva, who blushes and smiles in embarrassment and admission.

"So, who's the ghost?" Doña Cuca asks.

"My name is Alicia Maria Mejias Mancowski Mann," I answer.

"I see."

"Yes. I am the deceased wife of Professor Carlos Mann of Leland University."

"An Americano now?" Doña Cuca asks.

"My husband is. I died before I could become one."

"Better to grow where your roots are planted, Bella Dama," she says.

I cross my arms, I don't like these opinions about my Mexican-Americano husband and am ready to spend my anger on the home of this curandera, as I did on the apartment of mi Carlitos when he began paying attention to that Joy girl.

Doña Cuca understands the power of my temper immediately and takes steps to control me. "If you care anything for the life of that man in there, who I sense is very dear to you, though not as dear as he is becoming to Eva here, then you will control your temper, Señora."

I turn and flit into the other room where I can calm myself by studying the sad face of Señor Popcorn. He definitely needs the help of this old woman, and so I concentrate on praying for him. Since he has found love again after the tragic loss of his wife and daughter, I'm asking the Virgin of Guadalupe that he may live long enough to find happiness with Eva Córdoba, the daughter of a man whose whole purpose in life is to murder him.

Could things be any more complicated? I wonder.

If only Carlitos were here to use his logics to sort this all out for me. And suddenly I realize that I have no idea where he is. Dios mio, something else to worry about.

Chapter 7

It's nearly midnight, and Señor Popcorn's condition is getting much worse. His eyes are half open; his face is covered with sweat. The flesh around his injuries is becoming very red. The blood, still wet in his wounds, is black and smelly. Even the leaves that Eva places on them so skillfully do not seem to help, and they have their own terrible odor.

I look at him from across the room, feeling guilty for being angry with him because he did not listen to our warning. But in spite of that I am also still angry with him, and where is Carlitos when I need him? I'm pissed off at my husband too.

The popcorn man stirs. His eyes are red and swollen.

"Alicia," he whispers, which adds new worry to my feelings because he senses my presence even though I am invisible. Is he that close to death?

I appear beside him.

"Do you like her, Niña?" he whispers through his paper-dry lips.

"Oh, Señor, of course I do. Such a lovely lady, so perfect for you."

"You think so? Good, then help me recover."

"*She* is helping you, Señor, and so is Doña Cuca."

"I know, and I am sure that their remedies will eventually cure me. But I am in such pain. Please, Niña. I need a little drink from the flask in my pocket."

"Pocket?"

"My jacket pocket, over there."

I look across the room and spot his sport coat, which he was wearing when he was shot. The curandaras have removed it from him and placed it on a chair in the corner.

"Be a good girl and fetch the flask for me," and now he begins to cough. It's terrible, loud, and hacking. I wait for the curandaras to burst into the room, but they do not. Why not? I wonder. Are they so wrapped up in preparing medicines that they are neglecting their patient?

Señor Popcorn's cough ends finally.

"Get me the flask, like a good girl, Alicia. Then I will have the strength to endure these foul- tasting cures of theirs."

I smile. "What's in the flask, Señor?"

"Tequila, the water of life, Niña. Now be quick."

I glide over to the coat and immediately see the flask bulging in his coat pocket. I reach in, retrieve it, open it with some difficulty, and then I bring it back to Señor Popcorn. I smile at him lovingly. Except that now he does not move at all. His eyes are staring at the ceiling. His shredded-paper lips are parted. I study his chest, which at least showed a hint of breathing only seconds ago. Now there is no motion whatsoever.

Oh no! He's dead; I'm sure of it. I drop the flask and hear the tequila gurgling out of it. The sound is magnified somehow, like the soul of Señor Popcorn escaping from his tortured body.

After a moment I realize that I must go to Eva and tell her. If there is anything they can do for him, they must do it now. Perhaps they have charms and things that can bring him back.

Doña Cuca is snoring in a chair in the center of the room when I get there. Eva is across from her praying the rosary. I'm very afraid to face her and tell her of the tragedy. But I must.

"I'm worried about Señor Popcorn," I say to her. "He isn't moving at all ... or breathing." Eva jumps to her feet and rushes to the bed of her love.

"Oh," she moans. "Oh, no." And she reaches for the side of his neck to take his pulse. "Oh, no! Doña Cuca, come quick. Doña!"

The old woman shuffles into the room. "What's this?"

"I can't find a pulse. Help me."

The old curandera places her hand in front of Señor Popcorn's nostrils to feel for breath. She scowls.

"Dios mio." She looks at Eva, and there are tears in her eyes.

"Pray with me, Gatita," she says. And she places her hands on the dead man's cheeks. She presses her fingers into his soft flesh, closes her eyes, lowers her head and begins to mumble prayers in a language I have never heard before. It is not Spanish, I assure you.

After a moment Eva leans across and presses her fingers on top of Doña Cuca's. She joins her in prayer in the same unknown language, which must be some kind of ancient Maya or something.

I glide into the corner and continue my prayers to the Virgin of Guadalupe when suddenly the room becomes very dark. There is no light at all. Anywhere. The wind picks up and I hear it howling through the pitch-blackness. It screeches through the walls and ceiling. There is a desperate rushing around of huge bugs and lizards in reaction.

Outside, a jaguar joins in with a wild cry, and I jump. The two curanderas do not stop for a moment, do not even flinch; they continue their prayers, which are now beginning to sound like some kind of chant.

Doña Cuca pulls away from the dead man as the wind picks up and more animal cries cut through the night. The old woman is chanting and singing and spinning in the middle of the room. And even though there is no light at all, I can see her because the wrap she is wearing glows with a deep blue light that brightens her shape.

She spins and dips and pounds her feet onto the floor. Eva turns away from the dead man and joins her, continuing the dance, bringing her own light with her. It's a soft pink glow from her cloak, and I see it drifting around and around the blue aura of Doña Cuca.

The wind grows stronger still. But the women stretch out their arms as though they are huge birds riding with it, soaring across the endless darkness. With a thunder crash, the wind suddenly ceases. Lightning blazes through the night, flashing a brilliant, blinding white! The curanderas drop their hands to their sides and begin to twist and wriggle like lizards in the rain.

They are so different from one another: Eva's face so very lovely with her auburn hair that catches the glow from her gown and flashes wildly around her face. The old woman is almost funny the way she moves. Their eyes are closed, but they do no collide with each other. They sense each other's presence and location, and so they dance on and on and on. And during all this time, there is no light at all except the sudden flashes of lightning and the blue and pink brightness coming off their dresses. It reflects in their hair, in their faces as it trails their movements through the room.

I have snatched Eva's rosary now, and I pray it as I watch the dancing go on and on and the women becoming weaker and more exhausted ... all night long ... through all the blinding flashes of lighting and the rumbles of thunder ... all night long, until dawn begins to spread a warm glow through the jungle and then throughout the house.

With the coming of sunlight Eva and Doña Cuca slump together, fall to their knees and collapse in exhaustion.

I stand and walk over to the bed, to Señor Popcorn. I reach out and touch him on the face with invisible hands. He is still cold and motionless. And then the corner of his nose twitches.

Then his whole face twists, and he turns away from me and blasts a great sneeze into the wall. It's so loud that it wakes the women from their slumber. He wipes his face on his dirty sleeve as he smiles up at me.

Eva comes running to him. She sees that his eyes are open, that he is breathing, that he is smiling. She immediately checks his wounds and sees that they are healing very well. There is barely a scar left where the bullets attacked him.

"Mi amor," she cries and kisses him hard on the lips. I jump up and down with gladness.

We turn to look at Doña Cuca, but she is dead to the world, lying on the floor, snoring her nose off. It is a wonderful welcome sound that fits with the soft breath of this morning's breeze and the buzz of the jungle that no longer holds the terror of night.

They have saved Señor Popcorn.

My heart sings.

"Amen," I whisper. "Gracias a Dios."

Chapter 8

"I will bathe him, by myself, behind closed doors," Eva Córdoba shouts. Doña Cuca laughs.

"I guess you've earned the right," she says. "Come, I'll help you fill the tub."

The two curandera-women leave the room, and I am left alone with Señor Popcorn. He is sitting up in his bed looking very dirty, but also very healthy at the same time.

"I'm so sorry, Niña," he says to me.

"For not heeding our warnings about your enemies?"

"That too," the old man says with a silly smile. "But mostly for not telling you about Carlitos."

"You know where he is?"

"I sent him on a mission."

My eyes narrow.

"If I had not used all my energy praying you back to life, Señor, I would kill you right now."

He laughs, and does not even cough as a result, proving just how healthy he is. "I sent him to the United States ... to Washington."

I frown. "There was no need for that."

"I had to, Niña. I am buying vast quantities of cornfields. And Carlos is my agent."

"You put your plan into effect before you were sure that Eva loved you?"

"I had to take a chance."

"So, now you are on your way to becoming the popcorn king."

"El Rey de Maíz. The King of Corn!"

His eyes sparkle, and just then Eva and Doña Cuca return carrying a large tub filled with steamy water.

"*I* will bathe him," Eva says defensively.

"I'm afraid you'll need my help," Doña Cuca teases.

Eva turns on her like a protective jaguar and snarls, and Doña Cuca scurries from the room. I too disappear, and hide in the rafters. I want to see this ... don't you?

Eva helps Señor Popcorn to his feet, which apparently is not difficult because much of his strength is restored. She helps strip away his old clothing, and I am amazed at the physique of Señor Popcorn. His body is like the Greek statue of an athlete ... an older athlete, yes, but still a very handsome one.

He steps into the tub, and Eva takes a large bar of soap, dips it into the water and begins to scrub.

"Ummm," Señor Popcorn sighs. "Thank you for saving me."

Eva smiles, takes a huge sponge, sops up some water, and squeezes it above Señor Popcorn's head. Water pours down all around him.

"The pleasure will be all mine," she says as she drops the sponge and begins to suds his hair. Without rinsing, she also scrubs his shoulders and his chest. When she is through he looks like a huge white dog, soapsuds from head to toe.

Again, Eva uses the sponge to squeeze great gushes of water all over his upper body, washing the foam down into the tub. Señor Popcorn enjoys it all.

"Now for the best part," Eva says, as she takes the huge bar of soap and plunges it down below the water ... between his legs. Her eyes are hot on Señor Popcorn who responds with a burning look of his own.

"ALICIA, YOU GET OUT OF HERE," she shouts as she turns back to look at me. I have forgotten once again that curandaras can see ghosts at all times.

"Enjoy yourselves," I say boldly, and I roll my eyes as I zoom from my spot on the ceiling and out the door.

#

We decide that, in spite of his miraculous recovery, Señor Popcorn needs more time to heal, and he still needs to hide out. So everyone settles in and decides to stay here a while. Doña Cuca doesn't mind. She is enjoying the company.

At this very moment, we three women are sitting around the kitchen table. Eva and La Doña are eating tortillas and beans, and Eva is telling me how she learned that she was a curandera.

"I was a schoolgirl," she says. "We were on the playground and a girl fell from a tree that hung over the concrete floor of the basketball court. Her leg broke and she screamed in such pain that I felt my body telling me to help her.

"I ran to her, placed my hand on the leg that was so badly twisted, and I held onto it and prayed. Moments later, when the school nurse came running to us, she saw me praying, saw the imprint of my hands on the girl's leg, saw that the break was not as complete as it should have been.

"'Where did you learn how to do this?' the nurse asked me as I helped carry the injured girl into her office.

"'I didn't learn it anywhere,' I said. 'I just knew.'"

"'As it should be.'"

"The nurse was a curandera too, a disciple of Doña Cuca actually. And so she sent me to this woman who was very old even then."

Doña Cuca scrapes the beans from her plate, gobbles them up and then gives us a nearly toothless smile. "But old as I was, I was still beautiful back then." She bats her eyelashes at us, "and I still am."

We laugh.

"I did teach Señora Eva many things," Doña Cuca continues. "But she learned most things from her own heart; her instincts were so true. I knew that if she wanted to, she could become a great curandera."

"But of course, my mother had other ideas." Eva adds. And then ...

"Oh, shit!" Eva's face suddenly freezes in panic. "My mother! She'll try to find me! I'm sure of it. And she's very good at such things."

She turns to me. "Alicia, we must be able to stay here a while longer. This is such a good place to hide, and Fernando still needs La Doña's care."

"I understand," I say, "How can I help?"

"Go to my mother's house. Keep an eye on her. Follow her in case she decides to search for me. Report back if she starts to draw close."

"I can do that."

I don't want to leave the popcorn man and this happy setting. But I know that I must aid my benefactor and the woman who now loves him so much.

We talk for a while longer, and Eva tells me many more things that will be useful in my efforts. Then I walk back to Señor Popcorn's bedroom where he is sitting in a chair, reading. He is still recovering, not as completely cured as I would like, but very much out of danger.

"I must leave you, Señor," I say. "I must keep an eye on Eva's family to make sure that they do not try to find you and attack you again."

I can see that the popcorn man wants to tell me that it is unnecessary, but I also note that he holds his tongue. He is smart enough not to challenge us about his safety any more.

He smiles up at me. "I am very happy to have such lovely women caring for me."

"Eva loves you, Señor. I'm certain."

He blushes and that warms me all over.

"Thank you for the role you played in everything," he says. "But when will you be leaving?"

"I think they want me to leave as soon as possible."

The old man nods. "Vaya con Dios then, Niña," he whispers. He takes my hand and I lean forward and kiss him softly on the cheek.

"Adios, Señor Popcorn."

I leave his bedroom, offer words of support to the curanderas, and then I fly away, back though the scary jungle, which is no longer quite so scary. I head right to the home of Señor and Señora Córdoba to begin my spying.

Chapter 9

Señora Yolanda Córdoba is a fine horsewoman just like her daughter. She gallops along the beach on her trusty red mare, while I ride behind her on Espanto Negro, my ghost horse. If La Señora were to challenge us to a race, we would leave them far behind, I'm sure. But the mare and the Señora do not even know that we are following them. So they ride quickly, but not foolishly, and we keep up very well.

Now, the trail turns from the beach and into the jungle. The trail is well worn, and so we continue to ride at a good speed until La Señora reaches a great rock wall that has gradually arisen along the western edge of the trail. Here there is a slight split in the rocks, and La Señora pulls up, gets down from her horse, and walks around in front of her.

"Don't be afraid," she tells the mare, "I know she frightens you, but you'll be okay, I promise."

Señora Yolanda leads the mare into a little clearing a short distance away from the rock wall. The horse is nervous, but La Señora ties her to a tree branch; she feeds her several carrots, and the animal calms.

The vines that climb over the split in the rock wall almost block it. Still, Señora Yolanda, with her youthful figure, manages to squeeze past them. I follow, having no problems with vines or rock walls or any of it. I simply pass right through them.

But now we are inside a great dark cave. After a moment our eyes adjust a very little bit, and we dare to move slowly into the blackness. I am a ghost, but somehow, I'm scared.

There's something terrifying here: strong smells that do not mix well together ... sweetness, yes, but also the stink of blood and the rot of death.

The floor of the cave slopes downward, and Señora Yolanda seems to be walking forever. We are now far underground. I am right behind her, of course, but she does not know it, and I have to be careful. If I become any more frightened, I might let out a scream, and you can imagine what that would do to Señora Yolanda.

We wander through the darkness until we run right into a solid cliff. Is this the end of the cave, I wonder?

No. Señora Yolanda presses her hand against the rock and it parts, creating an opening, which she squeezes through, and I follow.

We are suddenly in a great underground room. At the center is a huge statue: an eight-foot-tall figure of a woman dressed in white lace robes with a garland around her head. She has a *death mask* for a face and a great scythe in her bony hand. Dozens of vigil lights brighten her with a flickering glow.

There are other, smaller statues of this same lady: with her hands outstretched, holding a knife, threatening wickedly. Also, we see statues of the Blessed Virgin and other saintly women who also stand witness. Several of them wear rosaries around their necks.

Fresh cut flowers are everywhere: in pots, in vases, in coffee cans. They fill the air with a sweet scent that mingles terribly with the smell of blood, which I now see pooled in dozens of cups and bowls in front of the great figure.

Even more horrifying are the smelly, rotting stubs of bone and flesh scattered everywhere in front of the statue. I study them and then become suddenly sick. They are fingers and toes, cut and left there to rot in tribute to the lady.

I know the woman of the statue. She is MICTECACIHUATL, Queen of the Land of the Dead. In some old way she is my protector. And for a moment I feel grateful that her terrifying face is there to scare away anyone who would seek to harm me.

Now, there is a sudden banging in the far end of this cave. A sharp swish follows like the harsh fall of a machete. Señora Yolanda jumps.

"¿La Bruja?" she calls. Witch?

"¿Qué es lo que quieres?" comes a harsh reply, and a very tall, very skinny woman, who seems to stand as high as the statue of Mictecacihuatl herself, comes forward to talk to us.

La Bruja's face is almost a skeleton, with hollow eyes and cheeks that make her look like the statue even more.

"How dare you bother me?" she asks. "What the hell do you want?"

Señora Yolanda trembles.

"You must help me again, La Bruja."

Again? I ask myself. Señora Yolanda's has sought the help of this witch before?

"Have you brought money?" La Bruja asks.

Señora Yolanda nods. She pulls a small purse from her pocket and hands it to the witch who takes it, looks inside, and smiles.

"And you are also prepared to spill your own blood again ... as part of the payment?"

"Oh yes," Yolanda says, though her eyes are very afraid.

"And sacrifice another of your fingers?" Yolanda nods again.

Madre de dios, I do not like any of this. But I say nothing.

La Bruja smiles and her teeth are so yellow and pointed that even they are frightening. "All right, then," La Bruja says, and she grabs Yolanda's arm and lifts her hand in front of her face. I nearly shriek. Yolanda's entire middle finger is *already* missing.

"It did work then, didn't it?" the witch cackles. "My spell did capture Enrique?"

Señora Yolanda nods. "He married me."

"And now you are prepared to give up another finger?"

All the blood has drained from La Señora's face. Thick beads of sweat form on her brow.

The fear in her eyes screams at me. And still she nods. "Yes."

La Bruja jerks La Señora's hand toward her, produces a knife from under her cloak, holds it up, and lets the flickering light shine off its blade for a moment. Then she grabs La Señora's ring finger and, with one quick slice, cuts it off and lets it drop to the floor.

La Bruja now pulls Yolanda's bloody hand over to one of the bowls sitting in front of the statue, and she lets her blood spill into it.

Yolanda rocks back on her heels and faints. I catch her and slide her gently into a battered old chair that sits in the corner of the room.

La Bruja stares into the space I occupy, but she does not see me. So much for her witchy powers. She claims to represent Mictecacihuatl, but she cannot recognize a ghost when she meets one face to face.

I glide into the far corner and wonder if I should expose myself to the witch in perhaps my most terrifying form. I think not. I am here as a spy, after all, and the first rule of spying is *do not be seen.*

#

Yolanda has regained her wits, has her hand bandaged by La Bruja, and now we have moved to another part of the cave. Here, a clear opening into the rock above creates a natural skylight that provides brightness for their discussion.

"Tell me where I can find my daughter and her lover," Señora Yolanda asks the witch.

The creature lets out a sharp cackle, reaches into her apron and pulls out a handful of small bones. She tosses them into the air and watches where they fall and the pattern that they make.

"Very interesting," says La Bruja. She studies them and then she gathers up the bones and tosses them again.

"Second opinion," she adds with a smile. "Same results."

"And what do they tell you?" La Señora asks.

"I can show you exactly where Eva and her lover are," answers the witch. "Follow me." We run down another dark passageway and come to a large underground lake whose blue-green water is surrounded by a wall of small stalagmites. They stand like dwarves who watch the witch and all that she does.

La Bruja smiles, bends forward and sticks a boney finger into the water. Ripples rush out from her touch, and within them we can see a pathway through the jungle.

Señora Yolanda and I gape in wonder, and I know that the witch is showing us the very road that Eva and Señor Popcorn followed to get to the home of Doña Cuca.

"Another point-of-view?" La Bruja asks and, with a simple flick of her fingers in the water, the vision shifts, and we are flying through the jungle seeing through the eyes of Eva and me when we drove to Doña Cuca's home in the Jeep.

"Perhaps Eva is there even now," La Bruja says, as she splashes again. The water becomes cloudy, then clears again to give us a view inside the window of Señor Popcorn's room. He and Eva are embracing right beside his bed.

"¡Bastardo!" calls Yolanda, "I'll get him for this." And then she smiles cruelly. "Better yet, I'll let Enrique's men get him."

She cackles like a witch herself and wrings her hands in a hungry way. La Bruja joins her in evil laughter that grows and becomes so crazy that I feel terrified.

"Wait a minute," I say to myself, "I'm the ghost here. I'm the one with supernatural powers, and it's up to me to do something about all this."

Forgetting my vow to do no more than listen, I fly into the lake, enter the soul of the water, and take over the ripples where La Bruja's hand still plays.

I shriek, and my ugliness fills the lake.

"DO NOT DO THIS!" I screech in a voice that rings across the caverns.

The women fall backwards. Señora Yolanda turns and scrambles back through the cave, down passageways, through dark tunnels out of the secret doorway, and into the daylight. Then she dives onto her mare and rides off in panic. But the witch falls to her knees beside the lake. She prays, and then returns to the waters edge to explore.

Perhaps she will find some false explanation for my ghostly appearance. Perhaps the witch will convince Yolanda that it's safe to visit the place where Eva and Señor Popcorn are hiding. Perhaps La Señora will send her husband's men to find the popcorn man and execute him.

I decide that I cannot take chances with any of this. The very best thing I can do is ride back to Doña Cuca's home. There I will warn Eva of the dangers soon to come. And so I glide out of the cave, climb onto Espanto Negro and challenge him to get to the home of the curandera as quickly as possible.

We are there in minutes.

He is a ghost horse, after all.

Chapter 10

It is afternoon when I rush into Doña Cuca's home. The old curandera is nowhere to be found, but there are many noises coming from the room where Señor Popcorn sleeps. Without thinking, I invisibly move through the wall and stop at once. The most thrilling scene I have ever known in my life is right there in front of me. Eva and Señor Popcorn are making wild love.

She sits astride him on the bed, facing him. She is totally naked, eyes fixed on his, riding him wildly up and down like a bucking vaquera. She gives excited little cheers and cries as she does. He is silent, barely visible, wrapped in sheets, his hands on her hips as she pumps upon him. Down … and then up again shaking and shimmying with each movement. Her hands move to her breasts, she squeezes them hard letting her nipples pinch out between her fingers. She is bright red with passion.

I am seeing her from the side, too thrilled to make a sound. Is this so exciting because they are such a handsome couple (even the popcorn man with his newly rebuilt muscles)? Or is it the act of love, which thrills me? I don't know, but suddenly I miss Carlitos so much that I find myself wishing that I were in his arms and I could ride him as Eva now bucks upon Señor Popcorn.

Eva turns to me, and she sees me because she is a curandera who can see ghosts. (Why do I always forget that?) I blush, but she smiles as she continues her delicious ride. She is beginning to move even more quickly now.

68

A great gasp comes from the popcorn man. Eve shudders, moving faster. Her body clenches, his jerks up and down and up again in wild rhythm. And suddenly they are both trembling and gasping and going faster and faster until, in the end, with a great cry, Eva falls forward on her lover and hugs him tightly as he cries out, "¡GRACIAS A DIOS!"

They both stiffen for a long moment, and then they melt together.

I stand wide-eyed, not feeling anything but desire for my Carlitos. Then Eva, so relaxed as she lies on Señor Popcorn's chest, turns her head to me, smiles again, and winks.

#

Now, an hour later, we are all running around. Doña Cuca has heard my warning and decided that we must move to her other house at once. Her second home is much deeper in the jungles of this state, Quintana Roo. It is much harder to find. The nearest village of any kind is called Tizimin.

Eva and Señor Popcorn are still in the afterglow of their lovemaking. Though they do their best to help Doña Cuca carry her bundles of herbs and plants to the Jeep so that we can be away as soon as possible, they continue to stop and kiss and look into each other's eyes and sigh and giggle. This is still beautiful, I think, but it is also starting to get annoying.

I have no idea how long it will take Señora Yolanda to explain things to her husband and have him send his killers after us, but I know that our time is short, and so I urge everyone along. Doña Cuca has been most generous with us, but most of the things we are packing are hers. She says that it has been so long since she has been in her old place that she cannot be sure she will have everything she needs.

Finally, I watch Señor Popcorn stuff the last great bundle of leaves and twigs and bark into the back of the Jeep, we add another box of Eva's clothes, and then he climbs behind the wheel. Eva sits beside him, still smiling in dizziness from her afternoon of love. Doña Cuca tumbles into the back seat with jars full of roots and herbs.

"A prayer for our journey?" she asks.

"Heavenly Father," Señor Popcorn prays, "Please help us make it through this wicked jungle and lead us to a safe place where the bad guys will not find us. And, oh yes, again Señor, GRACIAS!"

Eva giggles at those words and swats him.

"Amen," La Doña and I answer, and finally, we are off.

Señor Popcorn drives the Jeep through the jungle following Doña Cuca's directions. Once again, there is a narrow dirt road ahead of us. Doña Cuca is quick to point out the *cenotes*, which are everywhere. These are deep sinkholes in the soil, almost all of which is made of limestone. The cenotes are often entrances into long rows of caves and underground lakes. I think of my visit to La Bruja and decide that her home must have been deep inside one of these.

The road is deserted except for the lizards and snakes that sun themselves on its surface and then move angrily out of our way as we plow through the sticky heat. We must get through Tizimin and then out beyond it for another dozen miles or so. That part of the journey may be difficult because the jungle treetops rise high above us and the humidity rises too. So does the thick layer of bugs that splash their bodies over the front windshield nearly blocking Señor Popcorn's view as he drives along.

Still we are happy: Eva has fallen even more deeply in love with Señor Popcorn and he with her. Doña Cuca will visit her old home that she hasn't seen in ten years. I feel good knowing that the day is coming when I will be with Carlitos again.

But the best thing of all, everyone agrees, is that the Jeep is air-conditioned.

#

The shooting starts two hours later as we pass through the far side of Tizimin. A small band of local policía gathers beside a bridge as our Jeep passes over it. There is no river here, just a wash that might run swiftly during the rains, but now there is nothing, just three men with rifles who begin shooting at the Jeep, trying to gun down Señor Popcorn.

The first bullets ping across the hood, and Señor Popcorn immediately ducks down. Eva does not move so quickly, and when the next bullet flashes through the side window, it strikes her. More shots follow.

The popcorn man looks at his love in panic. But I can see that the bullet has only grazed her shoulder, though her blood has splattered onto the seat and her lover.

"I'm okay, Fernando," Eva says, "Just keep moving."

And he does. He drives across the bridge and up the road. But la policía have a car too, a battered old Crown Victoria cop car. They climb into it and come after us.

The road is straight, so it is simply a race. A brand new Jeep Grand Cherokee against an aging cop car. There is also an added ingredient: the man driving our Jeep is skilled in the chase, and even through these boys know the roads, Señor Popcorn knows how to make a getaway. He floors it, our heads jerk back, and he leaves la policía in the dust.

Half an hour later, Señor Popcorn thinks we are far enough ahead, so he pulls off to the side of the road so we can care for Eva.

Our car is loaded down with cures of all kinds, so Doña Cuca has something she can put on Eva's wound. Señor

Popcorn pulls a flask from his coat pocket and offers Eva a swallow of tequila to help ease the pain. Then, he takes four big gulps himself, and looks on in sorrow as the operation begins.

Doña Cuca opens the girl's blouse, then uses her knife to dig the bullet out of her shoulder.

Eva bears the operation much better than her lover, who cries out as the blade enters Eva's wound and digs out the bullet. Even when the curandera wraps Eva's shoulder in leaves that will help the healing and draw out any poison, the girl is strong, but the popcorn man whimpers.

The operation is performed in the back seat of the Jeep as we sit by the side of the road. Señor Popcorn is so focused on his love that he fails to see the old cop car creeping up. La policía pull up beside us. Eva is the first to see them. She looks out of the side window just as Doña Cuca completes her work.

Eva gasps as the cop car driver pulls out a pistol and aims it directly at her face. Señor Popcorn concentrates so hard on the operation that he is aware of nothing else.

Now he glances up, but it is too late for him to do anything.

The driver of the cop car is about to blow Eva's beautiful face across the jungle. But just then, the cop recognizes her. He knows who she is. He drops the gun, slams the car into reverse, makes a squealing backward turn, and speeds off to Tizimin.

Everyone in the Jeep catches their breath and says a silent prayer of thanks.

There is wonderful news but also terrible news, I decide.

Eva has been saved. As the curandera's healing works, she will recover. But these policía *recognized* her, so they must know that her father is Enrique Córdoba. That is the bad part.

Soon, Enrique and Yolanda will know exactly where we are. And then the battle will really begin.

II
Carlos

Chapter 11

The butler says, "There's a Dr. Carlos Mann of Leland University to see you, sir."

He has gone to the far room, speaking in a clipped British accent, and after a moment there's a mumbled response that I can't quite hear.

"It has to do with de Cervantes … a new business venture," the butler adds. "Dr. Mann says you'll want to know about it."

I'm waiting in the entryway of the Córdoba estate in Cancun. There's more unintelligible mumbling, and then the butler comes back into the entryway. He arches his eyebrows, checks me out from head to toe, gives me a judgmental smile, and says, "Mr. Córdoba will see you now."

"Thanks, Jeeves," I answer.

"Jennings, sir."

"Sorry. I thought all butlers were named Jeeves."

He's not amused. "Right this way, Doc," he answers. I wince.

I follow Jennings into a great room with large luxurious couches, a grand piano, and original paintings hanging on every wall. It feels like an art gallery.

Enrique Córdoba stands in the center of the room, staring at one of the paintings. He's tall, well built, with a pencil-thin mustache and classic gray hair. He wears a pair of pleated tan slacks and a white linen shirt.

"Dr. Mann," he says holding out his hand to greet me, but he sure looks like he doesn't trust me.

"Señor Córdoba."

We shake. Jennings bows and makes his exit.

"So you represent Fernando de Cervantes, is that right?"

"Not really, but he's asked me to convey a message."

"He's run off with my daughter, you know?" Córdoba growls, and he looks like he wants to punch me in the mouth.

"I heard that his home was attacked," I answer. "And he felt that he had to go into hiding."

"With my daughter."

"It's my understanding that she wanted to go with him, that it was her idea that they hide."

Córdoba shakes his head and gives me a wry smile.

"Do you have a daughter, Señor? I see that you wear a wedding ring."

I'm a little unnerved by his question.

"My wife died in the third year of our marriage," I say. "We had not yet been blessed with children. I wear the ring as a tribute to our love."

Señor Córdoba's smile lessens. "A romantic, eh? Not that you're a lucky man, Doctor, but at least you've been spared the heartbreak of daughters."

Hell of a start to a conversation, huh?

"As for Fernando de Cervantes," Cordoba continues, "he's a criminal, wanted by the Mexican Government for drug trafficking. I could have you arrested for being part of his organization."

I smile. He's not going to intimidate me with this shit.

"I'm not part of Señor de Cervantes' organization; I merely came to deliver a message."

Córdoba stares at me for a long moment, then he sighs.

"Forgive me. I've just learned that my daughter has been injured in a shooting. Do you know anything about it?"

"No, I don't." (Talk about bad timing.) "Is she all right?"

"Yes, but only because the morons who were trying to gun her down finally recognized her. They reported that they had shot her but that, fortunately, it was only a slight wound."

"Who did it?"

"La policía in the town of Tizimin. They were trying to kill your boss."

"He's not my boss," I answer. "But ... I'm sorry about what happened to your daughter."

"She's wounded, still hiding out with de Cervantes, and now you're stupid enough to come here with some kind of message from him."

"He loves your daughter, Señor."

"And to prove it, he's putting her life at risk."

"That may be *your* doing."

Córdoba turns and gives me a killing look. Then he begins pacing the floor. His hands are behind his back; his head is bowed. He turns to me and stares. I recognize the expression. In his soul, he's scared.

"All right," he says, "So, let's hear what Señor de Cervantes has to say?"

I take out a neatly folded piece of paper, open it, and read from the notes I've prepared. "He says that he loves your daughter, Señor. And that she loves him too."

Córdoba's look is outrage, but he says nothing.

"He says that he would do anything to have her hand in marriage ... with your blessing, hopefully."

That makes Córdoba even angrier.

"In order to make it happen, he is prepared to turn over his operation to the government and let you do whatever you want with his crops."

"He's talking millions and millions of dollars worth of illegal drugs," Córdoba says.

If I answer him in any way it could make me some kind of accomplice, I think. So, I don't respond at all. Instead I just continue reading from the note.

"In return, once the land is cleared, he wants it back. He's entering a new business venture, and he intends to direct all his resources toward it."

"And the new venture is legitimate?"

"Corn. I've been to the United States and discussed his plans with the US Department of Agriculture. They are interested in encouraging his efforts under NAFTA."

Córdoba eyes the corner of the room, and I see that there is a bar there. "Would you like a drink, Doctor?"

I nod.

We go to the bar. He pours me a shot of tequila and one for himself. "I think your boss is insane," he says.

"He's not my boss," I repeat. "But I know he's deadly serious."

"Deadly is the operative word."

"Not if you and he can come to an agreement," I clink glasses with him and down mine in one swallow.

"Everyone could benefit," I say. "The Mexican government could say that they closed down the biggest drug operation in Mexico. The other drug dealers would be frightened by your success. The world would benefit from his plans to expand the growing of corn in Mexico; global warming would be lessoned by the addition of much more clean fuel into the marketplace. Mexico's economy would be strengthened, and our poor people would finally be able to afford tortillas again."

Córdoba smiles as though he's impressed. "You understand the dynamics of the corn market then, Dr. Mann."

"I've done my homework," I say. "I have formal documents to show you. Letters of intent from the United States government, letters of support from corn growing cooperatives. I'll be happy to go over them with you."

"There's no need," he says. "I represent Mexico. I don't negotiate with criminals ... especially when they've taken my daughter prisoner!"

I ignore the comment and lift my glass to him so that he will pour me another shot of tequila, but he doesn't. So, I take the bottle and pour one for myself.

"Think about it this way, Señor," I say. "This is an opportunity to do something good for Mexico."

I down the tequila and pour myself another. Córdoba glares at me and then, suddenly, he smiles.

"Dr. Man*cowski*," he draws out the letters of my name suggesting that I'm something other than what I claim to be. A sour look twists his face. "You teach Logic at Leland University, do you not?"

"Sí, Señor."

"I studied the subject a little in my youth. So, here's a syllogism for you, Doctor:

- *If* the Mexican government will not bargain with drug dealers
- *And* Fernando de Cervantes is a drug dealer
- *Then* the Mexican government will not bargain with Señor de Cervantes.
QED

"Have you enjoyed my tequila, Dr. Mann?"

I just stare at him.

"I hope so, because now I must ask you to leave. I will rescue my daughter from your boss in my own time and in my own way. Then I will see that he does not live long enough to ever see her again."

"It's a mistake, Señor."

"No. I don't think so. It is you, Doctor, Señor Popcorn, and unfortunately my daughter who are making the mistakes. But don't worry. I intend to rectify them all.

"Good day, Señor."

Chapter 12

I've returned after my disappointing meeting with Enrique Córdoba, and now, as I approach Señor Popcorn's vast hacienda, a ghost comes flying through the walls. She zooms up to me and begins hugging and kissing me before I can even see who she is.

"Carlitos, mi delicioso taquito, mi pequeño héroe."

I'm embarrassed and wonder what the hell Señor Popcorn's guards are thinking. Then, I pull back and gaze into the dark Mexican eyes of Alicia's old friend and fellow model, Sylvia Morales. God, she's hot! The guards wish they were me. I'm sure of it.

"What're you doing here?" I ask.

"Thought you could maybe use my help," she says.

The same maniac who murdered Alicia slit Sylvia's throat a few years ago. She wears the big scar across her neck rather proudly. She doesn't mind mixing it up at all.

"So, you know that you've come at a very dangerous time?"

"I do, Carlitos. The ghost network is vast, and they told us of the dangers to Señor Popcorn and his new lady love."

"Do you know where they are?"

"In the hut of an old curandera many miles into the jungles beyond Tizimin."

"Can you take me there, and to Alicia?"

"Better you go to Tizimin and I bring her to you."

"Why would you do that?"

"I fear that Enrique and his men will follow you, Carlitos. I fear that you will lead them to the home of the old curandera, and they will overwhelm the place and kill everyone, even Eva."

"So I'll have to bring some troops with me then?"

"Sí, Señor."

I pull out my cell phone and call Señor Popcorn's lieutenants Miguel Carillo and Victor Estephan, as Sylvia and I walk up to the hacienda. She lets me open the great door for her, and then glides in ahead of me.

Miguel and Victor are with us in minutes, and the three of us open a bottle of brandy and get into some serious planning and drinking.

"There are policía in Tizimin," Miguel says. "Enrique can supplement them with his own anti-narcotics troops and have quite a force."

"Why would he want that many armed men?" I ask.

Sylvia smiles. "Because he'll anticipate that you and Señor Popcorn's soldiers will come to Tizimin and try to defend El Patrón."

"But we don't know where he is."

"I can tell you, Carlitos," Sylvia says. "But, as I say, I'd better not. Better to let Eva and Señor Popcorn stay behind and be safe when the shooting starts."

"Even at that, I think you'll have to sneak into Tizimin," Miguel adds. "No point in banging and clanging your way there so that Enrique can get a good count of the number of men we have … and then outnumber us."

Victor has been listening to the conversation, and now he speaks up.

"We have trucks that go through the region. Their cargo is disguised as shipments of hemp. We can load men into those trucks and make them part of the transport. Enrique will know that the trucks belong to us, he may guess that we have men in them, but at least he won't know how many."

"I was hoping I could get there in a hurry," I say.

"Safer for you to ride in the back of one of the trucks," Miguel answers.

Sylvia grins. "I don't think Carlitos's sense of urgency has anything to do with troops and battles, Miguel."

She gives him a naughty kiss on the cheek. "Carlitos wants to get to Tizimin so that he can find his wife and make love to her. Am I not right, Dr. Mann?"

I smile and shrug.

Miguel's eyes widen. "For the sake of love, Doctor," he says, "I'll take you there secretly myself."

#

So, now I'm in a little hotel room in Tizimin, state of Quintana Roo, Yucatan, Mexico. The place is clean enough, but really small. Miguel has dropped me here after a hell of a motorcycle ride on side roads, dirt trails, and nearly non-existent jungle paths. Needless to say, no one knows I'm here.

I've showered, shaved, put on a clean white linen shirt and a new pair of jeans. And now I stand trying to sort out all the pills and toiletries that I've laid out on the top of the small dresser.

I want them to be neat and orderly so that when Alicia finally shows up they won't distract her ... or me.

"You look so handsome, mi amor," I imagine her saying.

Yeah, right. I showered until I ran out of water, brushed my teeth till my gums bled, and I still don't feel good enough for her.

"And you smell very nice too."

That actually *did* sound like her voice.

I look around and, of course, she's not there.

"Body wash and the sweet smell of Carlitos; what more could a girl want?"

I spin around again. I can't see her, but now I'm starting to catch on to her game.

"Talking invisibly, Alicia?"

"Sometimes it's the best way to talk, mi amor."

"And if I catch you, can I give you a good spanking for it?"

"You have never laid a hand on me, Carlitos. Don't forget, I have quite a temper."

I feel a sharp crack across my ass. It tingles.

"How do *you* like that, Señor?"

She slaps me again, but I manage to catch her invisible wrist and hold onto it as she slowly materializes in front of me.

"I hear that you want to see me. Is that correct, Señor?"

I nod and release my grasp.

"Then see," she says as she puts her hands on her hips and stands there, allowing me to drink in her beauty. She's wearing a broad, full-length, jaguar print dress with a neckline that plunges down to a wide, black, patent leather belt. Her matching shoes have inch-high platforms and 6-inch heels. A satin jacket with rolled-up sleeves completes the exotic look.

I lick my lips.

"You like what you see?" "Ummmm."

Alicia glides up to me, reaches for me and …

SLAPS ME HARD ACROSS THE FACE.

"What was that?"

"Punishment for not letting me know that you were leaving me for so long."

"But Señor Popcorn insisted."

"And since when does he keep you from telling his secrets to your wife … especially when she's a ghost?"

She slaps me again.

"You could have saved me from so much misunderstandings," she says.

84

"I'm sorry."

"You had better be. I told you I have not yet learned to control my passions."

"Your *passions*?"

"Sí. Anger is a passion, is it not, Carlitos?"

I smile. Now we're getting somewhere. "Are there other passions you haven't yet learned to control?"

"I think you know the others very well, Señor."

She steps back, gives me a sexy smile, and removes that leather belt. I sigh as she continues to study me.

"Well?" she asks.

"Well, what?"

Uh, oh. She wants me to take something off too, and I know that she has so many more layers than I do. Still, I undo a few buttons of my shirt.

She giggles and slides out of her jacket.

I'm starting to like this. I unbutton the rest of my shirt and leave it hanging open.

Alicia slides out of her jaguar print dress and reveals a delicious bra and panty set in matching jaguar print. She cocks her hip assuming one of the poses from her modeling days. WOW!

I undo my cuffs and drop my shirt to the floor.

"Ummm," she sighs as she moves toward me.

"You always were rock hard, mi amor." And she trails her fingers over my chest and abdomen before she reaches behind her and unhooks the back of her bra.

"Only for you, babe," I answer.

I unzip my jeans and let them hang there.

Alicia leans forward and lets her bra fall, catching it so that she's holding it against her breasts. She smiles.

"And only for you, mi amor." She slowly lowers the bra, revealing her perfect breasts. She lets the bra fall away, and now she's standing there nearly naked, staring boldly into my eyes as they devour her entire body.

I slam my jeans to the floor and step quickly away from them. All I have left is a pair of tight gray bicycle briefs that can barely contain my excitement.

My eyes are locked on hers as she takes in all of me. She's obviously enjoying every muscle that I've worked so hard to maintain.

"You *are* beautiful, Carlitos," she sighs.

"Como eres, Alicia." I whisper. As are you. "But now it's your turn."

"Yes, it is," she answers. But instead of losing those jaguar skin panties, she glides up to me, reaches for the sides of my briefs and drops them to the floor.

I spring to attention.

"First, let's see what we can do with *this*, okay?" she giggles.

"Oh, yeah!"

Chapter 13

I wake the next morning to a hard pounding at the door of my hotel room. Alicia is wrapped in my arms. Ghosts don't sleep, I think, but she sure doesn't looks like she's awake.

I nudge her, and she opens those pretty eyes. "One more time please, Carlitos," she begs.

Amazing!

The pounding on the door gets louder. "Who is that?" she asks.

"Pssst, it's Miguel," comes a whisper from outside.

"What's the point of whispering, pendejo?" I shout at him. "You've just about knocked the fucking building down."

I stagger to the door and open it for him. Alicia goes invisible. "The men are here, Doc," he says.

I don't like the nickname, but what the hell. "How many?"

"You gonna let me in?" he asks.

"Oh, yeah."

Miguel staggers into the room, and grins. "Was your pretty ghost-wife here last night?"

I roll my eyes. "Never mind that. How many men are here?"

"I'll bet she's as gorgeous as ever, huh?"

I shrug. "You *know* she's gorgeous."

"After so many years?"

"Damn straight. How many men, pendejo?"

He giggles. "She's almost as sweet as my Marie Elena, I'll bet?"

"How god damn many men did you bring with you, Miguel?"

"Oh, that, twenty plus one."

"Plus one? Who's the one … you?"

"No. I'm part of the twenty."

"Who then?"

"Señor Popcorn."

I can't believe it. After all the care we've taken to protect him, Señor Popcorn's has decided to show up anyway.

"Alicia!" I call, and she appears. Fortunately she's chosen a more modest outfit for the morning. Now she's wearing jeans, flats, and a black t-shirt with the words *Angel Wannabe* splashed across her chest.

"Did you know about Señor Popcorn coming here?"

"Sí, Carlitos," she says. "Please don't be mad. Sylvia tried to talk him out of it, but he said his place was here with his men. I came with him, protecting him all the way, ready to transform myself into a leopard and defend him if I had to. All I had left when I got to you were my spots which you saw on my gown and on my …"

"Never mind that," I interrupt quickly. "What happened when you got him here?"

"Miguel's men had just arrived. I left Señor Popcorn with them and came straight to you."

I shake my head in exasperation. Alicia doesn't seem to have become any more logical now that she's a ghost. On the other hand, *if* Señor Popcorn had come to our room last night, *then* our evening of lovemaking might not have happened. So, maybe she used pretty good logic after all.

"Señor Popcorn is safe, I assure you," Miguel says. "He's surrounded by twenty of his best compadres … make that nineteen. I'm here."

"Any word on Enrique?"

"Sí. He and ten of his agents are on their way in a small convoy. They hope to pick up another four policía when they get to Tizimin."

"So fourteen against twenty."

"Except for one other thing, Doc," Miguel adds. "We picked up some radio chatter telling us that Maclovio Renta and another ten of his men are on their way here too."

Maclovio Renta, El Mago, the wizard, is Señor Popcorn's archenemy. He's the guy who destroyed the popcorn man's great house just outside of Mexico City only a year ago.

"Just what we need," I add, "a whole other force going up against us."

"I don't know, Doc," Miguel says with a smile that's almost pure evil. "I've been looking forward to meeting up with El Mago again. I've got a score to settle with him, remember?" And he holds up his right hand, which has no fingers. The wizard had them all chopped off in our last encounter.

#

Over the next three days the village of Tizimin is treated to tension like it's never known before. Señor Popcorn and his men are secluded in a little hacienda at the edge of town. Enrique and the assorted feds are in an old hotel on the main square. El Mago is nowhere to be seen. If we didn't have Miguel's ongoing assurance that the wizard and his troops were here, I'm not sure any of us would believe it.

Still, we often crisscross the town square on various errands, and occasionally, we catch sight of la policía who eye us suspiciously but do not stop us or say anything at all.

My nights are filled with Alicia's desperate lovemaking. I've come up with a new obsession, possibly to take my mind off of the upcoming showdown. Here's how it came about.

"Oh Carlitos, you are so sweet, and so wonderful," my wife tells me after our second night of lovemaking. And then she looks shocked and whispers, "Oh, no!"

"What is it?" I'm trying to remake a bed that has just about fallen apart from the power of our passion.

"You are too good, Carlitos, and that's a big problem."

I know I'm not too good, but I decide to humor her. "How come being good is a problem?" I ask.

"Don't you see, my love? I am being kept out of heaven because of my anger. While you, Carlitos, if you die, will go straight there. There will be no grand reunion in the afterlife. You will be in Paradise, and I will be in Purgatory ... and I don't mean the bookstore."

I laugh. "I've committed my share of sins."

"Oh yes. But the church has such strange rules." She pouts and bites her lip. "Who knows what's really a sin according to them. Like, you know, you can kill your wife and go to confession, but if you divorce her there is no confession or forgiveness. You go straight to hell."

"I doubt that God is that illogical."

"Believe me, Carlitos, any God who would allow such rules must have some very strange ideas."

So, now I start obsessing all the time. I don't want to put myself in any kind of danger because death might mean going straight to heaven and losing Alicia for a large chunk of eternity. I shouldn't allow myself to follow such illogical thinking, but since Alicia's terrible death made me so obsessive, I do it all the time.

I continue my meetings with Señor Popcorn and his band, but I'm unsure of myself, unsteady, and that can be deadly. The days drag by; the tension mounts. It's a week later, and suddenly, there's an intervention.

At exactly high noon, a Mexican woman struts out into the middle of the street and begins shouting. She's dressed in wide gaucho pants, a black silk shirt, a red bandanna, wildly painted cowboy boots, and an equally crazy hat. Two gunbelts crisscross her chest, and she carries a rifle.

"DAD, FERNANDO," she shouts, "COME OUT HERE AND TALK TO ME!"

It's Eva Cordoba.

"I thought you convinced her to stay out of this?" I growl at Alicia.

"I tried," she responds. "So did Sylvia. I thought we had her convinced, but she's a woman, she does what she pleases, and during a life and death struggle, she does what she thinks is *right*."

"And it's right to run into the middle of the street and get gunned down?"

"It's right to try and stop your lover and your father from killing each other."

"I MEAN IT, YOU TWO," Eva calls. "COME OUT HERE!"

There is a long silence and then slowly Señor Popcorn's men file out of the hacienda, and behind them comes El Patron himself. They walk slowly toward Eva who turns to them and smiles. She moves confidently through the crowd of gunmen, takes Señor Popcorn by the hand, leads him to the front of the crowd, and stands beside him. He puts his arm around her.

"FATHER, COME OUT HERE AND TALK TO US!" Eva shouts.

The doors to the old hotel across the street open, and la policía and Mexican anti-drug agents form a wall of protection for Enrique Córdoba.

The tall handsome man walks past his troops and up to his daughter and the man he has been trying to apprehend for the last fifteen years.

"If you turn yourself in right now," he says to Señor Popcorn, "the government will go easy on you."

"He's offered to give up the drug trade, Papá," Eva says. "He's agreed to turn to a life that will help the Mexican people and the world. He needs to be exonerated."

"That's up to the courts," Enrique says to her. "Are you going to come peacefully, Fernando, or do we have to take you by force?"

"I WON'T LET YOU TAKE HIM!" Eva almost spits the words at her father.

Guns cock on both sides as I make my way belatedly through the crowd and up to the three principals now standing in the center of the street. Opposing gunmen are lined up on every side.

Eva does not know me, but she smiles when I arrive. Her father is less receptive. "We don't need any faulty logic right now, Doctor," he says. "This is a legal issue."

"I can see that," I answer. "But *if* the President of Mexico has the power to commute sentences, and he does, right?"

Enrique nods impatiently. We can hear more guns being cocked all around us.

"And *if* the Mexican government has the power to seize land and then restore it to its rightful owner, and they do, don't they?"

Enrique nods again.

"*Then* it's possible to find a legal solution that will satisfy both parties."

"Maybe," Enrique mumbles. "Risky, though."

"For me, not you," Señor Popcorn answers through gritted teeth.

"It can work," I say, "all we have to do is ..."

And just then a bullet zings right over my shoulder. I fall to the ground. Three men rush in front of Enrique to protect him. Señor Popcorn's men do the same. I scramble out of the street as bullets blast, and everyone runs for cover.

Señor Popcorn has already lost four men and the rest of them have ducked down behind the cars that are parked on one side of the street. The feds are across from them, hiding behind the planters in front of the hotel. Occasionally someone races out and fires at his opponents. But too many men are falling. Even though there are no clear shots for the opposing gunmen, men who should be under cover are beginning to die.

Miguel nudges me and points to the window over the market. Gunfire blasts from it.

"El Mago," he curses and bolts for the door of the market. The men in the window spot him and riddle his body with bullets. He falls, calling out the name "Marie Elena."

Four more of Señor Popcorn's men rush into the market and up the stairs. As the shooting continues in the street, it's joined by a barrage of gunfire from the window above the market. Then silence settles everywhere.

We wait, not daring to move.

The door to the market opens and El Mago's men burst into the open. They have submachine guns and they take out half of Señor Popcorn's remaining men. Then they charge across the street and annihilate the feds.

Enrique and one of his deputies are all who are left. They run toward us, easy shooting for Señor Popcorn's men.

"Hold up," the popcorn man calls, and he rushes out directly into the line of fire to get Enrique.

It's now six of us: Señor Popcorn, Enrique Córdoba, Eva, two other men and me facing El Mago and at least twenty gunmen.

"Give up that pendejo, Fernando," El Mago calls. "My fight's not with you today."

Little by little, more of El Mago's men move out of the market and take up positions all around us.

"We'll let you and your lady friend go free," El Mago calls.

"Just give us Enrique."

I shake my head and turn to Señor Popcorn. "You don't believe him, do you?"

The popcorn man just laughs.

"Then, how the fuck do we get out of this one?"

Señor Popcorn smiles. "Sometimes, amigo, you have to be more than logical. You have to be *creative*." And he reaches in his shirt pocket, pulls out an iPhone, and hits one button in the middle of the screen.

The old hacienda where he and his men were staying ... EXPLODES!

Out of the ashes, an M1 ABRAMS TANK comes rolling along. On either side of the massive machine are columns of men and women dressed in jungle camo combat gear. They are each carrying an assault rifle except for those at the very head of the brigade who are armed with rocket launchers.

"An overwhelming show of force," Señor Popcorn cheers as Renta's men scatter at the sight of the oncoming assault.

The popcorn man turns to Enrique and gives him a crooked grin. "You think you're playing with kids, amigo?"

Eva's father is not amused. He stands and dusts himself off. Then he holds out his hand to his daughter.

"Eva!" he commands.

She looks from her lover to her father and back again. Anger and tears are mixing in her eyes. Suddenly, Señor Popcorn picks up one of the pistols that is lying on the ground and points it at Enrique.

"No!" Eva screams. Enrique steels himself.

Señor Popcorn fires directly over the fed's shoulder, nailing one of El Mago's few remaining soldiers who has decided to finish the assignment even though it will cost him his life ... which it does.

As I look out across the square I can see Señor Popcorn's soldiers rounding up the last of El Mago's men. I'm sure The Wizard has escaped as always. Disappearing is one of his very best tricks.

The popcorn man now stands. Enrique is staring at him, dumbfounded. Señor Popcorn tosses the pistol away, shrugs at the man he had hoped would be his father-in-law, and then turns and simply walks away.

In a moment Eva goes running after him.

Chapter 14

A shaving mug comes sailing at me. It hits hard, and bounces off my gut. I'm upset for two reasons. First, I've just done 200 crunches, and you'd think, after a workout like that, the cup would *shatter* against my abs. It didn't. Second, Alicia's pissed at me again … for no reason. Okay, there *is* a reason; I know what it is, and it's time to face the music. But before I can, she wings two ornate glasses at me, followed by a small hand mirror and then a bowl full of sponges that's been sitting on the floor just outside the shower.

The sponges just bounce off me, but the big porcelain bowl that contained them raps me good on the head and then shatters all over the floor.

"What do you mean you want to go back to California, Carlitos?" Alicia flashes into an angry presence in front of me. She's wearing high heels, tight jeans, and a red t-shirt with the words: ***Don't F*** With The Ghost***, spelled out across her nipples. She's not wearing a bra.

"I got a letter this morning telling me Dr. Danielson died."

Alicia flips from fury to real sorrow in an instant. "He was such a good man, and he was your friend. He gave you your PhD and your job, and all the rest, did he not?"

"Something like that," I say with a sympathetic smile. Alicia never did understand the workings of the university.

"But it doesn't matter," she says stomping her foot and looking around for something else to throw. "We have been here only a month, and Chinatown is still after you."

"Not Chinatown," I answer, "just one crazy Chinese chick."

"A crazy Chinese chick who is also very powerful."

I sit down on the edge of the bed and stare at the floor for a moment.

"I can't stay away forever. If Charlotte Burke becomes the new Dean of the Philosophy Department, we'll have some latitude. But if she doesn't, the department could give me a very rough time."

Alicia walks up and stands in front of me, she cocks her hip, folds her arms across her chest, and begins to tap her foot.

"Tell me how, please?"

"Well, for one thing they could fire me."

"No, they could not," she warns as she arches her eyebrows.

"Okay, probably not," I say. "But I might end up teaching more classes, working longer hours, doing less of the things I like to do, you know."

"No, I do not know those things. But I do know that there is someone in Chinatown who wants to kill you and another person there who wants to marry you even though you are already married to me. We can stay here. You can work for Señor Popcorn. It is very simple."

"Except that I'm a teacher, not a farmer. I'd go nuts here."

"Better nuts here than dead there, mi amor."

I get up and walk across the bedroom and out the front door to get some fresh air. It's a beautiful morning and the grounds of Señor Popcorn's residence are magnificent. A macaw flits over to the palm tree that arches just outside the door. The bird squawks at me angrily. Guess Alicia even has allies among the birds. No peace out here, so I come back inside to face her.

"Look, I'm going back to the university, that's it. So, let's stop arguing; we have a wedding to plan."

Alicia plomps down on the bed and bites her lip. I can see that she's fighting to suppress her anger. And then she smiles, thank God. Hopefully, she's decided to focus on the wedding.

"I'm glad that Eva and the popcorn man will be married very soon," she coos. "I'm also glad that Señor Enrique surprised everyone by going along with all of Señor Popcorn's plans." And then she pouts. "But I'm unhappy with everything else. I want you to stay here in Mexico where we belong."

I sit down next to my wife and take her hands.

"I just can't do that. I need to attend Danielson's funeral, at least."

"I can understand that."

"I need to take over my class before the university decides that they don't need me."

"I may even be able to understand that."

"And besides, Tiger Joy has moved on to other things. It's been a month. How long can she stay mad at me?"

Alicia sighs.

"That I do not agree with. Tiger can stay mad at you for the rest of her life, and her soldiers can continue to hunt you until you are dead."

I look into Alicia's beautiful dark eyes, and I realize, unfortunately, that she's right.

III
Carlos

Chapter 15

I'm staring into nothingness … white nothingness … pure white.

Through it comes a vision, soft, fluttering: Alicia's eyes. "Am I dead?" I call out to the ghost of my beautiful wife.

"Almost," she whispers. "Almost dead."

"Good."

"No, Carlitos, not good."

I can feel her presence through the emptiness. And then she is all around me, enveloping me, caressing me, comforting me.

"I want to stay with you forever," I whisper.

"No, mi amor," she sighs. "You cannot."

It's all whiteness and the sweet caress of Alicia, and then there's the wrenching sound of heavy metal tearing, as though a car door is being ripped from a vehicle.

My head explodes with pain. "Alicia!"

Beyond the whiteness I can make out shadows, faces, figures moving, looking in at me. "Jesus!" someone mutters.

"ALICIA!" I call out.

She sighs. "You cannot be dead, Carlitos. You cannot stay with me in the ghost world for very long. There are new rumors that they have plans for me."

"They?"

"Those who run heaven and earth … and also purgatory."

Pain crackles through my body. My muscles are on fire the way they were at the end of my prize fights in Mexico, only this is so much worse. This is unbearable. I'm trying to move, or maybe someone else is moving me.

"There's still a pulse," a distant voice says. "He's still alive."

The whiteness returns. Alicia returns.

"Will it be good?" I ask her.

"How can it be good if I am away from you?"

Alicia's voice fades. Her gentle touch gives way to brutal pain. A red light swirls beyond the whiteness. Sirens are screaming. I'm screaming.

"We've freed him!"

The voices obliterate the whiteness.

"Careful now ... onto the stretcher."

I'm lifted through a sea of pain and land gently onto a gurney. I feel myself moving through the sun-baked street. Behind me I catch a glimpse of the mangled wreckage of the limo I was in as I rode to Dr. Danielson's burial.

Ironic, huh? I'm heading to someone else's funeral when some asshole comes barreling through the police barricade. For a second I flash on the front end of a silver Lexus as it screams toward me. There's a young Chinese kid driving it full throttle. He's actually smiling, like he's drugged up and on some suicide mission.

At that moment of absolute panic, I can remember Alicia's warning: "Her soldiers will continue to hunt you until you are dead." Then, there's a massive collision, a blast, bone-crushing pain, and the whiteness. Thankfully, with it comes oblivion; I feel nothing. I only hear my ghost wife whispering.

"Do not die, Carlitos. If you do, you will lose us forever."

Chapter 16

Hello, I'm Abigail, reads the nametag on the pretty Asian nurse who greets me the next time I open my eyes. There's something very familiar about her.

I'm aware of deep throbbing pain that's still everywhere in my body, but it's hidden under a blanket of narcotics. I see all kinds of tubes going into a PICC line that runs into my arm. One of them may be a morphine drip.

Abigail flits in and out of focus, I lose her, and I'm out of it again.

This time the nothingness is black ... dead black. But there are sounds. Things are being placed on a tray next to the bed. There's that little tinkle of medical instruments, the clunk of bottles, a spoon maybe dropping something into a glass of water?

My eyes pop open and the nurse is much closer now. Even though I'm doped up, Alicia's warning sets off sirens in my head as I read the fine print on my nurse's nametag.

Hello, I'm Abigail.
Abigail Joy, R.N. Leland Medical Center

That's right. My nurse is one of the Joy sisters.

Everything seems so surreal, the harsh brightness of the overhead light, the whiteness of the cabinets and walls, the fact that Nurse Abigail is wearing three-inch stiletto heels and red fishnet stockings. Her curvy shape weaves in and out of focus as she struts across the room, stoops over, and takes something from the counter. Then she turns, notices that my eyes are open, and smiles. "Oh, good, Dr. Mann," she coos. "You're just in time to watch. This'll be a lot of fun ... for me, not for you."

She moves right up to the bed and I see she's holding a terrifyingly long syringe. On the table beside the bed are a glass of water and a bottle of blue crystals that she's mixed into the water. The label on the bottle is small and I really can't read it. I squint, trying to concentrate. What the hell does it say?

STRYCHNINE!

Great. Just my luck.

I should be screaming now, but I'm not. Instead my obsessive-compulsive disorder kicks in, and, to hide from my growing terror, I start spooling through the things I know about the deadly poison. My parents kept a box of it in our little home in Mexico ... to kill rats. I remember the warning label saying something like:

NOT TO BE TAKEN BY HUMANS ... poisonous powder that acts within minutes ... If ingested, victim will experience terror, pain, muscle spasms, convulsions, stiffness in the arms and legs, arching of the back and neck, inability to breathe ... and soon death!

Nurse Abigail turns toward me and I focus on her nametag once again: Abigail Joy! Even in my drugged out state I know that this has to be one of Tiger's plans. She didn't get me with the car crash, so now she'll have one of her sisters do it with poison. Tiger always did like torture.

I'm surprised she's not here to watch.

"It's a little hot in here, don't ya think?" Abigail says as she sets the syringe on the edge of the table and undoes the top two buttons on her blouse. It pops open revealing the kind of expensively enhanced breasts that so many of the Joy sisters have purchased.

Abigail fans herself with her hand. "Murder is so damn exhausting." She grabs the PICC line, takes the syringe again, and moves it toward the line. She's going to add the strychnine directly into my IV, pumping the poison quickly into my system. But it won't kill me fast enough; I know that much. First, there'll be all the torture that Tiger is so fond of.

"At least I can give you something nice to look at as you go into convulsions," Abigail chirps as her voluptuous cleavage hovers over me. I strain to reach up and stop her, but I can't. My arms and legs are strapped to the bed.

"Had to tie you down, honey," she says. "Strychnine death is always so violent … all that thrashing around."

The syringe is moving toward the PICC line. I'm about to scream my damn head off. But suddenly the needle swerves away from the line as though it has a mind of its own. It struggles up into the air and seems to be fighting with Abigail as it jerks back and forth. Finally, it dives straight into *her* arm.

"WHAT!" Her expression contorts with the deadly realization that she's injected herself with one of the most painful poisons ever.

She drops the syringe, staggers back to the phone and screams into it. "Emergency, emergency! Room 701, emergency!"

Abigail eyes me frantically. Still, she realizes somehow that it will be a few minutes before the drug takes effect.

"You'll pay, you bastard," she calls as she grabs the syringe, reaches for the mixture of strychnine again, plunges the needle into it, and then draws in the poison. She brings the dripping needle toward me once again just as the door to the room flies open. Abigail is lifted up off the floor and thrown unceremoniously through the door and into the arms of two big male nurses who see the needle still in her hand. They instinctively dodge it as they pin her to the floor. One of them hovers over her as she begins to thrash.

"Poison! Strychnine! Help me!"

The second male nurse rushes to me.

"I'm the one whose been poisoned," Abigail calls. "Not that son of a bitch. He tried to murder me."

The nurse looks at her and then over to me. He pulls back my covers and sees the restraints. "I don't think so," he says.

"God damn it!" Abigail calls. "He twisted the fucking needle back against me, shoved the poison right into my arm," She realizes too late that her words are an admission that she's the murderer. But it doesn't matter now. She's raging. "Save meeeeee! He tried to kill my whole family, my mother and father, all of us!"

She arches her back violently, tosses her head from side to side, and gasps for breath. The first nurse is trying his best to restrain her.

"You okay, Dr. Mann?" the second nurse asks. I nod, "Better take care of her."

"Will do." But as he leaves me, I know that Nurse Abigail Joy is in for a whole boatload of suffering ... even if she does survive.

Chapter 17

Darkness again. Then through it moves my lovely wife. She's dressed in a short nightie. Her look is hungry. I'm still groggy, but she sure holds my attention.

"You saved me, didn't you?" I ask.

"I could not let you die at the hands of this Joy nurse, Carlitos," she answers. "I told you, you must stay alive." And now she sidles up to me with a look that suggests she has more than restful slumber on her mind.

"I have to keep you whole," she sighs. "I have to keep you well."

"You're doing a great job."

"Of course. But I can do more."

"Rest?" I ask. I am, after all, still drugged, still aware of all the painful bruises and a headache that's never ending. But at least it's all dulled down by the meds, more like "I don't care about the pain" than that it isn't there. On the other hand, this vision of my wife is something that I do care about.

"I will guard you, Carlitos. There will be no more Joy nurses with their poisons coming into your room."

"Thanks for that."

"Yes, and besides we have to talk."

"About?"

"Things …" she coos.

Alicia glides even closer to me in that sexy nightie. Her model's legs are on full display. In spite of all the drugs and pain, I'm really turned on. The nightie has an empire waist that enhances the kind of natural breasts that the Joy girls could never buy.

"Why are you wearing that nightgown?"

She giggles and bats those big dark eyes. She bites her lip, dances a little, doesn't answer. "Alicia?"

She pirouettes, then leans above me, bending down, kissing me: a ghost kiss, very solid, real, and wet.

"Alicia!"

Her long fingers slip her hair behind her ear. She glances away, and then back at me. "Sexual healing," she signs.

"For whom?"

"Both of us, Carlitos. I can make love to you so spiritually that you will not feel any strain at all, just happiness and relief. Then you will sleep as never before."

Damn! That sounds good.

"But I am allowed to say *I told you so*, am I not?"

"Yes, you are," I admit.

"Good."

She licks her lips. She licks *my* lips.

I reach for her and pain shoots up my arm and into my chest.

"No reaching, Carlitos. Perhaps I should tie you down the way that Joy nurse did."

"No need."

"Sí," she whispers, and just to prove the point she lowers the front of her nightgown. Her breasts jump out at me.

I try to reach for her again.

"No, mi amor," she sighs. "Like this."

And suddenly she's floating above me, this half naked vision of my wife. She glides out of the nightgown and lowers herself onto me, over me, through me, becoming transparent, becoming one with me, until all I can do is *feel* her. But man, do I feel her, everywhere, especially in all the places that count. I don't have to move a muscle to have the hottest ghost sex I've ever known.

It's amazing.

#

I wake the next morning to see a young doctor studying me. "Good morning, Dr. Mann," she says. "I'm Debra Shapiro."

She's younger than I am. That's disconcerting. Short, with a cute brown bob, thick glasses, and studied, perfect diction.

"Did you have a good night's sleep?"

Oh yeah!

"The consensus is that you're on the mend," she says, "maybe out of here in another few days. How would you like that?"

"Very much."

"There will be a lot of rehab, of course."

She's wearing a white lab coat, a black pencil skirt, and sensible black shoes. She keeps looking from me to my chart and back again. She smiles whenever our eyes meet.

"Food's okay?"

"Having a hard time keeping it down."

"Try. It's very important: food and rest." I nod.

"You're very lucky," the doctor continues. "Your injuries weren't nearly as bad as they could have been. And that business with Nurse Abigail! All the doctors are talking about it. How *did* that syringe end up in her arm instead of yours?"

I shrug. "My guardian angel."

She smirks and squeezes my hand. "Better keep him close."

"Her."

"Girl guardian angel, huh?"

"Yep."

"I'll bet you two have a lot of fun together?"

"You have no idea, Doctor."

Dr. Shapiro gives me a broader smile. "Stay well," she adds, then squeezes my hand again, turns, and squeaks from the room in those sensible shoes.

As soon as she's gone, Alicia appears. She's pissed.

"There will be no more flirting with young lady doctors, mi amor, or with evil nurses who are trying to kill you."

"Agreed."

She sighs and sits down on the edge of my bed. Her eyes tear. "Now I must tell you something very sad, Carlitos."

My heart sinks.

"I must go into rehab myself, I am told."

"What do you mean?"

"I don't know. But the ghost network contacted me two days ago."

"Did we do something wrong?" I ask. I can't believe it.

"*We* did nothing wrong. But perhaps *I* have been doing something wrong all my life."

I can't imagine what. Can you?

"The purgatory ghosts tell me that we must meet with them to talk about it."

"*We* must meet?"

"Sí, mi amor. They want you there too. It's quite an honor, you know, for a living person to be invited to a ghost meeting."

It may be an honor, but I start to panic. "Does this mean that you're moving on?"

"I already told you that, mi amor. But there may be a way to slow things down. Soy una chica muy inteligente." She blushes, too embarrassed to say the words in English.

"Yes, you are a very clever girl," I say, "*my* clever girl."

Alicia's bites her lip. She blushes even deeper and gives me that sweet look of hers. "Oh Carlitos, I will find a way for us to stay together, I promise." And then she's on me again.

Covering me with kisses and making my body long to regain its strength so that I can show her how much I appreciate her love.

Chapter 18

Two months and a lot of painful rehab later, Alicia and I have still not had our meeting with the Purgatory Ghosts. But Dr. Shapiro's words have proven to be true. I'm back in my classroom on the Leland Main Quad.

It's Logic 101, the first day of the new quarter, and students are filing into the room. And then I spot Amy Joy, and I motion for her to come up and talk to me. She does.

"Hi, Dr. Mann." She smiles nervously. She's wearing her usual short plaid skirt, Leland sweatshirt and tennis shoes. She looks cuddly. (Sorry, Alicia, but she does.)

"Glad you're back," she says. "Sorry about the … you know, the accident."

"Me too. But thanks for the call to Señor Popcorn to gain us that time in Cancun."

"I thought it would help. Maybe you should have stayed longer."

"I had to come back with the new dean and all. How are you holding up?"

She shrugs and tucks her hair behind her ear just the way Alicia does. "Not too well. I've got this huge debt to work off."

"What kind of debt."

"Tiger tells me I'm responsible for the fees Doctor Hoi was willing to pay for Veronica."

"The FBI shot Hoi, and Mother and Father," I say, "and you're supposed to make the contribution he isn't alive to make?"

"Sick, huh? I'm Tiger's secretary now. I do whatever she tells me to, whether I like it or not. And that including some very *special* projects."

"What kind of special projects?"

"I'd rather not say."

I look around the class; all the students are involved in their own conversations. Even though we're at the front of the room, and our talk is deadly serious, no one is paying much attention. Thank God.

"Why don't we talk about it after class?" I ask. "Maybe I can help."

"I don't think so, Dr. Mann. I'm already in deep shit for contacting Señor Popcorn."

"How'd Tiger find out about that?"

"She had one of her boys beat it out of me. While she watched."

"Jesus!"

"Yeah, rough." Amy looks around and sees that the class has fully assembled. "I'd better go back to my seat."

I check the clock on the back wall. We only have a few seconds before the class is supposed to start.

"Amy, I'll do anything I can to help you."

"Better not, Dr. Mann," she sighs. "With all the pressures Tiger is putting on me, even I can't be trusted these days."

She turns to go, then shuffles back to me and hands me something soft and silky. "An invitation," she murmurs. There's a very troubled look in her eyes.

I stuff whatever she's given me into my coat pocket without looking at it. Then I refocus on the class and try to take my mind off of Tiger's deadly plans by starting to sort the students in my usual OCD way: blonds, brunettes, redheads, sweatshirts, t-shirts, blouses, jeans, cargo pants, skirts. What the hell am I doing?

Someone clears his throat. Tom Johnson, my teaching assistant. He's reminding me that we're already a couple minutes into class time, everyone's assembled, and I haven't said a word.

I refocus.

"Is anyone feeling illogical today?"

It's my standard opening, and it gets a laugh. So, I launch into my classic First Day Lecture, which I know cold. It's a well-rehearsed performance really, designed to get me through session number one without too much thought or effort.

And thankfully, it works.

Chapter 19

I return to my little off-campus apartment that evening, suspecting the place to be torn to pieces after my latest close encounter with Amy Joy. The first few times this happened, I thought the Joy Lum Clan was trying to scare me. Then I realized that it was just the ghost of my wife and her evil temper.

But today everything is orderly. I make my way into the bedroom. Alicia's ghost sits on the edge of the bed, surrounded by hundreds of pictures of our life together: when we were children growing up in Mexico, our high school days as soccer stars, my adventures as a young professional boxer, some of Alicia's modeling photos, my graduation from the University of Guadalajara, our wedding, and our first years in America.

Alicia is sobbing. I enter the room and want to console her, but she picks up a little digital clock from the nightstand and throws it at me.

Yep. That's closer to what I expected.

She tries to scream. But she's sobbing so hard that she can't really raise her voice. It comes out more like a sob:

"Go back to your Joy girls, bastardo!"

"¿Qué tiene de malo?" I ask softly.

"What's wrong?" she responds, standing and moving toward me. Her hands are trembling.

Still, she reaches into my coat pocket, and pulls out the soft silky thing that Amy gave me. It turns out to be a pair of silk panties probably belonging to Tiger Joy. They're tiger striped anyway.

Alicia holds them up. And I see the words, "Come Up and See Me Sometime," embroidered across the backside in lace.

Alicia waves the panties in my face. "*These* are wrong."

I wonder how she even knows about them. But then Alicia starts sobbing even harder, really crying now, until she's such a mess that she coughs, chokes, and ends up blowing her nose in the lacy lingerie. Then she just collapses against me, dropping the panties at my feet.

"¿Es éso lo ùnico malo?" I ask. Is that all that's wrong?

"No …"

"Then tell me."

"Oh Carlitos, I was trying so hard," she says. "I thought that I could stay with you because you were so unwell and needed my protection."

"Thank you," I say and hug her. She melts completely.

"Yes, but my time has run out, your protection has run out, and now we must go to that meeting with the Purgatory ghosts and find out what evil they have lined up for me."

Alicia pulls back and looks up at me. Tears stream down her face.

"I'll have to go to heaven and leave you behind where these evil women can feast on you."

I'd laugh at her choice of words except she's saying she has to leave me.

"I can't let you go," I respond.

"Who can say 'no' to heaven, mi amor?"

"I don't know."

"No one; that's who. So, pick up those sinful panties, throw them in the garbage where they belong, and let's go."

"Now? Where?"

"To the Purgatory Bookstore where those ghosts are waiting to break our hearts again."

#

115

We slip into the store just before closing time, my invisible wife and I. And, as we ascend to the third floor, I remember the first time I came here and what a frightening experience it was.

Now, as I hear the crusty old gal who runs the place lock up and leave for the night, I'm terrified again.

Then the lights go out, and I hear it … a low, soft, mournful tune, the kind a young woman might hum to herself if she were dying.

The hair on the back of my neck stands on end. "Alicia!"

As I turn the corner of the staircase I can see dusty boxes of books stacked everywhere. A few more steps up the stairway and I see the front window that looks out onto University Avenue. It's a big picture window, and silhouetted against it is a thin wisp of a girl. She's the one who's humming as she tangles her fingers through her hair. She adds soft, breathy words to her song.

"My youthful life is snatched away."

The figure before the window begins to glow. It's a sickly blue-green pulse of light that reveals a slow-moving rot that's traveling up the girl's arms from her fingertips to her shoulders.

"Dark gray death is where I stay."

The rot moves over her shoulders, down her body, across her tiny breasts, which are barely covered by the shards of a tattered t-shirt. The rot shrivels those little nubs into nothingness.

The girl's legs are crossed in a lotus position and now the rot spreads over them and down to her toes.

"So I invite you. Come and play."

Suddenly, the green ooze sweeps up over her face illuminating it and turning the Goth girl's empty look into a grinning, evil death face as she screams the last words of her lament:

"Play with me IN DEATH!"

Instead of falling backward it terror, I just smirk. It's only Jenny Beck teasing me. "You can't scare me, Jenny," I say.

The ghost slouches over to me, and resumes her more traditional form: pale white complexion, stringy black hair, anorexic shoulders and a new black Goth t-shirt that spells out the word: **BOO!**

"Always worth a try," she says as she holds out her arms offering a spooky but cheerful embrace. I go up to her, and give her a hug. She sighs happily, so I pull back to look into her eyes. As usual, dark make-up has turned them into hollow pits. A spider-shaped barrette gathers the left side of her hair. Then the barrette springs to life, and a real tarantula crawls back behind her ear, drops to the floor, and scuttles off.

It startles me, and I jump.

"Gotcha," she giggles when she sees the fear flare in my eyes. "Couldn't resist. I am *so* cool." She pumps her fist triumphantly.

"Yes, you are," I answer.

The scrawny girl beams and then steps aside to make way for the head of Ghosts Anonymous, Carlyle August.

"Dr. Mann, how very good to see you again," he says.

Sometimes I think he's the ghost of Cary Grant, except that I know he's actually a high tech guru who made millions before driving his cream colored Ferrari just a little too fast on highway 280 and ending up dead.

Alicia materializes beside me and holds out her hand for him to kiss. He does and then looks up at her.

"Alicia! I'm pleased to see you too, my dear," and then he gives her a hug that's a little too enthusiastic for my tastes. I am reminded again just how crazy he is about my wife. It's the kind of shit I have to put up with because I married this goddess. Every guy who meets her falls in love with her.

"Greetings, Alicia," says the ghost of Friedman. The old safecracker wavers into visibility right beside Carlyle. "And Dr. Mann," he says turning to me, "hello. Come, join our little soirée."

Friedman gestures to the table by the window. Yet another ghostly silhouette is sitting there now, one that is perfectly proportioned.

"Hi there, gorgeous." That's Royce Brilliant.

"Hi," Alicia answers demurely.

"I meant your husband, not you, chica," Royce says with a laugh. He's the handsome remains of a gay biker.

"Whatever," adds Jenny Beck, as she moves in beside Royce, and the others all take their seats around the table.

Alicia and I sit across from Carlyle. And, in spite of the happy greetings, it doesn't take long to notice that there's a decided pall cast over the proceedings. Carlyle is especially sad, and I start to realize why. He has to give my wife the bad news.

"I have very *good* news for you, Alicia," he lies as he tries to force a smile.

"The judges have decided to *help* you with your problem. Now you'll be able to make much better progress."

Alicia looks at him quizzically, and Carlyle looks embarrassed.

"Okay, they don't think you're making any real progress and they've decided to do something about it."

Alicia begins sobbing at those words. "I know," she murmurs, "my temper still takes control of me."

Royce scoots in next to her and wraps his arms around her, offering the kind of comfort only a gay man can give to a beautiful woman.

Carlyle looks at me sadly, as though asking for forgiveness. "They've arranged for the ghost of Sigmund Freud to help your wife, Doctor."

Alicia gasps. "And who is he?"

"The Father of Psychoanalysis ... whose cigar is just a cigar?" Friedman answers with a chuckle. But my wife just looks on in confusion.

"How can he and his cigar help me?"

"The people upstairs think he'll be able to help you gain some anger management skills, sweetheart," Carlyle answers.

I give him a funny look, and he shrugs. "Sorry."

"I would think Skinner would be better with anger management," I say.

"Freud may know more about the subject than any of us think," Carlyle responds, "and the people upstairs have always been impressed with celebrity."

"If he uses psychoanalysis with Alicia, it could take years and years," Friedman says.

"I like years and years," my wife answers, trying to quell her tears.

Carlyle lowers his eyes, "Except ... that the treatments are to be held at his home."

"Where's that?" Alicia grabs my hand and squeezes it nervously.

"Vienna."

"Across the sea? For years and years?" Alicia turns and buries her face in my shoulder. "I won't go."

"I'm afraid you have no choice, dear," Carlyle says as gently as possible.

Just then the big clock at the Los Altos Methodist Church begins to strike midnight. The first loud gong shakes the little bookstore.

"When do I have to leave?" Alicia asks.

"Right now, I'm afraid." Carlyle whispers.

"No way," I hiss as I get to my feet and glower at Carlyle from across the table. My hands are fisted. I'm ready to try and beat the ghostly crap out of him.

The church bell continues to toll. Alicia runs to me and holds me tightly.

Carlyle looks at us nervously, but before he can say anything, we hear the unfamiliar clip clop of horse's hooves on University Avenue.

"Oy vey," murmurs Friedman. "Their agents have come for her."

We all move over to the window and there, in the street in front of the building, is an old, imperial carriage from the days of the Austro-Hungarian Empire.

Four royally dressed guards, carrying well-polished rifles, step down from it and march toward the entrance to the Purgatory Bookstore. They glide directly through the doorway without opening it. They're ghosts, after all. When they reach the top of the stairs, they approach the table and my wife. One of the soldiers, an arrogant young man, addresses her.

"Frau Mankowski?" he says.

"Sí."

"Come with us, please. We are here to take you to Doctor Freud."

I clench my fists and move on the young man, but he lowers his rifle and sticks it right in the center of my chest.

"Don't move!" Carlyle warns me. "Ghost bullets can kill."

Alicia pushes the rifle away from me. The guard lets her do it. "At least a good-bye kiss," she pleads.

"Of course."

Alicia comes up to me, puts her arms on my shoulders, then glides her long fingers up my neck, and tangles them in my hair. Her tongue teases my lips, and I invite it into my mouth. It's the most passionate kiss she's ever given me, and she's moaning as she does it. My eyes are closed but I'm hoping that the ghosts have turned away to give us a few seconds of privacy.

Somehow I doubt it.

"Ummmm, mi amor," Alicia sighs gliding her fingers back into her own long black hair and twisting it like a little girl. "I'll see you soon," she whispers. "I hope."

The guard clears his throat, and he and the others step up beside her and march her out of the Purgatory Bookstore and out of my life before I can find a way to stop them.

I have no idea when or *if* I will ever see Alicia again.

Chapter 20

It's the very next day, and my longing for Alicia is unbearable. Still I've managed to get to class and sit behind my desk. I stare blankly at my students as they enter the room. Amy Joy sneaks up to my desk and stands nervously beside it.

"Did I get you in trouble?" she asks. "How?"

"With Tiger's panties ... you know, the invitation?"

"Let's just say they didn't help."

"Alicia get mad?"

"Yes, but it doesn't matter. She's been sent off to Vienna for some anger management training ... from Sigmund Freud."

"You won't see her again then ... until ..."

"Who the hell knows?"

"I'm so sorry," Amy sighs. "I didn't mean to ruin your last night with your wife, but Tiger, you know, insisted."

"You're just her little messenger then?"

"Among other things," Amy says. "But what should I tell her?"

"About what?"

"About whether or not you'll come up and see her sometime?"

"Sounds like it's an invitation to an execution ... my own?"

"Maybe, or maybe she'll just torture you."

"Great. And if I say no?"

"She'll just torture me, instead."

"This is nuts."

"Well, she is, isn't she? A full-fledged maniac."

I see Amy eyeing the back of the room, and for the first time I notice that a very muscular young man is watching us intently.

"Your keeper?" I ask.

"He's supposed to be my bodyguard."

If I weren't so heartbroken over the departure of Alicia and aware of Tiger's intention to kill me, I'd go up to that kid and beat the crap out of him right here in the classroom. I'd probably get fired for it. But it just might be worth it.

Still, I decide to do the most prudent thing I can think of.

"Tell Tiger I'll be up to see her in a day or two."

"Cause, right now, you're too broken up about the loss of your wife."

"Right."

"She may just buy that. Thank you." Amy nods, I smile, and she heads back to her seat. As far as I'm concerned, there's no sense in trying to find out what Tiger's next move will be. All I can be sure of is that it will be painful.

I look up and see that my students are still entering the classroom. Along with them comes Dr. Charlotte Burke.

"Hi, Carlos," she says as she makes her way up to my desk. She's wearing a gray business suit, diamond earrings, and a nervous smile.

"The dean wants to see you," she says.

"Applebee?"

"The little shit," she affirms.

The selection committee overlooked Charlotte even though she clearly had better credentials, and they made Oliver Q. Applebee the Dean of the Philosophy Department. Charlotte hated the guy when he was her colleague, and now that he's suddenly become her boss, she likes him even less.

"I have a class to teach," I say.

"I'm here to take over for you."

"Whose idea is that?"

"Applebee's."

"Okay then. Know what he wants to see me about?"

She shakes her head. "I don't, but Lupe Bravo is with him."

"The old witch?"

"The same."

"I thought she'd go back to Mexico when her husband died."

"No such luck," Charlotte answers. "Maybe she's here to bitch about that article you wrote last winter ... the one that's winning all the awards."

"It's certainly not the kind of thing she or her husband would approve of."

"Not at all."

"You know what ..." and after a moment of tense reflection I just whisper, "Fuck it. Fuck Lupe and her husband. Fuck Oliver Applebee. Fuck them all."

"No thanks." She winks at me. "You'd better get going though; wouldn't want to keep Lupe waiting."

Chapter 21

I glide past Applebee's cheery receptionist and right into his office. Our new dean is sitting behind his desk talking to Lupe Bravo. Lupe's a scrawny old Señora who's wearing a dress featuring dozens of brightly colored parrots.

Applebee gives me a concerned look as I enter, and I can see that his news will not be good. Then Lupe jumps to her feet and rushes me. She swings her purse at me and hits me so hard that both of us nearly fall down.

"¡Cabron!" she shouts. "¿Cómo le puede hacer eso a tu marido?"

"How could I do *what* to your husband?"

"No te hagas el inocente. Tú sabes lo que hiciste."

"I'm not playing innocent. I don't know what the hell you're talking about." Lupe is about to charge me again. But fortunately Applebee steps between us.

"Can't we just sit down and talk about this rationally?" he asks.

"No hay nada racional sobre el delito de plagio." There's nothing rational about the crime of plagiarism.

"Plagiarism?" I ask. "Now I know you're nuts."

"And who are you to make such accusations? You criminal!" Lupe answers. Suddenly she's speaking perfect English. It's only when she gets excited that she automatically reverts to Spanish.

I turn toward Dean Applebee. "Can you tell me what the hell she's talking about?"

Applebee shrugs. "Apparently you copied your entire paper, the one that won all the awards, from one of her husband's early works."

"How the hell could I? I was there when I wrote the whole thing. Besides, his political philosophy is diametrically opposed to mine."

"Not originally," Lupe snorts. "When he was a young man, he was a romantic, a Christian, a socialist almost. He believed that we must take care of the poor and the downtrodden."

"So what happened to him?"

"As he grew older he began to realize that humankind can only survive if the poor learn to take care of themselves ... pull themselves up by their bootstraps, so to speak." She does the whole *pulling up the bootstraps* gesture proudly, as though she really believes it.

I bury my face in my hands. "This is ridiculous."

"Is it now?" Lupe asks. "Then how do you explain this?" and she goes to Applebee's desk, picks up an open book and pushes it in front of me. The book is worn, looks like something from the early twenties, but the article it's opened to is called, *Revelations on the Rights of the Poor— by Pedro Bravo*.

I study the piece. It's mine, word for word.

I look up at the strained face of the old woman, glance over at a very stern Dr. Oliver Applebee, and then back at Lupe.

"Looks more like your husband copied from me."

"Impossible, of course," Applebee mutters. "Pedro Bravo died two years ago. You wrote your paper six months back."

"Maybe he's into time travel."

"¡Cabron!" Lupe hisses.

"Mrs. Bravo, please try to control yourself," Applebee says.

Lupe could use some anger management training herself, I think. Too bad, we may have to wait till she's in the afterlife before she can get it.

"So, just how do you explain this book?" Applebee asks.

My OCD mind starts churns out a conspiracy theory. These guys are in league with Tiger Joy and this is her latest attempt to get me, only this time it's not murder, just public humiliation. Lupe, Applebee and Tiger Joy, an unlikely combination to be sure. I know Tiger's motivation. But what's theirs?

"Do you remember Pedro actually writing this article?" I ask.

"In fact, I do." Lupe smiles. "It was in Mazatlan. The sky was blue. He was so romantic, so full of idealism. Our nights were scenes of joyful passion."

"And you remember this specific work?"

"Of course," she answers. *"Reflections on the Need for Revolution."*

"My article is called, *Revelations on the Rights of the Poor.*"

"Yes, that's what it was, *Revelations on the ...*"

"Rights of the Poor," Applebee finishes for her.

"Yes, that's it."

Shit. I try a new tack. Maybe I'll give everyone the benefit of the doubt. "So, what can I do to clear up this little misunderstanding?"

"This is no misunderstanding," Lupe hisses. "You've stolen my husband's words and ideas and besmirched his name."

"Besmirched?" I can't help but smile at her choice of words.

"She's serious, Carlos. And the faculty board has to consider taking action."

I stand and put my hands on my hips. I spent too much time as a prizefighter to take this sitting down. "What kind of action?"

"Dismissal from the university."

"What?"

"I have already filed charges," Lupe says, crossing her arms and grinning defiantly. "I'll ruin you."

I stare at Applebee.

"That's not our intention," he says. "However, until this matter is settled, you've been put on mandatory leave without pay. Dr. Burke will take over your classes."

"What happened to innocent until proven guilty?"

"Yes, well, this is academia and we have our reputation to protect. Please clear out your office and refrain from any further contact with your students."

Lupe looks very pleased with herself.

"My assistant will give you a package," he says. "It will tell you what you can and cannot do. Your faculty privileges are also suspended."

"What about my medical benefits and Dr. Greer?" He's the shrink who's treating my OCD condition.

"Yes, you can continue to see Dr. Greer and get treatment for the effects of your recent accident. Otherwise, the campus is off limits."

"Great." I shake my head. "Can I go now?"

"Please do," Applebee answers.

"Ms. Bravo," I say as I turn to the old woman, "I'm sorry about this misunderstanding, but I guess I'll see you in court."

She sneers at me. "Professor Mancowski, I'll see you in HELL!"

Chapter 22

"New job, Carlos?" I hear a honey voice ask.

Whoever she is, she's right. I'm down on my hands and knees sorting records into the lower cabinets of Torquemada, "The Best Used-CD-DVD-Record-&-Tape Store in Silicon Valley®."

I've been out of work for almost two months at this point, and yesterday I received a letter from the university telling me that I have been officially removed from the faculty for the rest of term. The letter went on to say that the university continues to explore Lupe Bravo's charges against me, and may reinstate me in the "unlikely event" (their words) that they find evidence to overturn their decision. Otherwise, within another six months, their decision will be permanent.

Things are already getting tight financially, so I'm helping out at the record store, which belongs to my friend Assad.

"On your hands and knees is where you belong."

The voice is laced with cruelty. I don't want to look at the source. And then I have to because she jams the toe of her high heel boot right into the front of the cabinet, blocking my efforts to restock the shelves.

"I could use a shoe shine while you're down there too, Carlitos. Want to *lick my boots*?"

I turn and look up at Tiger Joy decked out in all her dominatrix finery. I haven't seen her in over a year. She's wearing knee-high leather boots topped by fishnet stockings, a latex skirt, and a form.fitting corset. There's a black leather choker around her neck, and on top of it all, her still very youthful, very pretty face—almost a teenager's face really, in spite of the bright red lips that curl into a vicious sneer.

She carries a riding crop.

"How does it feel to be out of a job, Chico?" Tiger taunts. I study the hatred in her eyes without saying a word.

"Imagine getting a PhD so you can work in a record store? You should be punished for that." And so she slams me across the back with her riding crop. My muscles tense; I close my eyes, and instinctively I grab one of her ankles.

I realize that if I grab the other I can probably rip her right in half.

"Go ahead, try something," she says, "and your precious little Amy will pay the price."

I stop for a moment realizing that I can probably kill Tiger right here and now. Then I hear a grunt and turn to see three of Tiger's elite bodyguards standing by the doorway. They're slim but muscular, intimidating anyone who has any thought of entering the record store ... even the local security guards. More importantly they'll probably be able to get to me before I have a chance to split their mistress in two. I let go of her ankle. Tiger coos in satisfaction. And then she goes all hard on me again.

"Minimum wage boy," she calls. "I'll bet that's what you're friend is paying you now, right? You should be ashamed of yourself, DOCTOR."

CRACK! That whip smacks me again. I don't even try to respond, just shudder for a moment. Then, I pick up another record and try to stuff it into the cabinet. She still blocks me with her foot. I move to the right, and she slides her foot forward continuing to block me. I look up that gorgeous leg, up the full length of that well-crafted leather boot (must have cost her a mint). I look beyond, past the fishnet stockings to the skirt and then past it.

"Do you like what you see, MISTER Mann? Want a taste? Why not come home with me for dinner. I'll feed you well, and when we're done maybe I'll serve you to my lovely pet, Sid."

I remember Amy's story about Sid Vicious and how Tiger tried to feed Amy to the beast. And suddenly Tiger's pounding on me with her whip and screaming: "YOU FUCKING MURDERER! YOU HELPED THE FBI KILL MY MOTHER! YOU SON OF A BITCH!"

She's absolutely right, of course. I close my eyes and feel the whip snap across my back again … and then again and again as Tiger begins to lose control and pound on me while she screams at the top of her voice.

"MURDERER! "BASTARD! "KILLER!"

"STOP IT!"

It's Veronica, Assad's wife, Tiger's adopted sister. Veronica is very, very pregnant, and she's dressed in stretch pants and a big white t-shirt with a bull's eye on it. The shirt is pulled tight over her baby-bump.

"Helen, what are you doing here?" Veronica's using Tiger's real name, which somehow stops Tiger cold. Veronica grabs her and spins her away from me. She uses her unborn baby as a weapon almost. She belly-bumps Tiger back against the record shelves on the far side of the aisle.

One of the goons has turned toward Veronica. He crosses his arms as thought he's about to move on the pregnant woman if he has to. It doesn't bother Veronica.

"Carlos has been through enough," she says.

"Has he now?" Tiger rolls he eyes. "Mother and Father are dead, and he's responsible."

"They're not even our real parents, Helen. They were about to sell me to a sadistic maniac."

"If you hadn't been so stupid," Tiger says, "you could have had a great life. They would have married you off to some Chinese Steve Jobs, and you could have inspired him to change the world."

Veronica's eyes sizzle back at Tiger. She knows she hasn't done as well as her sisters in school, but in many ways she's proven to be as strong as any of them.

Tiger doesn't care. She starts pouring on the sarcasm. "You had to go to Leland, take logic from this dipshit, who was too honest to give you a good grade but not honest enough to write his own fucking essay."

"He didn't copy that paper from anyone," Veronica says.

"Don't defend him. He was going to flunk you, you stupid bitch!"

Veronica flinches and then lowers her eyes. "I know he would have flunked me. But he did NOT steal that paper from Pedro Bravo."

"Well, the university apparently thinks so."

There's a long, hard, nervous silence in which I finally struggle to my feet.

I walk up to Tiger, take the riding crop from her hand, and break it across my knee. Then, I wrap my arm around Veronica and lead her into the back office. I never say a word.

After a while we can hear Tiger taking what's left of her crop and start break things. She vents her anger on hundreds of those rare vinyl records. Her pretty young face is twisted into a bitter sneer. Her bodyguards stand at attention in the doorway. Shopping mall security arrives. They peer through the window, see what's happening, and decide that it's more prudent to just move away.

Chapter 23

Now that I've lost my professorship at Leland, I'm looking hard for a suitable new position. But, in the mean time, I've taken two part time jobs to keep up the payments on my Los Altos apartment. I have to hang onto the place. I share it with Alicia's ghost, and when Alicia finally returns from Vienna, I want her to know where to find me.

My first part time job, as you know, is at The Torquemada Used Record Store. My second job is as a busboy at La Meremma, an excellent little Italian restaurant on University Avenue. Part of the appeal of the job is the fabulous free dinners I get every day.

It's 12:30 PM now, and I'm clearing a table where some hurried businessman spilled clams marinara all over everything. What a mess.

As I sop up the sticky sauce and begin to gather up the plates, I start paying attention to a conversation at the table behind me. A man and a woman are proposing a toast ... to *me*.

"To Carlos Mann," says the guy. "He finally got what he deserved."

"Amén," the woman answers.

It's Oliver Applebee and Lupe Bravo. I recognize their voices, not to mention their attitudes. My hand tightens on an empty wine glass, and I almost break it.

"You have no idea how humiliating it's been to work in his shadow," Applebee says. "Carlos breezes in here from across the border with that slutty little wife of his, and old man Danielson practically turns the department over to him. Carlos got his PhD in nine months; do you hear that? Nine months instead of the usual three years. He's on the faculty before any of us can say a word about it."

Applebee takes a sip of champagne, savors it for a moment, then makes a nasty face and continues. "He's the one Danielson sends on those high profile speaking engagements … you know, at those luxury resorts … all across the country and around the world: Stockholm, Edinburgh, Rio de Janeiro; meanwhile, I'm left back on campus buried in fucking paperwork."

"And now this essay of his," Lupe picks right up where Applebee left off. "Award after award. He's drawn all the attention away from my husband, as if no other Latino scholars exist."

Now it's Lupe's turn to take a good slug of wine. "And Carlos isn't even really Mexican," she adds. "Mancowski? I don't think so."

Applebee reaches across the table and takes Lupe's hand reassuringly. "The university still wants your husband's papers, you know," he says.

"And they're going to get them now that this Mancowski person has been put in his place."

"I've always hated the bastard," Applebee continues, "but more than that I hated that wife of his … always cozying up to Danielson. I remember the first faculty party we went to. My Kathy dresses in the sweetest white lace dress I've ever seen. It has a high collar and yellow lace all along the edges; she looks like an angel, and I know she is going to make a wonderful impression on everyone. Then in walks Mrs. Mann in a skirt and blouse, to a formal party. But it doesn't matter what she's wearing on top, because she isn't wearing anything underneath. Those cheap boobs of hers might as well have a sign on them that says 'Hey, look at us!' Every time she moves she puts on a show, and then she always turns her eyes discreetly away, so that the men she's talking to can soak up the view. I wouldn't be surprised if she pulled old man Danielson into the bedroom and gave herself to him just to get that degree for Carlos."

At this point I've heard more than enough. I'm shaking with anger. Still, I try to make myself calm. I repeat a few silent prayers for self-control, and then I go up to their table. I stand there for a moment studying the man and woman who cost me my job. Lupe is having lasagna for lunch; Applebee, crab cioppino. Their bottle of champagne sits in a bucket at the front of the table. It's almost full.

"Is there anything *else* I can get for you?" I ask calmly. Applebee's jaw drops when he sees me. Lupe gasps.

"Here, let me adjust your plates," I say politely. And then I quickly tip Lupe's lasagna right into her lap. In less than a nanosecond I do the same with Applebee's cioppino.

"Oh, wow, can't imagine how that happened," I say as I see the red glop and chunks of fish spilling down the front of their clothes, into their laps, and over their shoes. "Let me help clean up the mess," I add, and I grab the bottle of champagne, shake it for a moment and use it to spray bubbly stuff all over the top of Lupe's parrot-infested dress ... and then onto her face. Then I spin and dump the rest of the wine over Applebee's head.

My enemies both sit there sputtering and cursing.

Before either of them can say anything too clearly, I bow.

"My compliments," I say and then turn and walk out through the kitchen. On the way I hand the empty champagne bottle to the owner of the establishment. I click my heels. "I've enjoyed working for you," I say. "Good-bye."

#

I head over to Torquemada and find Assad and Veronica standing in the middle of the store. There's a man with them, a real nothing guy in a gray business suit. He has an iPad, and he's entering data into it as they talk.

Assad looks up at me nervously as I enter. Then he comes over and whispers, "You'll need to take a few days off, Carlos. This is the insurance adjustor, and he suggests that we shut the place down while they figure out the extent of the damage."

Veronica walks up beside him. "Tiger," she says to me. "I'm so sorry."

"I'll pay you for the time off, of course," Assad adds.

"No, you won't," I answer with a smile. "I'll pay you for the damages."

I'm suddenly feeling an almost humorous detachment from my life as it crumbles around me.

Assad gives me a concerned look. He knows I don't have any money. "Come back in a few days and we can talk about it," he says.

"I'm going to pay for the damages," I repeat. The insurance adjustor looks at me and nods. "There will be a huge deductible that you can contribute to," he says.

"I will."

"No, you won't," Assad insists. He grabs me by the arm and jerks me away from the insurance guy.

"Get out of here now, Carlos, or the insurance company won't give us a cent."

"I'll take care of the costs," I say.

"But you just lost your job; you have no money."

"Trust me, I'll make it right," I say. Then I pull my arm out of his grasp, turn, and head out of the store.

#

There's an old saying in boxing, "you have to know when *not* to get up," meaning after you are knocked down you should wait and see if you are so badly beaten that you should stay down.

Fortunately or unfortunately, my coach and mentor, Uncle Pablo (aka Tio Chulo—Uncle Pretty Face, the middleweight champion of Sonora) never believed in that saying. His advice was "always get to your feet no matter what." And at this point I decide that's what I need to do. I've been down long enough.

#

An hour later I'm sitting in a beautiful new high tech office building on Page Mill Road. "Dr. August will see you now," says the receptionist as she strides into the waiting area.

I jump to my feet, and follow her. I'm nervous, knowing very well why I didn't pursue this connection before. Andrew August is the brother of Carlyle, the owner of the Purgatory Bookstore and head honcho of Ghosts Anonymous. Carlyle is a great admirer of Alicia and the last guy I want to be indebted to. Still, at this point I have few alternatives.

When I enter his office, Dr. Andrew August smiles warmly at me. He's still very much alive, of course. We shake hands.

"Carlos, we've been trying to reach you for days."

"I've been out pursuing new career opportunities," I say.

"Why do that? We need you here, man."

"You need logic professors?"

"We need you for something else," he says as he pats me on the back and leads me out of his office and down the hall.

He stops in front of a pair of mahogany double doors. He pulls out a set of keys, looks back and forth down the hallway, and then opens them.

"Check this out," he says.

When he flips on the lights, I gasp.

Inside is a display of the most unusual computer peripherals I've ever seen. Amazing colors, crafted of a strange metallic plastic that's been molded into wild fantasy shapes. On the left, a display of cobalt colored hard drives, terminals, and other devices are arrayed across an enormous table. Above the display, bold lettering proclaims: MINOS.

Across on the opposite wall is a similar set of computer hardware, but this one in shaped more ruggedly, colored dark red, and named ARES.

Sitting between the two is a display of other computer devices, this time in a spring yellow- green color. Above this set-up is the name DEMETER.

"We are developing new lines of market-specific, bulletproof data storage and inscription systems," Andrew tells me. "MINOS and ARES are already in place."

I stop and think for a minute. Knowing a little bit of Greek mythology, I deduce, "Minos and Ares, for Banking and the Military."

Andrew nods.

"So I suppose Demeter is agriculture."

"Agribusiness," he corrects.

"Okay," I say. "I know a little bit about that."

Andrew walks up to the Demeter exhibit, picks up a wireless mouse and begins moving it around on the table. The display on the iMac in the center of the exhibit shows charts and graphs of world agricultural production.

"Look at this," he says, and he calls up a series of images of Mexico. "Mexico has been a great agricultural power ... one of the best in the world. The current drought has severely limited its productivity, but we think Mexico can become an important player again."

"Interesting," I say. "So, you know about my trip to Washington on behalf of Fernando de Cervantes?"

"Señor Popcorn?" Andrew responds. "Know all about it."

"Did you read my paper, *Revelations on the Rights of the Poor*?"

"I did. You're no communist. You're not in favor of vast communal farms."

"A more balanced approach," I say.

"You're perfect for us. We want you to fly to Washington, talk to the Department of Agriculture, some of the same guys you've already impressed. Help convince them to adopt DEMETER protocol. Part of our pitch will be that we're planning to expand into NAFTA and sell our systems to Mexico and Canada. You'll be in DC to help us talk about your native country."

His eyes are bright with enthusiasm, and I know that this is more than a favor he's doing for me. This is his attempt to help sell his dream.

"Will you do it? We'll pay you well."

Could I have walked into a better deal? I ask myself. Then, just for the hell of it, I shake my head. "No."

His face drops. "Are you serious, why not?"

"Don't like the name."

"What?"

"If you're going to sell these systems to the Mexicans you have to change the name of the agricultural system to XIPE TOTEC, or as we pronounce it *shee-PAY-toh-teck*."

He frowns. "Who the hell's that?"

I give him a deadpan stare. "The name of the *Aztec* god of agriculture."

He laughs. "Meet me at San Francisco International at ten tomorrow morning: American Airlines, First Class check in. We can discuss naming conventions on our flight to DC."

And just like that I become a well-paid consultant for August Technologies.

Chapter 24

Two weeks later, I walk into my little apartment, and the place immediately breaks my heart. It's so damn lonely.

I've just returned from a highly successful trip to Washington. Not only has XIPE TOTEC become the name of August Technologies' new agribusiness product, but we've made a huge sale to the Department of Agriculture. In the process, I've re-established my relationship with some of the most powerful people in agribusiness. Still … I can't escape this new feeling of loneliness.

"Las cosas están mejorando, mi amor," I whisper as I go from room to room. Things are getting better.

"¿Pero, dónde estás?" But where are you?

I open the door to Alicia's closet. Since she's been in Vienna, I've turned the little room into something of a shrine. I've rearranged her clothes and pinned her nicest pictures up on one wall: Alicia dancing, laughing, loving, and being herself. Her best magazine ads are in here, and they're all so damn sexy. I'll admit it; some nights I used to come in here and get drunk. All that sweet-smelling perfume, sexy lingerie, and dreams of Alicia. I always wake up in the middle of the night with a rotten taste in my mouth, a splitting headache, but a smile on my face.

Six years ago, when she was still among the living, Alicia posed nude for me. It was our anniversary and I'd offered to give her anything she wanted. We were just getting started and didn't have much money. But I still needed to do something special.

So, I'm setting the table, getting ready for a beautiful roast chicken that Alicia has worked so hard to prepare. "Is this your present for me?" I call to her. She's in the bedroom. But then she comes waltzing out wearing this gorgeous lace wrap and nothing else.

"Good God!" I say.

"You like?"

"Do I?"

"Wonderful, because it is part of my present for both of us."

"Not just the great meal."

"Well, that is for both of us too, and the love we will make tonight, mi amor."

"Amen to that."

"But I want you to do something else for my birthday."

"Anything you want."

She's flitting around the room, twirling the wrap, sometimes opening it, but only when she's facing away from me. She's teasing me with that incredible body of hers.

"So what is it?"

She tightens the wrap, tucks it in and reaches down and pulls a magazine from under the end table.

"This!" she says and she hands me a copy of *Playboy* magazine, *the* copy of *Playboy* magazine, *Mexican Playboy*, the one she's in.

"You know what's wrong with this book, don't you, Carlitos?"

"You always complained that Señor Popcorn wouldn't let you pose nude."

"Sí, I have all my clothes on all the time. What fun is that?"

"You want me to take pictures of you in these *Playboy* poses?"

141

"Sí, I know the poses."

"But naked?"

"Won't it be fun?"

"Damn straight!"

So, I get out my camera and snap away, and we eat chicken and drink wine, and make love, and take pictures of Alicia naked, and sing and dance and make love again. And now I have all those pictures pined up in the closet. I've draped that same lace wrap in front of them just in case anyone else happens in there.

But tonight, my first night back from Washington, I find myself very drunk. I've dumped my luggage, taken a quick shower, slid into a pair of sweats and now I'm lying on the closet floor already into my second bottle of sangria. I'm staring at those pictures and talking out loud to this vision of my beautiful dead wife who has disappeared from my life yet again. I hate to admit it, but I'm actually crying.

And then there's a knock on the door.

Chapter 25

It's Amy Joy.

She's dressed for the nighttime: little black dress, high heels, a shawl wrapped around her against the California cold.

"You're drunk, Dr. Mann?" she says as soon as I open the door.

"Not enough."

She looks me up and down. "Can I come in?"

She replaces her look of concern with one of purpose. I stumble backward.

"We want to take you out to dinner this evening."

"We?"

Amy looks rather nervous. "Some of us from Chinatown."

"Will your sadistic bitch of a sister be there?"

Amy looks away for a long moment, then back at me. "She's the boss, isn't she?"

"And she'll give you a big bonus for just delivering me to the restaurant?"

"Very big."

I shake my head and smile. "Guess we should go then, shouldn't we?"

Amy looks down at her hands, fumbles with her fingers for a few moments and then brushes past me into the bedroom. She enters Alicia's closet. She sees it all: empty bottle of sangria, naked pictures of my wife, her pretty underthings laid out in a tragic display.

When Amy returns to the living room, she looks very sad.

"What'd you expect?" I ask.

She shrugs. "Could be worse."

"Actually, I've just returned from a very successful business trip to our nation's capital."

"Then why all this?"

I lean back against the wall and slide onto the floor. I hug the sangria bottle to me. "I haven't heard from Alicia in months. She's gone, and I'm starting to doubt that she's ever coming back."

"So, you should come have dinner with us. Get your mind out of the closet."

I hesitate.

"Your wife will never know, and after what you've been through you deserve a little fun."

"Where do you want to go?" My speech is slurred. I'm still sitting on the floor.

Amy looks down at me with those Alicia eyes, and she is absolutely delectable. "MacArthur Park. We have a reservation for 9:30."

I smile, "Sounds good."

I get up, set the bottle of sangria on the table, and watch as it rocks back and forth for a moment before it finally comes to rest … upright.

"Un momento por favor," I say.

She giggles. "You're speaking Spanish, and I'm Chinese."

"Standby," I say, and I go into my closet and put on the new suit that I bought for my Washington meetings: gray, tailored, new shoes, starched white shirt. I wear it open-collar. When I turn to face Amy, her eyes sparkle brightly.

"You look great," she says, "and we *are* going to have fun."

"Is that a paid political announcement from your sister?"

Amy looks troubled for a moment, then takes me by the arm and leads me out of my apartment.

#

I haven't been to McArthur Park in years, but the place still looks the same. I'm arm in arm with Amy as we enter, and now a devilishly handsome Chinese kid makes his way through the crowd and up to us.

He smiles warmly, gives Amy a hug, and then shakes my hand.

"Dr. Mann," he says, "My name's Al. Glad you could come. Helen is in the back waiting for you."

"Oh boy."

If I hadn't just come from two very successful weeks in DC, I might not be up to this. But other than missing Alicia so much and still being a little drunk, I have to be feeling better about my life and my future.

Al smiles happily, turns and says, "Follow me."

He leads us through the crowd and into a secluded room with an enormous banquet table.

Tiger is presiding over a large contingent of handsome young Asian men and women. I recognize one of them as her twin sister Florence, aka Bunny. This girl is the exact opposite of Tiger, a true submissive, raised and trained to be innocent and serve the needs of dominating men. On the other side of Tiger, beyond three more handsome young men, I recognize someone else. It's Nurse Abigail who tried to poison me in the hospital. I'm really surprised to see that she's recovered.

The whole scene is starting to feel like a nightmare. All the young men are dressed in black suits with black shirts and ties. They all wear sunglasses.

All of the women are dressed in party dresses, just like the one Amy wears: black, low cut, expensive.

We take our seats. I'm directly across from Tiger who seems to be having a great old time.

"Thanks for joining us, Carlitos," Tiger purrs.

I flinch as she calls me by the pet name that Alicia uses.

"No problem, Helen," I answer. "Haven't seen you since you tried to beat me to death in the record store."

"Yeah," Tiger responds. "That was fun, wasn't it?"

I don't answer.

"We wanted to invite Assad and our sweet sister Veronica to join us this evening," Tiger says, "but Amy talked us out of it."

Amy looks down at her hands and is suddenly more uncomfortable than ever. "Amy's paying Veronica's tribute, you know," Tiger says.

"Tribute?"

"Sure. It's customary in our family. The husband pays for the privilege of marrying one of our sisters. Dr. Hoy offered two hundred thousand dollars for Veronica; you must remember that."

I do. I topped him in the bidding.

"Well, now that Dr. Hoy is no longer with us, thanks to you, Amy has to work off the tribute. How long do you think it will take for a pretty young lady like Amy to work off a two hundred thousand dollar debt?"

I don't answer.

"How about *the rest of her life?*"

The whole table erupts with laughter … except Amy and me.

"She's my private secretary now," Tiger continues. "And she's given a handsome salary, which she uses to pay back the family. Fortunately, she's also eligible for bonuses. For example, tonight she earned quite a bonus just for delivering you here."

"She told me," I say. "Why do you think I came?"

"Of course. Amy has decided to follow an old Chinese proverb," Tiger continues, "the one that says '*whatever it takes.*'"

There's more embarrassing laughter.

The waiter comes, takes our order. I ask for the fillet mignon, and Tiger is only too happy to oblige. I skip the wine though. More wine on top of the bottle of sangria I've already downed? I don't think so, not if I'm going to be able to get out of this alive.

#

The meal is over and we're eating dessert. Everyone else is having after-dinner drinks. I'm going with coffee and bread pudding.

Tiger reaches across the table and takes my hand; she fondles it, studies the huge graduation ring from the University of Guadalajara, and of course, my wedding ring. Abigail, Bunny, and the boys ooh and aah. Amy looks away.

"I have a nice surprise for you," Tiger says, "a gift actually." She turns to her sister. "Amy, if you will."

After a moment, Amy places a small narrow box on the table. It looks like the box for a bracelet or a necklace. I can tell by the look on Amy's face that she finds this part of the evening especially distasteful.

"Go ahead, open it."

I do.

Inside the box is a leather collar, very fine black leather with a solid gold nameplate riveted into the middle of it. Embossed on the nameplate is a single word: "SLAVE".

"Interesting," I say pointing to the collar. "I assume you have a matching item, Helen."

"Of course, I'm wearing it right now."

Around Tiger's neck is a black leather choker. She reaches up, turns it around, and I see that there's also a nameplate on hers, but this one says: "MISTRESS."

"Does the relationship appeal to you, Carlitos?" she breathes.

I check out the onlookers, and suddenly my OCD kicks in. Tiger's boys are all well trained bodyguards. The fact that there are ten of them should be something of a compliment, I guess. They are studying me now. Some of them are smiling, others are looking at me intently, ready to pounce. I wonder for a second just how many I could take down if I decided to bolt. Most of them I hope. I can already guess which of them would move first. I'll bet the whole routine has already been orchestrated, and this one guy looks like the sacrificial lamb who would take my first punch and …

"Dr. Mann." It's Amy. "You're tripping again." Then more loudly she adds, "May I put the collar on you?"

I come out of my OCD distraction, look into her eyes, and see that tears are beginning to form. I don't want that, don't want Amy to get into any more trouble than she already is. Still, she did just betray me by bringing me here, didn't she?

"Can we wait a bit?" I ask.

Tiger waves her hand in fake generosity. "No rush. There's so much more for us to talk about."

Amy looks relieved as she sets the collar aside.

"Now, I have a *real* surprise for you, Carlitos," Tiger says. "Ready?"

I smile. "Why not?"

"Amy?"

With that command, Amy gets up from her chair, walks over beside Tiger and takes the seat next to her. One of the young men had been sitting there. He's a great big kid with broad shoulders and a merciless grin, the last guy I'd want to fight. And now he stands and walks over behind me. Not much doubt what he's there for.

"I'm sure you remember your wife's closest friends, don't you, Carlitos?" Tiger asks.

"Her two best friends are both dead," I say. "Sylvia Morales and Chula Contrerras."

"You *are* a good husband," Tiger gushes. "I can't want to see how you perform when you're my slave.

"Amy?"

The girl reaches for a small Chinese puzzle box that has been sitting on the table beside Tiger. Amy works the puzzle and opens the box to reveal yet another, smaller box, this one inlaid with carvings of dragons. It's the kind of box I know very well, because Alicia was imprisoned in one once. It's a ghost trap.

Amy twists the trap in just the right way, and the ghost of Alicia's friend Chula Contrerras slips out of it and takes a seat beside me. She looks troubled and angry.

"Pendeja," she curses at Tiger.

"Mind your manners, Miss" Tiger says, "or we'll stick you back in the box with your parents and toss all three of you into a warehouse somewhere in the middle of the Gobi dessert."

"She has your parents are in there too?" I ask Chula.

"Sí, ghosts don't take up much room, Carlitos."

"I understand," I give her hand a squeeze. She gives me a pained smile in return.

"Tell him," Tiger commands.

Chula gives her a nasty look and then turns back to me.

"I'm sorry, Carlitos, but I must bring you some very bad news."

"About Alicia?"

"Sí."

"Is she all right?"

"She is that. She seems to be enjoying herself in Vienna very much now."

"Was Freud rough on her?"

"She was rough on herself when she was with him, but he may have helped her."

"Good."

"Yes, very good, except that she's been so lonely."

"She's not the only one."

"Get to the point please," Tiger hisses, and I can tell that she's looking forward to something really unpleasant.

"Yes, the point," Chula says. "The point Carlitos is that Alicia has made acquaintances."

"Oh, for Christ sake," Tiger calls. "Mother, can you join us and help Chula tell her story?"

With those words the ghost of Mother Joy (who—yes—I'm responsible for having the FBI gun down) shimmers into the chair on the other side of me. She's dressed in her usual tight red silk sheath with the large slit down the front to reveal the finest cleavage money can buy. There's also a slit up the side that shows perfectly proportioned legs.

"Both Chula and Mother have just returned from Vienna," Tiger says "Mother, tell Carlitos what Alicia is up to."

Mother crosses her legs toward me and offers a smile that's pure evil. No doubt about it, she gives me the creeps.

"Well, as you are well aware," she begins, "Your Alicia is lovely. She's the toast of all those balls that the Hapsburg ghosts keep holding at Schloss Schönbrunn after midnight when the palace is no longer open for tourists."

"Schloss Schönbrunn?"

"The summer residence of the Holy Roman Emperors." She gives me a look that says *don't you know anything, asshole.*

I shrug. I'm not an expert on the Holy Roman Empire, and I'm really much more concerned about my wife.

"Does Alicia seem happy?" I ask.

"She was crying a lot when I first met her at one of those Hapsburg parties," Mother says. "But then she met someone, you know, and suddenly …"

"What do you mean she *met* someone?"

"She did, and it saved her. She's so in love now."

I reach for Mother's arm, and just as quickly the guy behind me grabs my wrist and pins it to the table.

I turn to Chula, who turns her eyes away. "Perhaps Alicia *is* in love," she whispers.

"I'm sure they're having lots of ghost sex," Mother continues so damn cheerfully. "I can practically guarantee it."

She knows her words are tearing me apart. Except I have to remember who she is and where I am.

"I don't believe you."

"Chula!" Tiger calls on my wife's friend to witness.

"I don't know that they're having sex," Chula responds.

"See for yourself," Mother says and she pulls out a book full of photographs showing Alicia in a great gilded hall, dancing with an extremely handsome young Austrian. And next, there is Alicia, kissing the guy ... passionately.

"Sorry, I don't have any shots of them actually *fucking*," Mother says. She's not the happy gossip anymore; she's a full-fledged bitch who wants revenge.

"You can't take pictures of ghosts," I mutter as my fists clench.

"Of course you can," Mother answers.

"How?"

"Ectoplasm," Tiger says. "Something you'll have to learn more about, Carlitos." Everyone breaks out laughing, though I have to admit I don't get the joke.

Mother goes on and on about the happenings in the Hapsburg court. She gives me a thousand examples of how Alicia has been unfaithful to me. Chula reluctantly nods here and there to confirm the truth of what she's saying.

By the time Mother is through, I'm limp. I can feel despair moving in.

It's then that Amy comes to me and puts her hand on my shoulder. She turns to everyone and speaks up strongly.

"Just back off, will you! Look at what you're doing to him."

Mother and all the others recoil in shock: Amy is seldom so assertive, standing up to all of them like this. They turn away. Many get up from the table and move to the far side of the room. Soon they are talking among themselves, paying no attention to us at all any more.

Amy raises my head and holds my face in her hands. She brushes my hair back, looks deep into my eyes.

"Oh, Carlos," she whispers. "I'm so sorry. But you know I love you."

I tense; this is not what I want to hear.

"Please. Carlos, look at me."

She pulls my face around to hers and her lips move to mine. She kisses me, and I let her. It's a long loving kiss, and I don't pull away. Until I hear a camera click.

"Thank you very much," Tiger says as she sashays around the table gleefully.

"Well done, Sis," Tiger answers. "I didn't think you could get him to do it."

"But I didn't mean to ..."

One of the boys sweeps Amy away before I can get to my feet and respond. But now Tiger is moving in on me.

"Surrender, Carlitos," she says. "Your ghost wife has moved on. You're mine now." She reaches across the table, takes the slave collar and brings it toward my neck.

The testimony about Alicia's infidelities, all the wine, the inappropriate kiss from Amy, and my incredible longing for my wife suddenly raise my anger to the boiling point.

"I WOULD NEVER ..." I roar in a monster's voice that I didn't even know I had. I jump to my feet and leap toward Tiger. But halfway through the move something slams into the back of my head, and the lights go out.

IV
Alicia

Chapter 26

This is Alicia, and I am very angry with this Dr. Freud. I want to ask him about returning to Carlitos, but all he wants me to talk about is my Mamá and Papá and growing up in Mexico.

I have materialized into his office wearing my passport photo dress, the one I wore when I had my traveling pictures taken so long ago. Carlitos says it makes me look businesslike. I want to look businesslike for this nasty old man, because I do not want him to know that I am going to try and trick him.

Dr. Freud thinks his job is to help me overcome my anger so that I can move on to the next world. He does not even believe in the next world. But he does not believe in ghosts either, even though he is one.

Dr. Freud speaks in the ghost language of German, which I understand even though I only speak English and Spanish. That is the way things work after you die.

I have traveled through many nights to get here. And since I have come so far, I know I will have to spend a great deal of time talking to this man whose job is to cure my anger so that I can leave my Carlitos forever. You can see why I need to trick him.

Dr. Freud's office is very nice, I think, for an old man. Lots of dark furniture: desks, tables, couches, and a nice thick carpet. He asks me how I feel, and I say sad because I have had to leave Carlitos.

"Even though you are a ghost, and he is not?"

"Sí."

He shrugs, says, "Okay," and then changes the subject. "Let's get to work?"

He gestures to the couch and says that I should lie down, which is something I do not want to do even though he is an old man. I don't like lying down on couches in rooms with men when we are alone.

"Please," he says, and he smiles. So, I do it.

"I want you to lie there, relax, and just let your mind go blank."

"That is very easy for me to do," I say, and I giggle a little.

The old man smiles. "It's a very comfortable couch," he says. "Just tell me the first thought that pops into your mind."

"Anything?"

"That's right."

"Well," I say, "I think this is a very comfortable couch."

"Wonderful," he answers. "Now we are getting somewhere."

We both laugh, and I decide that the old doctor is not as grouchy as I thought; certainly not as grouchy as my Mamá and Papá became when I was five.

"Papá was a good man," I say.

"Go on."

"He was a good man in spite of her."

"Her?"

"Dolores Consuela Modesto, his girlfriend. I helped introduce them."

Freud waits for me to say some more, and suddenly I am back in my village in Mexico, and Papá and I are getting ready to go down to the general store one Sunday after church. I am just a little girl, and he tells my Mamá that we are going on a date. I'm only five, and I am dressed up in the prettiest dress I own, the only one that I did not get after my big sister wore holes in it, the one my father bought me for my birthday.

"My mother is not happy that we are leaving. I think she is jealous because I will be spending time alone with my father on a Sunday afternoon, when *she* wants to be with him. She's already angry as she brushes my hair. She grits her teeth and pulls the brush through my curls so hard that it hurts."

Dr. Freud takes out a cigar and lights it. He looks at me and then looks away. He half closes his eyes and nods. I start to think he is asleep, but I go on anyway because I am enjoying this memory of my father, even though my mother was very angry with me at the time.

"So, Papá and I go down to the village store, and as we walk along I can see boys trailing us.

These are boys that hate me already, even though I am only five. They like to beat me up and make fun of me just because they enjoy it. Sometimes when I am alone they run up to me and knock me down or punch me. I am usually dirty and wear raggedy clothes that were once pretty when my sister wore them.

"Papá has a job outside of town and has to get up early every morning and drive a long way. So he is not around during the day when the boys pick on me. He is not there to defend me, as he should be. I have no brothers, no uncles or boy cousins, and my sister thinks she is a princess.

Mamá does not care. So what can I do?

"But now these bully-boys will not run up to me; they will not pick on me because my father is with me, and he will stop them.

"Papá is handsome, did I say that. Big and strong, and he scares those boys, so they keep their distance."

Smoke is now billowing over me as I lay on the couch in Dr. Freud's office, and I pretend that the layers of smoke are really the streets of our little village with the rows of houses and shops and the range of grey mountains in the distance. I turn to the doctor and I see the ghost-smoke swirling around his head as he sits and listens and nods.

"Papá and I are at the doors of the village store, and we enter. And right across from the doors is a counter, and behind it is a cooler with bottles and bottles of soda pop. My mouth waters even now as I think of it.

"Papá reaches into his pocket, pulls out a handful of coins, and points to a bottle of soda.

The fat man behind the counter reaches into the ice and pulls out a drink for me. 'Muchas gracias, Papa,' I say and curtsey, smile, and take a drink. It tastes so good. Cherry. My favorite. And then a very pretty woman steps up beside my father and says, 'You have a lovely daughter, Señor.'

"At first I feel very proud and extra pretty, and besides the cool drink is making me happy, and the bubbles are making my nose tickle. And then I start to giggle, and so does the woman, and so does Papá."

Dr. Freud smiles and nods with his eyes half closed, as though he can see the picture that is floating above my head in the smoke, and he is enjoying it too.

"But soon I do not feel so happy," I say.

"Oh?"

"This pretty woman is taking Papá's arm and getting closer to him than I want her to be, and he is not trying to pull away from her. He turns to her and talks happily, and she is laughing and getting even closer, and now she is whispering things into his ear.

"I do not like this. This is my father, and he said he was taking *me* on a date, but now I think he has forgotten all about me. This woman is taking him away from me. And when he is not looking at her, she glances at me, and even though she is smiling I can tell that she does not even like me. Her smile is false.

"Now, I am afraid. I want to go up to my Papá and say something, but I do not. Like the silly little girl that I am, I just drink my cherry soda and say nothing.

"The woman's lips are right in Papá's ear now, and I think she is kissing him inside his ear, but then …"

Dr. Freud is a patient man, because he does not say a word, does not even look at me, just waits for me to say the next thing. But I am silent for a very long time because, in the smoke that floats above my head, I can see what happens next, and I am feeling like I want to die.

"Back in the little store, I slam the bottle of pop onto the floor on purpose. It breaks and splashes red sticky stuff all over my shoes and socks, all over my legs and my dress, and I begin to cry.

"Papá rushes up to me, away from that woman, and for a moment I see through my tears that she has crossed her arms in anger, but then she starts play-acting, running up beside my father and taking out her little handkerchief and helping him dry my shoes and legs. She dabs the handkerchief on her tongue to make it wet and then rubs it on my legs, but what she is really doing is rubbing her spit all over me … uugghh!

"'It's okay, sweetie,' she clucks over and over again like a big-breasted chicken, and I can smell her roses perfume. I am getting dizzy and feel like I want to throw up … all over her. But I do not. I let Papá dry my tears. I let that woman rub her nasty spit on my legs and my dress even though I know it will not get the stains out.

"'Don't cry, Niña,' Papá says, 'Do you want another bottle of soda?'

"'No!'

"I cross my arms and stomp my foot and pout.

"'Candy, por favor,' he tells the storekeeper, and the man pulls out a big box of candy bars and holds the box in front of

158

me so that I can pick one. I grab the biggest, chocolatiest bar in the box, and my father pays the man, and I am grinning now as Papá lifts me up onto a stool so that I am facing away from him. Then, he takes that woman by the hand, and leads her back into the store.

"I am facing away, but there is a mirror there, and I watch as Papá laughs and talks with the woman, and soon, before I am even half way done eating the candy bar, that woman is kissing my Papá on the lips … right there in front of a big bushel of red peppers."

Dr. Freud nods almost as though he expected this, and he is not surprised when I say that I am angry when my father takes me home and tells me not to mention any of this to my mother. Papá promises that if I do not tell her, he will take me to the store again next week.

"And soon we are going *every* Sunday, and now I know that the woman's name is Dolores, and *she* buys the candy and the soda for me, and my Papá takes her into a little room in the back of the store, and the storekeeper talks to me while they are gone … about how hot it is, about how pretty I am, about whether I would rather have chocolate or ice cream treats.

"Soon, Papá and Dolores join me again, and Papá is always a little red, and Dolores is very breathless and sometimes her lipstick is brand new, like she just put it on again because they were back there kissing. Still, I skip home, into the chilly air around my Mamá, even though it is over 100 degrees inside our house."

I start to cry, right there on Dr. Freud's couch. I am remembering a terrible day. Not the terrible/wonderful day that Carlitos saved me from those boys who were beating me up.

This is a *really* terrible day because there is no Carlitos to save me.

The old ghost doctor is hidden in smoke. I can barely see him now, but I stare up into those wispy clouds above my head and I can see the angry face of Mamá, and she is screaming at me.

"'Tell me about her.'

"'About who?'

"'Your father's puta,' she says, and I do not know what the word means. I guess my mother can tell by the confusion in my eyes.

"'The woman he told you not to tell me about.'

"'Dolores?'

"'Dolores! Is she prettier than I am?'

"'No, Mamá, she is not prettier than you are, but she *is* prettier than me.'"

Dr. Freud laughs. I am surprised. But my mother does not laugh. She slaps me.

"'You are all plotting against me!' she says, 'you and your father and this ... this Dolores!' She says the words like she is spitting out a spoiled piece of pig meat, and then she slaps me again. And suddenly she is hugging me and holding me and telling me that she is sorry, and rocking me back and forth, and then she jumps up, grabs my hand, and runs out of the house dragging me along with her right to the little store.

"'Where is this Dolores?' she asks the storekeeper as we enter. And the guy looks at me with anger in his eyes because I must have told Mamá ... which I did. And then Dolores is there, standing toe to toe with Mamá, and I think they are going to punch each other the way boys do. But Mamá does something far worse than punch Dolores. *She spits in her face!* Then, she turns and drags me out of the store after her ... all the way home.

"Papá and I rush out of the house that night after my mother has yelled and screamed and thrown things at him for having a girlfriend and at me for being part of his secret. And he turns to me and says, 'You have ruined things for both of us, Niña. No more sweets for either of us from now on.'

"And from that day on, every Sunday my father takes my mother out after church and marches her around the town plaza in her finest dresses, and she always carries a parasol and shows off, especially for Dolores who looks at us all (especially me) in great anger.

"They never like me again, any of them, not Papá, not Mamá, not Dolores, not the storekeeper, not the little boys in the street who keep beating me up for the whole next year. I am angry with all of them too. I think that maybe I deserve it for some reason, but then I think, what was I supposed to do? Did I want to be part of this crime against my Mamá? I do not think so. I am innocent but feel guilty anyway.

"Sometimes I beat things up just as the boys beat me up. My favorite victim is my little bicycle. I yell at it, kick it, and throw things at it. But one day, when the neighborhood boys and girls are beating me up again, and I am feeling full of hate but also guilt because I was part of a crime against my Mamá … finally, Carlitos comes along from another village, out of nowhere, out of my dreams, and he rescues me …

"FOREVER!"

Chapter 27

"What will you do this evening?" the ghost of Dr. Freud asks as I lay on the couch so tired from telling my story.

I shrug, "Haunt a nice hotel, I guess."

He gives me a fatherly smile, much more fatherly than Papá did after I told Mamá about Dolores.

"You should get out and have some fun. It will be good for you."

I sigh. "I am feeling too sad," I say.

"The Hapsburg ghosts throw lovely parties," he tells me. "There's one tonight at the Hofburg."

I make excuses: "I do not know these Hapsburgs or their Hofburgs, and besides, I have nothing to wear."

Freud pulls his glasses down and looks up at me over the top of them. "You are very beautiful, Señora. I don't think you'll have any problem meeting people. The palace is close. You could just follow the crowd, or I can give you a map."

"A map would be nice … and clothes?"

Dr. Freud smirks. "You're a ghost. Steal something when you get there. These are ghosts from long ago, so the clothes will be from the golden days of the Empire."

"Which empire?"

"Whichever one you want," Dr. Freud says with a little laugh. "The Austrian Empire, the Austro-Hungarian Empire, or the best one of all: the Holy Roman Empire, which wasn't Holy or Roman, but it was a lot of fun anyway … especially for the Viennese."

I smile. I thank the old doctor, and decide that visiting a ball in a great palace would be much better than haunting some old hotel no matter how nice it is.

Four hours later I am standing inside a ballroom at the Hofberg Palace listening to a song that everyone says is the *Blue Danube Waltz*. Ghosts of women in lovely ball gowns and men in dressy uniforms are spinning past me. They are almost flying, and I wonder where people learn to dance like this. It looks very dangerous but also very wonderful.

I have followed the old doctor's advice and stolen a gown from the museum, which is inside the Hofberg Palace. No one else is wearing one like it. And that makes me feel special. I am studying a handsome young ghost who stands across the way from me. His hair is golden blond; his eyes dance; his nose is small. He comes up to me.

"Wearing Sissy's gown, are we?" he asks.

I bat my eyes at him without saying a word.

"¿Sabes quién es Sissy?" he asks me in Spanish even though I would understand ghost-German. Do you know who Sissy is?

I look up at him through my eyelashes like some flirty party girl and say nothing. "She was the last great Empress of the Austro-Hungarian Empire."

"So?" I ask in perfect English.

"And she's also my mother," he answers. "You're wearing her dress."

"Is that not allowed?"

He laughs. It is a great loud laugh like an actor on a stage, but I can see that he is not mocking me because after he laughs his face is sweet.

"Would you like me to help you find something more suitable to wear, Señorita?"

"Señora, sir."

"Oh, so you are married?"

"Sí." My heart breaks all over my face. Tears form in my eyes.

"But, your husband is still alive?"

I nod, and sob and feel my breasts heaving as they never have before. It is the dress, which lifts them up and embarrasses me. Why are these people not more modest?

"You are beautiful … but so sad," he says. "I know just what you need to cheer you up." And with that he grabs me around the waist and twirls me out onto the dance floor.

I am flying, spinning, moving at a hundred miles an hour, and my feet follow him so naturally, because he knows exactly how to do this dance.

"What dance is this," I ask as we fly, "and what is this song?"

"*Tales of the Vienna Woods*, a Viennese waltz."

"I have waltzed, but never Viennese."

"So, tell me, where are you from, Señorita?"

"Señora."

"Yes, Mrs. Where are you from?"

"Mexico."

He throws his head back and breaks out in another great laugh. "My uncle was the Emperor of Mexico."

"In Mexico? An Emperor? Some time ago, maybe?"

"You didn't study your Mexican history very well, Señora."

I bite my lip and feel stupid. But still he is so very sweet.

"It's a tragic story," he says, "too tragic to tell a beautiful young woman on a night like this."

"Some other night then."

"When you are not wearing my mother's gown."

"Yes But tell me what would you like me to wear, Señor?"

He cocks his head, smiles at me, and then another great laugh fills the ballroom. It bounces off the many beautiful chandlers overhead. But the angels on the ceiling do not seem to mind.

The waltz ends. My handsome Austrian twirls me to a stop, and my Sissy dress comes gladly to rest.

"Thank you, mein herr," I say.

"Are you flirting with me, Mrs …"

"Mann," I answer. "Mankowski."

"Polish?"

"Yes, my husband is three quarters Mexican, one quarter Polish."

"We conquered them too, you know?"

"The Polish?"

"Yes, liebkin. Actually, we *annexed* them."

"Is that better or worse?"

"Better. No war. We Austrians prefer never to do battle if we don't have to."

"Then how do you conquer, Señor?"

"At our best, through love and marriage."

I like that, and I smile even more happily. He stares at me with those light blue eyes. His little nose is cute. And then his lips approach mine.

Oh dear. What am I doing? What would Carlitos say? What would he do? I scramble away from this Austrian and rush out of the ballroom, back to the glass case where I stole Sissy's gown. I quickly return it, put on my passport dress, and then run from the palace like Cinderella from a Disney cartoon.

Chapter 28

"Was it a pleasant evening?" Dr. Freud asks me as I enter his office the following day. "And did you meet anyone interesting?"

"Yes and yes."

"Anyone I might know?"

"Some Austrian."

I go over to the doctor's couch and sit on it. "That's all of us," he says.

"Not me." I answer, and then I lay down.

"Looks like you're ready to begin our next session."

"I am. Do you want more of the same story?"

"Just tell me the first idea that pops into your head and go from there."

I pause for a very long time. He waits, tipping his head in curiosity. And then finally I confess.

"I thought my mother would forgive me if I told her what I saw." I begin. I can feel my face turning white and the blood draining from me. This new memory is terrible.

Dr. Freud doesn't even look concerned. He just settles back in his chair and gets that sleepy look again.

"I am seventeen now," I say, "and deeply in love with Carlitos who has made a respected woman out of me. No boys or girls try to beat me up any more. For one thing Carlitos has become a professional boxer and goes around Northern Mexico beating everyone else up. No one messes with his girl. That's me. I love it. I am also captain of the girls' soccer team because Carlitos has taught me the sport so well."

Dr. Freud lights a cigar. I'm surprised and startled by the sound of his lighter as he flicks it. For some reason I feel very nervous this morning. Still I continue.

"My heart now has a small break in it because I learn that Carlitos will be going to college at the University of Guadalajara … on scholarship. I will not be able to go. I am admitted to the very small technical college, but what good is that? There will be no Carlitos, only the grown-up boys who used to pick on me. Luis is one of them. He thinks that he can make time with me in the absence of my love. He must not realize that I still remember the time he tried to put his cigarette out on my forehead when we were six years old.

"I'm so very sad one day that I decide to go for a run, out in the country beyond the village where there is a little cantina called El Lobo. The place is two miles outside of town, and the day is hot, but I run and run to get away from the idea that next year I will only see Carlitos on holidays.

"Now I am coming to the cantina. It is already starting to get dark, and I know that I have to turn around and go home. But then I recognize a little pickup truck in front of El Lobo. It is a red Toyota, *my father's* red Toyota, and there he is, coming out of the cantina, and with him is Dolores Consuela Modesto.

"I am so angry when I see this that I turn right around and run the other way: back to our village, back to my home, and, as I jog down the street, I pass Carlitos again, and he waves and smiles at me happily, like nothing is wrong. It is like he and my father do not know that they have destroyed my world again. So, I do not return my boyfriend's smile. Instead, I run home and go straight to Mamá, and I tell her everything … everything.

"She does not even seem to care that Carlitos is leaving me. She jumps right on my words about Papá and Dolores.

"'I will kill the pendejo!' she screams at me and goes to the kitchen drawer and takes out a big butcher knife because she is going to butcher Papá who every Sunday now for years and years has been parading her around the town square showing all his compadres how beautiful she is ... Papá who buys her pretty clothes that he cannot afford, who works two jobs at once, both far outside of town, so that he has the money to do those things. Mamá is *still* very beautiful.

Everyone knows it. All the men admire her, and yet Papá is back with Dolores.

"At suppertime my father comes home, but there is no sweet smell of tortillas or enchiladas or even rice and beans. There is the stink of boiling cabbage and my mother's anger. As soon as he opens the door, she rushes at him with that knife, and takes a big swipe at him through the air and cuts a great wound in the side of his face right under his eyeball and blood splatters out of it all over my Mamá.

"'¿Te has vuelto loca?' he screams at her. Have you gone crazy? But she gathers herself and charges him like he is a bull ... with the knife out in front of her. Papá has played bullfighter many times as a kid, I think, because he dodges her and then catches her by the arm. But Mamá is a fighter too, and she tosses the knife into her other hand and jabs it right into his side. More blood: on the kitchen floor, on the table where we eat, even blood flying up onto the crucifix on the wall.

"Papá twists her around and spins her to the floor, so that her hair falls into a puddle of his blood. He pulls the knife away from her.

"'What the hell's going on?' he yells.

"'Dolores!' she yells back at him, and she spits in his face.

"My father's side and his shirt and the floor underneath it are all red with blood. But at her words, at her spit, he rolls from her, throws the knife away with all his might, and it sticks into the wall right beside the bloody crucifix. Then Mamá and Papá just stare at each other.

"Like an estúpido, I rush into the room, grab a towel and try to cover Papa's wounds. But Mamá turns to me and yells, 'Tell him what you saw, Alicia!'"

I must be very excited in the telling of this memory to Dr. Freud, because now I am standing up without even remembering how I did it. I am walking back and forth across the floor in front of Dr. Freud who says nothing. But his eyes are asking me, "Did you tell your father what you saw?" and so I answer, "Oh, Dios mio, I did. I did."

Dr. Freud stands and walks up to me very slowly. He directs me back to the couch, lowers me into it, and I fall and lay on my side sobbing.

"Mamá hates me then," I say. "Papá hates me, Dolores does too. But Carlitos loves me. My parents blame me for everything that happens from then on, which is nothing. My mother stays with my father and never mentions the name Dolores or anything about her again. My father continues to see Dolores and I see them together openly now. But they never seem happy; even when they don't know that I am watching, they are sad, going through the motions of being lovers just like Mamá is going through the motions of being a wife. But she hates Papá, and she hates me and she even hates my sister who, as usual, knows nothing about anything.

"But there is joy in my life too because of Carlitos. We have another half year of high school together, and it is so wonderful: proms and dances and making-out on the beach. (I am throughout all this still a good Catholic School virgin, though I do let Carlitos take off my shirt some times and kiss my naked breasts. But that is all; I swear it.)

"Still, when I get back to my home, the house is full of *dolores*, which is the Spanish word for pain. My parents are never happy again even until this day."

I am crying miserably now, and Dr. Freud lets me. He walks back over to his chair, and I can barely see him as he picks up his cigar and takes a puff. The smoke drifts into the air above my crying eyes, and it seems to form the image of a person, but what person?

"With whom am I so angry?" I ask aloud in perfect Catholic School English. "No se; I do not know." And then I burst into tears again, and I cry until the session comes to an end.

Dr. Freud does not say another word.

Chapter 29

Clip—clop. I hear it. Clip—clop.

There are horses' hooves out in the plaza. They sound like the ghost horses that came to Los Altos and brought me to this place where I am so unhappy.

In my sorrow I haunt Saint Stephen's Cathedral, the great church that stands at the center of Vienna not far from the Opera House and the Hofburg Palace.

The cathedral is very large, very dark and dreary, but *I* am also dreary. Why did I leave Carlitos and come to Vienna to suffer like this?

I have been drifting around the church, no longer crying, but sighing all the time. My ghost- sighs scare the few old churchgoers who come here so late at night. They hurry out as if they've seen a ghost. Which they have not, they've only *heard* one.

I drift up to the huge dome and stare at the angels painted all around me. Is this what I want to be, I ask myself, an angel praising the Lord? I do not think so. And then I wonder if what I am thinking is a sin? I grin angrily. If it is not, then, how about this:

I would rather be down on my knees worshipping my Carlitos. Giving him all the love he deserves. Adoring him. Yes, forgive me, Jesus, but I want to be back with my love. Dr. Freud's questions and this city are hurting me so much.

Clip—clop. I hear the horses' hooves again.

171

I soar higher, to the bell-tower of the church and look down onto the plaza in front. And there is a coach down there. But this is not the scary coach that brought me from Los Altos to Vienna. This is a golden coach with beautiful white horses and a driver who is red-faced and happy. The coach doors open and out tumble three ghosts. At least one of them is very drunk. There is a fat little man, a shapely young woman, and last of all, my Austrian dancing partner from the Hofburg. They are all dressed very nicely as though going to another ball.

My Austrian stares up at the great spires of Saint Stephan's. I know he cannot see me, and yet he calls out, "SEÑORA MANCOWSKI!"

I am sad and feeling dreary, like this cathedral. Still he was fun, was he not?

"Señora Mancowski!" he calls again as he makes his way through the great heavy doors and down the main aisle of the church.

"Señora!"

His ghost boots clomp around as he searches for me.

"Señora Mancowski! We are off on a wonderful new adventure, and we *demand* your company." He laughs his great laugh, and I am feeling a little better because he is here and because of that laugh. So I swoop down in front of him from the heights of the bell tower.

"Señor Austrian."

"Bella Dama," he answers when he sees me, and he bows deeply. "I thought I'd lost you. I had to go to Dr. Freud to find out who you are."

"You know Dr. Freud?"

"Only by reputation. He didn't seem to want us to meet. I practically had to beat it out of him."

"You beat him?" I ask. "For what?"

"Your whereabouts."

"But how did he know where I would be?"

"He didn't. He simply said that you were feeling sad, and I decided this was the saddest place I could think of."

His great Austrian laugh booms through the whole cathedral again almost mocking God. I'm not sure I mind. I'm very angry with God myself at this moment.

"You must join us on our adventure," he says.

"And what adventure would that be?"

The shapely young woman steps forward. I can tell that she is British as soon as she starts to speak. I have seen many British movies in my lifetime after all.

"It's a surprise, Mrs.," she says, "a great and wonderful surprise. So leave these unhappy saints 'n' angels to themselves, and come party with us!"

"Fiesta!" I cheer automatically raising my arms above my head and dancing in a circle ... and then guilt punches me in the stomach, just as mí Carlitos would punch another fighter hard and cruel.

Oh, no! I think. What would Carlitos say to all this?

The Austrian sees my sudden sadness. "What is it, beautiful lady?"

"My husband would not approve, Señor."

"He would want you to be happy, would he not?"

"I suppose so."

"And he would know that there is nothing scandalous in a ghostly adventure?"

"I guess that depends on what kind of a ghostly adventure it is, Señor."

"How scandalous can ghosts be anyway?" he asks.

I wonder if the Austrian has ever experienced ghost sex. Maybe not, I tell myself, though I do not believe it. Still, *nothing scandalous*, he says, which I do not quite understand, but somehow it makes me feel better anyway.

173

"Wunderbar," I say, and I bat my eyes at him. I cannot help myself.

"Sí, muy bueno," he answers as he picks me up and spins me around.

"But, Señor," I say, "I cannot come on your adventure unless you tell me one important thing."

He smiles. "In exchange for your company, I will tell you anything you like."

"What is your name?"

He frowns. This apparently is the one thing that my Austrian gentleman does not want to share. He looks at his friends. He shrugs, they shrug. Then the young woman speaks up again.

"My name is Clarissa, Mrs.," she says. "This extremely drunk old fellow is called Sebastian.

An' our handsome friend is named Rudy."

"Yes," my Austrian says with a smile. "Call me Rudy."

Rudy. Not an Austrian name, I think. How wrong I am.

"This way, ladies," Rudy says as he leads us up and into the carriage. The inside is even more beautiful than the outside, with velvet seats and gold ornaments and decorations everywhere.

"Ready, Alicia?" he asks.

"Where did you learn my first name, Señor?"

"Alicia? From Doctor Freud."

I smile. "So, he *wants* us to be together?"

"Perhaps he does," Rudy answers. But I can tell from the look in his eyes that Dr. Freud does not. And for a moment I wonder why. But before I can think any more about it, the whole coach and all of the horses lift up off the ground, and we soar through the chilly night across the city, over great parks and palaces. And now the wind seems to grow stronger. It begins to knock the carriage sideways and we sway back and forth. We have are own ghost balance, of course, which is usually very good, but when we pass under a bridge the carriage almost flips upside down, and Clarissa lets out a scary squeal. Still it is fun, I think. I giggle, Rudy laughs, and Sebastian turns green and almost vomits. But he does not.

At last we come to a small open field on the outskirts of Vienna where there is a little carnival doing its best to stand against the wind.

Large white sheets with painted images of bearded women, strongmen, monster snakes, and other wonders flap in the wicked breeze. The carriage stops on the edge of the field, and we all get out and follow Rudy as he leads us into the wind. He marches between dirty wagons where brown bears, a mangy lion, a pack of wild dogs, a painted zebra and other unfortunate animals stand sadly facing into the growing gale.

The crowd is sparse. Stilt-walkers strut among the few patrons and almost fall over whenever the wind blows strong. A grossly fat lady on a rocking chair sits on a stage in front of a ratty purple curtain. She pulls her wrap around her, shivers, but still manages to laugh frighteningly. When she sees us, she calls out to Rudy, "Come give us a quick kiss, mein herr … before the wind blows us all away."

Rudy turns to her and tips his hat. "No gale on earth could get *you* off the ground, fräulein," he calls.

"Dummkopf," she shouts as she makes a nasty gesture toward him.

Rudy just smiles at her, turns back into the wind and keeps marching ahead.

Suddenly there is the harsh growl of a tiger that is kept in a great cage at the very end of the row. The tiger is too well fed, too handsome, the wagon too clean and bright to really be part of this carnival, I think. But Rudy pulls his coat tight around him and walks right up to the monster. He tips his hat to the tiger, and the beast snarls and licks its lips hungrily in reply.

"Some other time," Rudy says. Then he spins around and begins fighting his way past booths full of games, magic wheels, rings to be tossed over the necks of nervous swans that are trying to stay afloat in small ponds, bottles that are being knocked over again and again by the wind instead of by the tennis balls that are meant for such things. He heads up to a dusty old yellow-orange wagon that shudders as the gale grows wilder. Lightning blasts. The air is thick with wetness, but still there is no rain.

A sign next to the wagon's small doorway flaps in the wind. It shows images of stars, moons, playing cards, and devils, and it says:

Hope—Pain—Fate—Destiny—Fortunes Told

"Wouldn't you like to have your fortune told, Alicia?" Rudy asks me.

"My fortune is that I am dead," I answer with a shrug.

"I know, Mrs.," Cynthia says as she grasps the edge of her gown before the wind can rip it off of her. "But wouldn't you like to learn the fortune of your husband … who we all know is living?"

"Yes, how about *that*?" Rudy asks.

"Excellent," adds Sebastian as he is suddenly grabbed by an angry gust and thrown so hard against the side of the wagon that the whole thing shudders and the door flies open.

"My husband's fortune," I say. "That could be very interesting." And I suddenly feel so excited that I jump ahead of them all, run up the short stairway, and into the darkness of the wagon.

Inside, small candles give off the only traces of light. They are in tiny candleholders that seem to be growing right out of the walls. We can barely make out posters that hang as decorations. They show the faces of strange playing cards, the outline of a hand with dotted lines over it, a head with sections of the bald skull marked off.

There is a small square table with five chairs around it. In the center of the table is a dark cloth covering something large and round, and looking very much like a soccer ball.

"MIRIAH!" Rudy calls, and there is a rustling from behind a small curtain that hangs just beyond the table. The rustling is even louder than the wind, which continues to shake the wagon as though it might pick it up and take us all flying into the skies.

"Come out here, lovely," Cynthia says as she lowers herself into one of the chairs and holds onto it to steady herself against the rocking motion caused by the wind, "we've a gift for ya."

I look around, I see no gift, and then I forget all about such things as another blast jars the wagon and, at that moment, a small dark woman backs into the room. She wears a heavy black cloak that covers her head and all of her hunched-over body. But when she turns toward us, I see that she is in fact quite young. Her eyes are pale blue, but her hair is jet black and falls in ringlets over her shoulders. She sits down and rides the wind-blasted wagon the way a captain would ride a ship in a storm. As she does, her image seems to shift, from young to old and back again. I am a ghost so I understand this shifting of human shapes, but even I am surprised by the way she continues to change her shape. Old, young; blurry, sharp; dark, light; still, pulsing; and through it all, her eyes never change. They are always those soft aquamarine pools. In spite of all her shifting, she is alive. I am sure of it.

"Greetings, beautiful," Rudy calls as he steps across to one of the chairs and drops into it with a loud crunch. He is very heavy for a ghost, I think.

"Ummmm," Miriah answers as she flashes her eyes at me. "Who have we here? Some ghostly beauty?"

177

Her voice is shifting too: sexy sometimes, and frightening others. "Introduce yourself, Bella Dama," Rudy says. "Tell her your name."

"Alicia Mann, Señorita," I say.

"Yes."

Miriah reaches across the table and takes my hand. Then she pulls me into one of the chairs and continues to hold onto me. I want to jerk my hand away, but somehow I cannot.

"You'd like to know about your Carlitos, wouldn't you, sweetheart?"

"How did you know?"

Miriah smiles, tips her head to one side, flits her eyes over to Rudy and back to me, but she does not answer. Then suddenly she tears the cloth off of the object on the table, and we see that it is a great crystal ball, bigger than a soccer ball. Within its circle, a pink glow pulses in time with the tipping of the wagon in the wind. The glow wants to hypnotize me, I think (brighter—darker—brighter—darker). I look to my companions and find that they are sitting comfortably on these rickety wooden chairs, in spite of our rocking in the wind. Except for Miriah, they are ghosts and can be weightless if they want to be. They can let the wind and its nasty games pass right through them if that is their wish. And for the first time tonight, they must all decide to do that, because they are suddenly stock-still. But, as the glow from the crystal ball reflects on their faces, I see that they are all watching ... me.

Miriah passes her hand over the ball, and I see an image forming in its center. It is a face: Carlitos. His look is confusion, pain, and anger. Then the face of Amy Joy joins him, approaches his. He closes his eyes; she kisses him. It is a long loving kiss. Carlitos does not fight against her passion.

"No!" I shout as I jump to my feet. "He cannot be doing that. You are tricking me."

"And why would I do that?" Miriah asks. "I would *like* to show you what you want to see. Unfortunately, the glass does

178

not lie. Your Carlitos is kissing another woman ... passionately. And what's wrong with that?"

"Everything!"

"Really," Miriah arches her eyebrows in a questioning way. "But you are dead, and he is alive."

The wind slams into the little wagon, and it tips halfway over before it falls back. But we do not care. We stay motionless within the tilting wagon. Rudy catches Miriah and holds her to him so that the one living person with us will not turn upside down. Rudy is a ghost, after all, and we have more important things to think about than the wind and its nasty games.

"Carlitos and I are married," I say.

Miriah reaches forward and takes my hand again. I don't want her to, but I do not seem to be able to pull away.

"*Till death do us part*, Beauty, you swore it," she says. "You are dead, he is not. The laws of the church are very clear."

"I don't give a damn about churches and their laws!" I say as I stand firm in the crazy rocking wagon. "I will find that Joy girl he is with, and I will make ribbons out of her."

The wind howls and so does Miriah. She howls with laughter as she says: "We will be glad to help you, won't we Rudy?"

My handsome Austrian nods with a smile that is almost sad. "I'll make my carriage available to you right now, Alicia, and it will whisk you right back to San Francisco where you can be as bloodthirsty as you want to be."

I nod and flash my nails at them, showing that they can also be claws. "Or ..." Rudy adds.

"There is no *or*," I growl with the wind.

"Of course not, Alicia ... *but* ..."

"There is no *but*, Señor."

"Certainly not ... *only* ..."

"Only what?" I ask finally, if only to make Rudy happy enough to give me the keys to his carriage so that I can drive it back to San Francisco where I will tear that Joy girl a new and uglier face.

"*Only* ... why not stay here with us."

"Rest, relax," Clarissa adds.

"Stop fighting," Miriah says.

"But this pinchi wind makes me want to fight," I say as the whole wagon, the whole carnival, the whole of Vienna is almost blown apart.

"Ah," Miriah says. She snaps her fingers and the wind ceases immediately. The silence is shocking.

"I have a place where even ghosts can relax," Miriah says. "You can sleep, gain refreshment, and face a new day with a new sense of purpose."

The pink light in the crystal ball begins slowly pulsing again. Rudy is glowing. Cynthia is humming some old lullaby. Miriah's image again begins to waver between a beautiful young woman with ocean blue eyes and an ancient crone who somehow seems to look more and more like La Bruja.

My eyes are heavy. All of me is heavy. In spite of the witchiness of what is happening, I allow Miriah to take my hand, and lead me toward the curtain behind the table.

"Softly, softly, this way," Miriah is cooing until:

Rudy clears his throat. "A-humm."

Miriah looks at him crossly for a long moment. Then she reaches into her pocket, says, "Oh, all right," pulls out a small packet, and tosses it to him.

Rudy eyes Cynthia, whose expression has suddenly grown hungry. Sebastian's fingertips begin to quiver.

"This way ... softly," Miriah whispers as she continues to lead me toward the curtain. I stop.

She pulls harder on my arm. I move in her direction, as she wants me to, and then I see Rudy opening the packet right there in front of me. White powder is now on the tip of his finger as he pulls it from the packet and moves it toward his nose.

I freeze.

"Is this what I am?" I ask them all. "I am the *gift* you spoke of, something to be given in trade for drugs?"

I can't believe it. I want to explode with anger, but I need to know more. So, I try to remain calm.

"Where are you taking me?" I ask as coolly as my boiling blood will allow.

"To the other side of the curtain, beautiful," whispers Miriah, who has shifted to her youthful image again.

"But what is back there?"

"A chamber ..." answers Clarissa.

"A chamber?"

"Oh yes," murmurs Miriah, who—together with the crystal ball, the pink glow, the humming of Clarissa, the trembling of Sebastian, and the soft eyes of Rudy—is very much trying to hypnotize me.

"A ghost chamber," Miriah repeats, "a wonderful chamber of peace."

"A CHAMBER OF HORRORS!" I scream, and I jerk my arm away from Miriah and fly out the door of the wagon.

Five gypsies are waiting outside for me: dark men in top hats and long black coats. They have scars on their faces; their eyes are hollow pits of nothing. Their fingers are long and grimy and reach out to grab me as I fly by.

I pound one with a kick of my footballista legs and zoom through the rickety caravan as the wind picks up as though it had never stopped.

I am racing with the wind, driving into it, under the same bridge that Rudy's carriage did. I fly low through the winding streets of Vienna.

"Let me help you, girl," an old crone cackles as she lunges at me from a darkened doorway. I swing away, but she's up on a broomstick and trailing after me. She speeds up and grabs at me again. I dart down an alleyway and rush into the wind at its fullest force. It nearly stops me dead as a dozen Viennese policemen with great black dogs come running after me.

I fly up into the air and through the open window of an apartment. Somehow, Miriah is there with a ghoulish version of Sebastian. He lifts a coffin in front of me, then slams it shut, almost catching me inside of it. Still I manage to fly past it and out another window and into the narrow, dirty streets of Vienna once more.

This chase is exhausting, and now Rudy's coach is plowing through the air after me. He is buffeted by a heavy wind that rocks his carriage this way and that. He opens the door and calls to me.

"Alicia, you don't want to run away; we have such sweetness in store for you."

Yeah, right, I think. Like I want his *sweetness*.

I duck around another corner and run right into the witch and her broom. I zip to the left, and there are those cops and their dogs. I spin around, and Miriah and a ghoulish Sebastian are rolling the coffin down the cobblestone streets toward me.

Witch, cops, coffin, carriage!

I zoom over a high wall into a great plaza. Dogs, gypsies, lions, men on stilts, tigers, and cops are milling around down there. I scream with all I have, and pull back into the nearest doorway.

The door opens, a hand reaches out, grabs me by the shoulder, and pulls me down into the blackness.

#

"You're all right here, ma'am," whispers a young woman's voice. The wind rattles the windows. Even though I am a ghost with ghost vision, I can barely see in this darkness. And suddenly there is a heavy pounding at the door.

"Open up in the name of the Empire!" someone shouts.

"No, we won't," the young woman whispers so that only I can hear. "Come with me, please." And she takes me by the hand.

I follow her as we fly across the room through the darkness and up a flight of stairs, up another flight, through several rooms, to a very small room in the very back of the building. There are no windows, but a fire flickers in a small fireplace. There is a bottle of ghost brandy sitting on a table with glasses all around it. There are also comfortable chairs that are inviting even to frightened ghosts. I sink into the one nearest the fire, close my eyes, then open them and stare out at the young woman who seems to have saved me.

"I'm Anna Maria Pessler," she says calmly. "You're safe now. This apartment backs right up against Dr. Freud's suite. No one will dare bother you here."

"Why not?" I wonder.

"The doctor seems to have some spiritual protection in the ghost world."

I think this is funny because the doctor doesn't even seem to believe in the ghost world, even though he himself is one of the spirits.

"They think I'm some kind of gift," I say, "someone to be traded for drugs."

"It's just the Crown Prince," Anna Maria answers.

"Which Crown Prince?"

"Crown Prince Rudolph, heir to the throne of the Austro-Hungarian Empire."

"Rudy?"

Anna Maria giggles, "If you want to call him that."

"He is an evil man, is he not?"

"No one knows for sure. He could have been great. He seemed to understand the needs of the people and of the times in which he lived. But in the end there were drugs, women, and suicide."

"He's dead now. He's a ghost."

"Perhaps one never loses the hunger for narcotics," says Anna Maria Pessler, "even after death."

"So, what am I to do?"

"Stay here tonight. We can talk if you like."

"And in the morning?"

"I think your enemies will be gone, and you can walk right next door ... to the office of Dr. Freud, to begin your next session."

This room is so deep inside the building that the whistle of the wind is very faint. The pounding on the door ceases. Dogs stop barking; carriages drive away. And in the end it is just Anna Maria and I, and the small fire, the ghost brandy, and our conversation.

"I was his patient, you know?" Anna begins.

"Dr. Freud's?"

"Yes." She brushes her cheek sadly, and I can see that she wanted to be much more than his patient. "He cured me of hysteria, terrible nightmares, and other things."

She pours me some ghost brandy, and we toast the good doctor. The warmth of the brandy adds to the warmth of the little fire, and at last I begin to relax.

"You were in love with him, were you not?" I ask. "Oh, yes.

"I planned to tell him. I knew he loved his wife. But it seemed important to let him know."

"He does want to know what you're thinking," I say.

"But I never had a chance to say it. On the day that he finally helped me see the cause of all my problems, I was so stunned that, as I walked from his office, I stepped in front of a carriage and the horses trampled me to death."

She smiles.

"And was that good?"

"Oh yes, because on that very day, I moved into this apartment and became his aide. He is such a silly old man, so preoccupied with his work, that I was able to attend to him … far better than his wife."

"And you have done it ever since?"

"Ever since."

The brandy makes me feel warm, so does the fire, so does the smile on the face of Anna Maria Pessler. There is really nothing more to say. So we sit there like two contented ghosts staring into the nighttime darkness. And all the while I try not to think of the images of Carlitos kissing Amy Joy that I saw in the gypsy's horrible crystal ball.

Chapter 30

I am flat on my back in Dr. Freud's office, staring up through the smoke at the person I am so angry with, the person who has caused all this hatred that is keeping me from becoming an angel ... even though I do not want to be one.

Dr. Freud has refused to talk about Rudy, or gypsies or ghost chambers. "Let Anna Maria help you with all that," he says.

So, instead I am looking into the past again, at my days in Mexico, trying to find someone so hateful that she left no forgiveness in my heart.

And suddenly the smoke is clearing and I am seeing my mother in our old kitchen in my hometown of San Lucero, Mexico. I am a little girl again, five years old, just after Mamá has learned of my father's infidelity.

My mother is yelling at me, about my Papá and Dolores and the terrible sins they have committed against her.

"I will make him pay for this," she says.

She is chopping onions, which is already making her cry; tears are streaming down her face. The more she chops, the sadder she gets and the angrier, until she is treating the last great purple onion as though it is my father's heart. She jabs her knife into it, and I almost expect to see blood come squirting out.

Mamá's face is so full of hatred that it has become very ugly, even though she is such a beautiful woman.

She jerks the onion off of the end of the knife and then, in one quick slash, she cuts the onion in two. I'm terrified for my

186

father, even for Dolores, but especially for me, because, after all, I am alone with a crazy woman who is holding a kitchen knife as though she is going to kill someone.

"That is not Papá!" I cry. "That is not his heart."

And my words seem to confuse my mother. Her anger turns back to sorrow; real tears begin to flow, even though the onion has already done so much to her (and she has done so much to the onion).

She does not like me. I know that. For some reason, she thinks Papá and I are partners ... with his girlfriend. Mamá jams the knife into the half onion that is sitting face down on the cutting board. She sneers at me the way only angry mothers can sneer at their daughters, and then she goes to the cupboard and takes out a bottle that is dark and blue with a death face on it.

"What is that, Mamá?" I ask.

"Just some native herbs. They're very spicy," she says. "Your father likes *spicy* things after all, doesn't he? Spicy food and spicy Señoritas." She says the words *spicy* with such hatred.

"I know. But the face of death is on that bottle."

"HE DESERVES TO DIE, EL CABRON!" she screams.

"Not to die," I say. "Please, Mamá, not to die."

She walks back to the cutting board and shakes her head with this most evil smile on her face.

"No," she says, "not to die, mija, but maybe just to *burn* a little, right?"

"Yes, burn is okay. Burn is better than die."

I say this because all this talk has me suddenly remembering my first meeting with Dolores and how I threw my bottle of delicious cherry soda onto the floor because she was taking my father away from me.

The bottle broke; the cherry soda splashed all over me. But that did not stop her. Dolores still took my father to the back of the store and kissed him again and again. Now suddenly I understand some of the things my mother must be feeling.

Yes. After kissing and loving Dolores, perhaps he does deserve to burn a little.

"¡EN EL INFIERNO!" My mother's eyes are wild now, and I am agreeing with her worst hatreds.

"But not in hell, Mamá. Right here at dinner?" and I smile the way she is smiling. I am sharing the same feelings.

Sharing feelings between mother and daughter is good, am I not right, even if we are plotting to burn my Papá's stomach with terrible spices?

So, I get down off my chair and walk up beside my mother and study the box of spices. "It says, 'tóxico,' Mamá."

"Well, yes," she says. "All very strong spices have that warning."

I know she is wrong. I look up at a box of cayenne pepper and see no face of death on it.

And suddenly I am very afraid for my father.

"It is my mother then I hate most of all, is it not, Dr. Freud?"

"Is that what you think?" he asks me.

Is my mother the person who has caused all my anger and hatred? I wonder. I am not sure, and Dr. Freud is not giving me any answers. He just looks at me for a very long time and says nothing. We wait together. And finally I ask.

"Is it time for me to go?"

"Do you want it to be time?"

"¡Dios mío! What I want is for you to tell me something … ANYTHING."

The old doctor chuckles. "If you want to go, you can go."

"No."

"No?"

I force myself to stop thinking about Mamá and Papá and Dolores and all my painful memories. And I say, "You must tell me about this Rudy person ... and about drug addiction and suicide."

Dr. Freud turns away nervously. I stand and stomp my foot.

"I am telling you my most awful secrets. You have to tell me these things. They are important."

He waits; he does not move, and I am trying to figure out what he will do, and finally he does talk to me: "The ghost who has asked you to call him *Rudy*" (he says the name as though he were eating a sour pepper) "is really the Crown Prince Rudolf Franz Karl Joseph Hapsburg, the heir to the Austro-Hungarian throne. Anna Maria told you that much, I know."

"How do you know?"

"Before you arrived, while you were still preparing for our session, Anna came and told me about your night."

"Then you know about the gypsies?"

He nods.

"And you know that Rudy tried to make me a gift to this Miriah, in exchange for ghost drugs."

"The young man is such a tragedy ..." Freud says as he shakes his head, "... for himself and for the whole world. He would have been the next Emperor, except that he died before his father did.

"His death completely unhinged the monarchy, and many say led to World War One ... and perhaps even World War Two."

I feel my stomach suddenly turning over nervously. Still, I ask the next logical question even though I think I already know the answer. "And how did he die?"

"Suicide," Dr. Freud says immediately. "There are many theories as to why. Some say his lover was pregnant and he killed her and then shot himself as part of a suicide pact.

Others think that he was an unstable young man to begin with, a heroin addict, given to fits of melancholy.

They say he went around asking beautiful young women to join him in suicide, which apparently his last lover finally did."

"And who says that he was so unstable?"

"I, for one, but some later historians also agree."

"But he is so charming."

"When he wants to be, but he seems to have such little regard for life and for the women who fall in love with him."

"I did not fall in love with him, Dr. Freud."

"You're lucky."

"But he has little of this regard for me anyway, because it seems that he tried to trade me for some cocaine."

"You got away though, didn't you?"

"For now."

Suddenly I am shaking with anger. "Why did you not warn me of all this? Why did you send him to me when he came and asked where I was?"

"You're a strong woman, Alicia. You can take care of yourself."

"I don't feel strong when I am with him, and I'm so alone here, and I miss my Carlitos so much, and he is apparently being unfaithful to me back in San Francisco, and ..."

Dr. Freud turns toward me. He puts down his cigar and comes over to me, takes me by the hands.

"Be careful, Alicia," he says. "Loneliness can kill you, even if you're already dead. Avoid the Crown Prince. Stay with Anna Maria; she will take care of you until your treatment is complete."

"All right," I say as I give the doctor a little smile, nod and then walk to the doorway.

Outside the sky is already growing dark. I look over at the doorway to Anna Maria Pessler's little apartment only a very few steps away. I wonder why I can't just walk through the wall between the two buildings. Something about spiritual protection for Dr. Freud, I guess. So, I must go outside. I check all directions just to be safe. It is something a ghost should never have to do, but I am feeling so cautious. Then I start out in the direction of the doorway only a few feet away. And, halfway there, someone comes out of nowhere, grabs me with inescapable ghost arms and throws me over his shoulder. I begin pounding on his back. I can tell by the fine quality of the coat he is wearing that this is the son of royalty; this is the son of the Emperor.

This is Rudy who has captured me again.

Chapter 31

His gorgeous royal coach arrives, and Rudy jerks open the door and throws me inside. He hauls me up onto the seat, spins me around, lets me pound on him with my fists for a very long time, and then says, "Alicia, Alicia what is this anger all about?"

"You tried to sell me into slavery," I shout at him and flash my long nails toward his face. I want to scratch his eyes out. He catches my wrist in mid air and holds it there.

"What are you talking about, Señora?"

"The gypsies!"

"What gypsies?"

"In the carnival."

He looks at me as though I am crazy. "Ghost hallucinations."

The words come from across the carriage, from the other seat where Clarissa sits in a fine ball gown giving me a pretty smile.

"No wonder she needs a shrink," Clarissa continues. "You're crackers, Alicia."

"Crackers?"

"Crackers, nuts, they're all the same," Rudy says as he finally forces my hands into my lap and dares to let go of them. "She just means that you're imagining things, dear."

"I did not imagine a nasty woman named Miriah who showed me Carlitos kissing his Joy girl in a crystal ball."

"Were we there when it happened?" Rudy asks.

I nod. "Of course."

"You must have imagined it," Clarissa says.

"There was no cocaine?"

"Oh, there might have been cocaine," Rudy answers with a grin, "but I usually don't have to buy it from gypsies."

"He's the bloody Crown Prince, Mrs.," Clarissa adds. "He can have all the cocaine he wants, whenever he wants it. Think about it. It's only logical."

It does seem logical, doesn't it? I think. Why would Rudy need to trade women to gypsies for drugs?

"You are saying that there were no witches on brooms chasing me through the night, no policemen with dogs, no coffins held open by Sebastian?"

Clarissa laughs and points to her fat friend who is slumped down beside her. "Does he look like he could *ever* hold a coffin?"

Groggy old Sebastian is still very drunk even before the beginning of the evening. I am stunned. Do I want to believe these new ideas? Of course I do. But should I?

"So then, where did we go last night?" I ask.

"You went nowhere," Rudy answers. "We visited you in Saint Stephens and invited you back to the Hofburg for another ball."

"And you declined."

"So we went alone."

"We don't know what you did," Clarissa says. "Sounds like you went a little batty, flitting around up there in the church rafters with the rats and the angels and who knows what else."

"But truthfully," Rudy adds, "it just wasn't as much fun without you, pretty lady. That's why we decided to kidnap you this evening and bring you along."

"Masquerade!" drunken Sebastian suddenly shouts out.

"At Schönbrunn Palace," Clarissa giggles.

"Not the Hofberg?"

"Schönbrunn is a much better place for a masked ball," Rudy says. "Brighter, far more spectacular. Of course, if you'd rather not come along, we can take you back to that dreary old church. You won't have any fun, but I guess you will be very, very safe."

"Oh, come on, Alicia," Clarissa says a she leans forward and slaps me on the knee. "Join us."

I realize that if last night really was just a bad dream, then Carlitos really did not kiss Amy Joy in some crystal ball. And Rudy is really a very nice man, and Clarissa is a good friend, and Miriah and the whole gypsy carnival may not have existed at all. Am I ready to believe that?

"Who knows what strange effects churches have on ghosts," Rudy says.

I remember them being very helpful in Sinaqua, Arizona. But still, I would enjoy going dancing and believing that my husband is faithful.

"Here," grunts Sebastian, and he pulls a big box out from behind the seat and hands it to Rudy.

"We've found a dress for you," Rudy says. "One that is very much in the Spanish style and very modest."

"We think you'll like it," Clarissa adds.

Rudy opens the box and turns it toward me. I catch my breath. Inside there is a gown the color of vanilla ice cream.

It actually looks like a cake with swirls of satin and lace, and tiny bouquets sewn along every layer. I wore many beautiful clothes when I was a model, but this dress is something better than all of them. It even has a long silk train, and I wonder how I can ever dance in such a gown. And yet it is so beautiful, so *Spanish* that I reach forward, slide my hand around Rudy's shoulders, pull him to me, and kiss him on the cheeks.

He blushes like a little boy, not like the crazy Crown Prince that Dr. Freud warned me about. "Come over here, dear," Clarissa says and she pulls me to her side of the carriage. Then she pushes Sebastian across to the other seat, reaches up, pulls a string, and drops a curtain across the coach. She and I are alone behind it.

"Change quick, girl," she says, and she helps me struggle out of my everyday clothing and into the beautiful gown.

Rudy laughs as he sees first one bulge and then anther poking into the curtain.

"I wonder what part of your body that is, Alicia," he jokes.

Finally all is complete, and Clarissa raises the curtain.

"There ya go, Rudy," she grins.

He gasps as I look up at him feeling very elegant indeed.

"Wonder what she'll do when ya give her the pearls?" Clarissa asks.

Rudy holds out a long narrow box covered in velvet. He opens it and I see three strands of giant pearls.

I smile as he takes them from the box and offers to put them around my neck. I lean forward and let him.

"I feel like a queen," I say.

"An empress, you mean."

"Not like someone in a ghost chamber, then?" Sebastian mumbles.

I turn and frown at him. Did he really say what I think he said? Did I mention a ghost chamber to any of them when we were talking? Would they know about it unless it was real and they were there?

Rudy freezes. Clarissa sucks in a deep breathe then reaches over and swats Sebastian.

"Will you stop with yer nonsensical babbling, ya old drunk."

Rudy laughs. And suddenly, before I can have another thought about any of this, the whole coach and all the horses lift up off the ground, and we soar through the warm night to the Hapsburg summer palace of Schönbrunn.

#

This is the most handsome place I have ever known in my life, a great, golden building that is wide and high and beautiful. There is a ring of carriages pulling up through the circle that leads to the front entryway. Every person who comes here is a ghost, and even the carriages and the horses are ghosts. We jump to the very front of the line. As we approach, Rudy hands me a pretty little mask that covers my eyes and nose. He puts on a much larger one that hides almost all of his face behind a devil's horny grin. Clarissa's mask is a pretty doll's face with snow-white skin and a big beauty mark on her upper lip. Sebastian puts on a full horse head mask as soon as we stop.

Rudy takes me by the hand and leads me from the carriage, through the doorway, and into a great ballroom. Mi Dios, what wonder is here! The walls are white with windows all along the side. Over the windows are arches of what I think must be solid gold. The floor is beautiful wood, cut in crossing patterns. Great chandeliers hang from the ceilings and above everything are scenes of angels and armies and heroes and ladies looking down on all these Austrians who are waltzing around the room.

In the front of the ballroom, up on a stage, is a small man with a wide moustache who leads a whole orchestra.

"Johann Strauss the Second," Rudy tells me as he points to the conductor. "His ghost, anyway," he adds, "and this is one of his most famous works."

"And its name?"

"*The Beautiful Blue Danube*."

And with that, Rudy takes me in his arms, and we are off flying over the dance floor. We dance around and around, moving too fast for me to focus on anything. The music ends, and we come to a stop in front of an enormous crystal punchbowl filled no doubt with delicious pink ghost punch. I am dizzy and still laughing from the sheer joy of twirling.

"For you, Bella Dama," Rudy says as he scoops out a great ladle of punch, pours it into a crystal cup, and hands it to me.

I raise the cup to my lips and, feeling suddenly very thirsty, drink it down. "More?"

"Oh, yes."

He pours me another, I sip it as he takes me by the hand and leads me up to the bandstand, where he motions to the conductor.

"I would like to request another of your finest works," he says. Strauss nods with a smile.

"*Wiener Blut*," Rudy says, and I burst out laughing almost spilling my punch in the process.

It is to me a very crude sounding name, is it not? Rudy starts laughing too, not even knowing why, maybe because he is such a ... a good friend ... I think ... I hope. Not the dangerous villain that Dr. Freud warned me about.

"*Wiener Blut* means Viennese Blood, you know," Rudy tells me, "or maybe the Spirit of Vienna?"

I nod as we move into the center of the dance floor. Many of the other couples join us. Each person wears a fanciful mask. There are doll-like girls and mysterious, featureless gentlemen.

But there is also an ugly witch standing far away from us, and I do not even want to look at her. There are masks and costumes of horse, bears, cancan girls, men dressed formally, an old Chinese gentleman, at lease five or ten devils, twenty angels, and over in the far corner looking coldly at me ... a gypsy woman. I turn away, not wanting to see her, not wanting to believe she is there. And Dr. Freud's words come back to me.

"Be careful Alicia. Loneliness can kill you even if you are already dead."

The music begins. Rudy takes the cup from me and tosses it back through the crowd where some soldier catches it and smiles as what is left of my drink splashes onto his face.

"I think he feels honored," Rudy says with another laugh. And then he takes my hand and we begin to dance. But this music is not what I expected. It is so beautiful, but beneath its beauty is such sadness, like so many things are about to be lost. It is a feeling that many ghosts share, I know.

We move slowly across the floor. In the far corner I spot a handsome angel who lifts his mask for a moment, and I swear I see Carlyle August behind the mask.

I turn to my right and a bawdy Paris princess whose gown is entirely, shockingly *topless* lifts her pink-cheeked mask to reveal the face of my good friend Chula Contreras. She forms a kiss with her lips and blows it to me.

What is happening? I wonder. I'm starting to feel dizzy. Is it the punch? Was there something in it?

Rudy pulls me tightly to him.

"I have missed you so much, mi amor," he sighs as he presses his hard body against me.

What?

I step back. He lifts his mask, and it is the face of mi Carlitos staring down at me. I rip off my own silly mask, throw my arms around his neck and kiss him passionately.

I look again; there is that handsome Mexican chin, that sharp nose, those blue Polish eyes. I reach up, press my hands to the sides of his face, and kiss him a thousand times on his cheeks. Suddenly, our lips are together again … parting … my tongue is in his mouth and I don't care; Carlitos has come to the ball to surprise me.

SNAP!

A camera flashes a picture, then a dozen more. "Thank you, Alicia," a very greedy voice whispers.

I look over to see the ghost of Mother Joy, dressed in a man's tuxedo with a top hat and tails. She has pulled her mask up to reveal herself. Beside her is a small man with a great camera.

I turn back to Carlitos to ask what Mother Joy is doing here, but he has donned his mask again. I pull it from him and see not Carlitos but the leering face of Crown Prince Rudolph who looks very hungry now ... for me.

I realize what has happened. The ghost of Mother Joy has many pictures of me kissing a man other than my husband. Oh, how she can hurt Carlitos with these pictures.

I spot the man with the camera running away from me. I pull free of Rudy and chase after him. The crowd parts to let me through, but every now and then someone leaps out to block my way and frighten me: a devil, a great black bear, Sebastian in his horse's head, the gypsy woman, and suddenly I look over and the whole orchestra has turned into gypsies. Señor Strauss has transformed into a wicked fiddle-playing gypsy conductor. The music becomes wild, maddening.

Everyone is dancing wickedly: devils, angels, crazy revelers dressed as animals, bare breasted women, men in tuxedos and top hats, stilt walkers, the fat lady from the carnival.

Rudy is running along beside me, shouting at me. "Kiss me again, darling, kiss me again!"

Everyone wants to watch us ... and take our pictures.

The man with the camera is now up on stilts, and he is running ahead of me in great long strides. He kicks over the table with the punchbowl, and the sticky liquid flies up in the air and comes spilling down all over my ice cream dress.

I pull off my mask and throw it aside, but as I rush by one of the mirrors I look and see that my own face has transformed into that of a gypsy with curly black hair, wide dark eyes and golden earrings. I feel dizzier and dizzier, but I am closing in on the stilt walker with the camera, and I must keep running.

Suddenly Mother Joy is beside me. She pulls up a fistful of pictures of me kissing Rudy.

"Carlitos will love these, you harlot!" Mother joy shrieks, and she tosses the pictures into the air and they fly everywhere, all over the room. Old men with monocles scoop them up off the floor, look at them, elbow their fat Austrian wives and point at the pictures, then at me, and they snicker.

I break through the doorway; the stilt walker is only a few feet ahead of me now. He waves the huge camera over his head like prize I am supposed to catch. I look back and there are dozens of ugly gypsy men right behind me, reaching for me with their grimy fingers ... gaining on me.

But I am gaining on the stilt walker and his camera too.

We round the corner of the building, and to my horror I see a raggedy red and yellow carnival wagon ahead of me. An enormous black horse pulls it. At the reins sits a gypsy man, dressed all in black. Across the side of the wagon in big letters are the words, "**GHOST CHAMBER!**"

"This way, my pretty," the gypsy man calls.

I am desperate, sick. My legs are feeling weak. The hands of the gypsy men grab for me. My ice cream dress is slowing me down.

"Over here," a voice suddenly calls, and I look across the road to the vast gardens of Schönbrunn Palace. Even in the dark, even in my panic they are magnificent. And right beyond the wagon is the opening of some kind of passageway into gardens of nothingness.

"Here, here," the voice calls again, and I see an angel dressed all in white, even wearing a halo and great golden wings.

I turn in her direction and feel one of the gypsies grab at the train of my ice cream dress, catch it, and yank at it. My shoulders jerk back where the train is attached, and then it pulls free, causing the man to fall backward tripping those that are behind him. I veer toward the angel, who stands in that dark entryway to nothingness. But the nothingness is the opening to a great maze of hedges that lead round and round. The angel grabs my hand and jerks me into it. I stumble through the maze hearing the crowd, all of them, Rudy and all the others, charge in after me.

But the angel is sly; she knows the maze. She winds me deep into passageways that lead away from the others. Finally, I am so exhausted that I fall onto the beautiful grass flooring of the maze, and I stay there. The angel cradles me. I look up into her eyes. She pulls her mask away. It is Anna Maria Pessler.

"Close call," she whispers, as we huddle in our corner of the maze and listen to the others pounding around in every direction but ours. We stay there for hours it seems, until the others give up, and one by one they leave.

"At least we have your pictures!" Mother Joy shouts to me. "You'll be mine another day!" Rudy calls.

"Masquerade!" Sebastian bellows at the top of his drunken voice.

A thousand other calls follow, including a sad warning from my friend Chula Contreras.

"Carlos is engaged to Amy, Alicia," she says. "He's leaving you for a real *live* woman."

"You'll never see him again," Mother Joy adds, "no matter what you do."

"Might as well just join me in a suicide pact," Rudy jeers. "It's what we were meant to do."

"Or find peace in the ghost chamber of our carnival," one of the gypsy men says.

At last I am so overwhelmed that I can barely move. The hours pass in sadness, until all the revelers are gone and the first light of dawn fills the skies. It is then that Anna Maria Pessler lifts me to my feet, takes me in her angel arms, and flies with me away from Schönbrunn and back to her apartment where she helps me into a more sensible dress and then prepares me for my next visit with Dr. Sigmund Freud.

Chapter 32

I am back on the couch with Dr. Freud. Anna Maria Pessler has delivered me to him. She tells him about my night of masked balls and horror.

I say that Carlos is about to betray me, and Rudy either wants me to go live in a ghost chamber that is part of a gypsy carnival, or join him in suicide. The last almost sounds inviting. But Dr. Freud does not want to talk about any of this. He is forcing me to remember the day when Mamá and I prepared a poisoned stew for my Papá.

I remember feeling hatred for Dolores, and because of her, for my father too. "Not too much spices though, Mamá." I say.

"Of course not, mija, just enough to make him good and sick."

Dr. Freud takes his cigar from his lips, looks at the burning end of it, flicks off some ashes, and settles back in his chair as I stare up through the smoke, and the images become clearer. I'm watching Mamá serving portions of her stew. There are four bowls, one for my sister, one for me, and one each for my Mamá and Papá. And now she adds those evil spices into Papá's dish. I watch her do it. And then I feel very evil and guilty. I am helping my mother poison my father.

As Mamá carries Papá's bowl to the table where he is waiting, I throw a handful of those evil spices into *her* bowl too.

How will she like that? I ask myself. Not very well, I know. And it makes me happy.

Oh, there is sickness in our house that night. Mamá and Papá sweat and shiver, and their lips turn blue. They take turns in our little bathroom relieving themselves of the evil that is in their stomachs. I try to comfort them. This is worse than I thought it would be. As my parents lie in pools of sweat together on their bed, crying out in agony, I cannot believe that I was part of this … that, in Mamá's case at least, I caused it.

Papá is the stronger of the two. The next day he is able to stand and take a few steps to the kitchen. He takes a sip of some milk that Mamá keeps for my sister and me, throws up immediately, and crawls back to his bed. I am left to clean up the mess. But I am willing because I deserve it. I have helped poison my Mamá and Papá.

And now Mamá is acting crazy. She lies in her bed sweating and screaming in pain, ranting about Dolores so much that my embarrassed Papá is unwilling to let me call the doctor. So, I call the priest. And the padre takes one look at Mamá and her hot, smelly, tortured body, and he gives her Extreme Unction, the last rites of the church, the sacrament of the dying. And then *he* calls the doctor.

And through all this I am miserable and afraid. I stay awake all night listening to Mamá's suffering. I only go out in the middle of the day to church where I pray for forgiveness and wellness for my family.

The doctor wants to know what they could have eaten that has made them so sick. So, I take him into the kitchen and show him the spices and tell him a lie: that I was helping my mother in the kitchen, and she asked me to get some spices for her, and I got her the wrong ones. The doctor reads the box and shakes his head.

"And how much did she put in the stew?" he asks. And I lie again: she did not put it in the stew because she did not think my sister and I would like it. So she just sprinkled a little into her dish and Papá's.

The doctor tells my sister and me to take cold cloths and put them on my Mamá's forehead and on Papá's. And we do this. We give them the medicine the doctor has said will help their stomach pain. And after four days of suffering and losing weight and throwing up, my mother and father finally begin to get well. He first. And then he takes care of Mamá with such tenderness that when she recovers she does not mention Dolores again … for many, many years. Until I (stupid girl that I am) see Papá and Dolores together at El Lobo, as I have said. And then I ruin her life again.

Dr. Freud's smoke is clearing. He takes his cigar from between his lips and studies it. "So, with whom are you most angry then, Alicia?" He asks. And I know. The smoke has cleared, and I am looking right at the person: a black haired little girl in a hand-me-down dress who helped her mother poison her father and then gave the same evil mix to her Mamá. I am staring up through the smoke at Dr. Freud's ceiling and seeing the person I hate most in all the world:

"¡Soy yo!" I say in Spanish thinking that using my native tongue will somehow soften the painful truth, but it does not.

IT'S ME!

Chapter 33

I finish my session with Dr. Freud, and I thank him.

"Would you like me to walk you to Frau Pessler's home," the doctor asks me, "for your own protection?"

"Oh yes," I answer, thinking that this is something he should have done last night ... but still it is better now than never.

"I have not been outside in nearly a hundred years," the ghost of the good doctor tells me.

"Then we will both be brave," I say. He answers with a smile.

The air outside the doctor's office is chilly. There is a nasty breeze flitting around the edges of buildings and threatening to bring mischief into the nighttime. But the walk from one building to the other is so short that we barely have time to notice, and I feel safe and secure on the arm of Dr. Freud.

"Anna Maria," Dr. Freud calls as he pounds on his friend's door. No one answers.

He is about to call again, when that wicked breeze kicks the door wide open.

"It's unlike her to be away at this time of the afternoon," Dr. Freud says as he leads me inside.

"Anna Maria?" he calls again. No answer.

"Let's just see about this," Dr. Freud mumbles, and he walks up the flights of stairway and into the cozy room with no windows, the one with the fire where I always feel safe. The fire is going, but Anna Maria Pessler is nowhere to be seen.

205

"She can't be far," the doctor says, and he lowers himself into one of the easy chairs near the fireplace.

I slide into the chair across from him, and we stare at each other for many minutes. Then the doctor stands.

"Anna Maria?" he calls yet again. "ANNA MARIA!"

I look at the old doctor's ghost and shrug. "Not here," I whisper.

Dr. Freud takes out a cigar and prepares to light it, then thinks better of it.

"She won't allow me to smoke in here," he says. "Even though it's ghost smoke and has no aroma. It can't kill us with cancer, can it? We're already dead."

He laughs, then slides the cigar back into his coat pocket and sits back down and smiles nervously at me.

We wait.

"I think you can go, Doctor," I say finally.

"She'll be right back, I'm sure. She wouldn't leave the fire burning if she were going to be away for long."

"And you really want your cigar."

Dr. Freud nods his head and smiles sadly. "Our addictions are all so deadly, Alicia: my tobacco, your temper, Rudy's cocaine ... Anna Maria's ..." he stops fast.

"Her what ..."

"Yes, well she should tell you about that herself," Dr. Freud says. "Very interesting case." "And as for my temper ..."

"We've almost cured you of that, haven't we?"

"I hope so," I lie.

"So I'll see you bright and early tomorrow morning then, Alicia?"

"Bright and early."

Dr. Freud already has the cigar in his mouth and the lighter in his hand as he starts to walk down the stairs, when a sudden fearful thought takes hold of me.

"Please tell me though, Doctor," I call after him.

"Yes?"

"Anna Maria's addiction, what is it?"

"Something quite worse than cocaine," he says, and he slams the door as he leaves the building.

The moment the door closes, terrifying laughter comes pouring from the closet off the room I am sitting in.

As frightened as I am, I go to that door and try to pull it open. It sticks and the laughter gets even louder.

"Damn you," I curse the door, and walk right through it … into not a closet but a whole other room: a musty old study crammed with bookshelves and books. And sitting around a table piled high with wadded up money, balls of cotton, vials of liquid, shot needles, cocaine spoons, mirrors, lines of white powder, bottles of gin and Austrian ghost wine, are Rudy, Clarissa, Sebastian, Miriah the living gypsy, and, sadly, Anna Maria Pessler herself.

Anna Maria has her sleeve rolled up, and she is giving herself an injection from a long thick needle … right in her forearm.

"This stuff's the best," Anna Maria slurs when she sees me.

Rudy picks up a vial and holds it up. "Rapture, Bella Dama," he says. "We all knew it was Anna's Achilles heel. Even Freud knew it. But the old fart just wouldn't admit it to himself or unfortunately to Anna Maria."

"She saved you, Alicia," Clarissa adds with a laugh, "but she can't save herself."

I gasp, pull away from them in horror, then fly back through the door and rush down the stairs and into the street. I know I have to escape, but Rudy is right beside me, and this time he stays with me.

The carnival wagon stands just in back of Dr. Freud's home. The giant black horse paws the ground impatiently.

"Right this way, girl," Rudy says gruffly as he gabs me by the forearm, "I've had quite enough of your chases."

"These are not chases, Señor," I say. "These are the actions of a woman who loves her husband and will bring him back here some day to kick your royal ass."

"Oh dear, Alicia," Rudy laughs. "Did you really say that? You *are* a street ruffian, aren't you?"

I try to jerk my arm away, try to escape Rudy's hold, and that is when Clarissa races up on the other side.

"Here now, Mrs.," she says. "Think of it as the beginning of a whole new life for you. You're a born entertainer, and so we'll provide you with a wonderful stage where you can thrill the crowds every evening at 9 PM."

Clarissa grabs my arm, and she and Rudy hold fast.

I dissolve into nothingness, and they dissolve with me. I bounce back to physical form, and they do too. They seem to be able to anticipate every move and follow it so that I cannot lose them as they drag me toward the carnival wagon.

Miriah rushes up to the door and opens it.

"In you go," she says as she unbolts a second great door made of some greenish stuff that almost seems to be alive. "This'll hold you … *forever*," she squeals.

Sebastian suddenly materializes beside her. He's holding a lifeless Anna Maria Pessler in his arms. Sebastian seems to be much more sober than I have ever seen him before.

"She'll make a nice addition to your collection too, don't you think, Miriah?" he asks.

"That she will," Miriah, answers. "That she will."

#

This wagon is what Miriah calls her ghost chamber. I see that one side of it is covered with a canvas that is meant to keep out the wind and rain and snow. When I am inside the wagon though, I see that behind the covering is a wall of something like glass only much thicker, with a green color that seems to swim as though it were alive. It makes everything on the other side of it blurry. Worst of all, it seems impossible for ghosts to pass through it. I know I try throwing myself at it a dozen times, bouncing off of it painfully, and then throwing myself at it again.

Suddenly this wagon containing the ghost chamber lurches forward. I hear the clip clop of horse's hooves. Only my ghost balance allows me to stand upright. Anna Maria lies at my feet. She's drugged, almost entirely asleep.

After nearly an hour of clomping through the cobblestone streets, she finally awakens. "Where am I?" she asks.

"We are in a gypsy ghost chamber," I answer. "Captives, together." Her face shows me the horror of her understanding.

"Oh no. Then, I failed you, Alicia," she sobs, "I failed Dr. Freud. I failed myself."

"You saved me twice," I say.

"But in the end …"

"Yes, in the end we are both captured, and there is no way out."

The wagon stops dead. The great horse gives a happy whinny and seems not to move at all. The inside of the wagon is dark. I lower myself to my knees, take Anna Maria into my arms and hold her.

"So, you are an addict even as a ghost?" I ask. She only sobs and nods her head.

In the corners of the wagon I can see ghost eyes appearing. A little girl in a pretty spring dress materializes. She is sitting on a small bench. Beside her, a little boy appears too. He reaches for her hand and gives it a squeeze.

In the opposite corner, a pair of lovers, only in their teens I think, stand holding fearfully onto each other. Their expressions are so sad, so lost. Others appear in the wagon.

Businessmen, women, an actor dressed as the devil, a nun. They all begin pacing around this ghost chamber growing more and more nervous, I think. And then the canvas suddenly drops, and through the strange green thickness of the window we see a small crowd gathered on benches outside.

A gypsy man steps up before the wagon. He holds a cane and he points to the window with it.

"Welcome to Madam Miriah's Ghost Chamber," he calls. "Here, for your pleasure, are the ghosts of sad creatures who roam the earth with no hope of ever seeing paradise."

We all sigh at once as we hear his words. The audience flinches. They hear us too.

"Gwendolyn," the gypsy man calls. And a sad looking young woman moves past me to the window and peers out through the green fog.

"No good news for you today, dear," the gypsy man tells her. "You're still our prisoner, still a captive of your sins."

Gwendolyn lets out a terrifying scream, and the audience pulls back in panic. Just what the gypsy man wanted, I think. This Gwendolyn must be a very dependable screamer, I think, as I watch her now throw her hands into the air and begin to moan. She tears at her hair. Others in the ghostly group join her. They beg for release; they call for their loved ones. The crowd shifts uneasily.

"Tommy and Marta," the gypsy man calls, and the two children walk hesitantly hand-in-hand up to the murky green window.

"We still can't find your mommy, dears," the gypsy man says with false sorrow. The children sigh.

"I don't think she's ever coming for you ... ever."

The children burst into tears and begin to wail. The other ghosts sob along with them. But the gypsy man laughs.

The crowd does not.

"Free these spirits," one woman calls. Others in the crowd agree.

"You wanted to see ghosts," the gypsy man shouts back at them. "Here they are. You got your money's worth. You wouldn't want us to let them go so that they could fly out into the world and haunt *you* … would you?"

The crowd is silent for a moment.

"Alicia," the gypsy man shouts to me. I don't move.

"Alicia, step forward. I have news of your husband, dear." I rise and run to the window.

"You know of Carlitos?" I call anxiously.

"Only that he is about to be married, dear, to a lovely young woman in Chinatown. You know her name, don't you, Señora? Tell us."

"Is it Amy Joy?" I shout back at him.

"Very good, Señora. Too bad we can't let you out so that you can attend the wedding." His face is so cruel as he says these words.

"I'll kill you!" I scream. "I'll tear your face into ribbons." The gypsy man laughs and turns back to the audience.

"See why I can't let them go, good people? They're threatening to kill me, and I'm sure that they'd do the same to you if they had the chance."

The curtain falls over the green blurry window. There is a touch of applause, and then we can hear the crowd shuffling away.

"Help us," the little boy and girl call together.

Gwendolyn bangs on the strange green window glass. But it is too late. Others mumble. But by now there is no one there to hear us. We are captives of the gypsies; just part of their little show is all. I return to Anna Maria, hold her close to me and begin to rock her sadly from side to side as we fade into the darkness, just as all the others do

V
Carlos

Chapter 34

"Comfy, Carlitos?" Tiger purrs.

She stalks up to my cell wearing a black latex mini dress with zippers all over it. They're up the sleeves, all the way down the front, across the tips of each breast. Her heels are sky high. The dress is incredibly short, making her legs look like they go on for miles. The effect is electrifying, and she knows it; I can tell by the smug little smile that curls her lips as she approaches. She continues to purr as she finally reaches the cage.

"Ummm, looks like Amy's done a grrreat job getting you in shape. You look so damn *hot,* mi amor."

I want to reach through the bars and rip her face off. She's using another of Alicia's pet names for me, like she thinks she can replace my wife. How shitty is that?

"Aw, still mad at me?" she pouts. "That's not nice."

I turn away from her.

"Carlitos, it's not my fault that your slutty little wife is fooling around on you. I didn't cause that. But I'm here to console you if you need it. So, why don't we just try to make up and be friends?"

I find myself actually growling back at her.

I've been in this cell for two weeks now. It's just me, a sink, a toilet, and a bunch of free-weights. Amy has been my caretaker. She comes in every day and delivers three good healthy meals: high protein stuff, full-grain cereal, fruit, and salad for lunch, steak and salmon for dinner. I eat everything she brings.

I'm so angry that I pump iron all day long ... nighttime too. None of that food is going to my gut; it's all being shaped by my anger ... probably into a hell of a physique. I just wish Alicia were here to see it. But nope! According to her friend Chula Contrerras, she's fallen in love with the ghost of a lecherous crown prince. So, I get more and more angry and do more and more reps with more and more weight.

That damn slave collar was around my neck when I woke up in this cell. One of Tiger's goons dropped me from behind in the restaurant, and she must have put it on me when I was out. I've done everything I can think of to get rid of it, and when I'm not pumping iron, I'm usually trying to cut it off with the edge of anything I think will do the job. (No knives allowed in my cell, of course. Tiger and her goons are too smart for that.)

Getting the collar off isn't easy. The thing is clasped so tightly around my neck that I have to slip my fingers under it and pull on it with one hand while I try to slice away at it with the other. So far I've barely made a dent.

Every afternoon Amy shows up with a leash, fastens it to the collar, and then leads me to a track out behind wherever-the-hell-we-are. I know we're no longer in Chinatown; too many big trees and open spaces.

Amy wears running shorts, high socks, track shoes, and a black cut-off t-shirt with the words *Zoo Keeper* emblazoned across the front in some kind of jungle lettering. All I'm allowed to wear are bicycle pants, if you can imagine it, and socks and running shoes ... all fucking day, every day. No shirt of any kind, even when it's freezing out.

Amy is pleasant, but robotic, like she's been brainwashed. I want to think that she's on my side and will slip me a note or say a few words when we're jogging along the track together ... while she's holding onto my leash. But that never happens.

She says nothing, never mentions that kiss we shared just before I sort of lost my mind in McArthur Park and was knocked unconscious. God, how I regret kissing her like that, knowing how Tiger operates, knowing how she could use it to manipulate Alicia.

"We want to encourage you to be more friendly, Carlitos," Tiger purrs as she stands just outside my cage.

I'll bet she can hear me grinding my teeth at those words.

"All any lonely girl wants is a little male companionship. Is that too much to ask?"

I turn my back on Tiger and walk to the far end of the cell where I sit facing away from her.

"Shame on you, Carlitos, and here I thought we could be friends. Come back. I'll take the collar off of you."

Now that's something I can appreciate. The damn thing is driving me nuts. I walk slowly back toward Tiger. As she sees me coming, she smiles and begins to sway and hum, half closes her eyes, as she does a sexy little dance for me. Her hips grind back and forth, and the latex clings and accentuates every curve in her body.

"You gonna take the damn collar off?"

"Sure," she sighs, "but first I'd like you to meet a friend of mine."

"Grrreat," I growl.

"Exactly!"

She claps her hands, and the door to the room swings open and a full sized Bengal tiger comes loping down the steps and right up to my cage. Must be the same one that terrorized Amy so many months ago.

Tiger pets the big cat when he arrives, and the monster immediately stills, soaking up the attention of his mistress.

"This is Sid Vicious," Tiger says.

"That's all I need," I say, "another sex pistol."

"Besides me, you mean, don't you?" Tiger asks with girlish glee. "Why thank you, Carlitos."

Then her eyes begin to glow and her face looks completely insane as she jerks open the door to my cage, and the big cat begins advancing on me.

"He hasn't been fed in three days," she calls as the tiger stalks me. "As much as I'd like to keep torturing you, Carlitos, Sid does need some lunch."

Sid Vicious roars, and I move back into the corner of the cell. "Goodbye, Carlitos," she sings.

But then I hear a gasp and another voice calls from the doorway, "Punch him in the face, Dr. Mann … HARD!"

It's Amy Joy who has just rushed into the room. As the big cat suddenly charges toward me, I give him a roundhouse right directly between the eyes.

The tiger falls like a sack of shit.

"He hurt my pet. You'll pay for this, Sis." Tiger calls to Amy. But I'm out of the cell and on her by then. I give her a left jab to the jaw, and she crumples to the floor.

But now good old Nurse Abigail comes running in with a poisonous hypodermic ready to dive into my arm. I give her a quick body slam, and she's down for the count.

Next come four members of the goon squad. But hey, I'm a champion boxer, and I've been eating red meat and pumping iron. I take them one at a time as they come through the door. A hard right to the jaw of each, and they're slumped all around me. Except for the last bruiser. He puts up quite a struggle, but in the end I don't mind. I've got all this pent up anger to get rid of. So, I just pound the living shit out of him.

"Come on, Dr. Mann," Amy calls as she pulls me away from my victims and leads me out the door and around the back of the building. As we make the turn I can hear the whir of chopper blades. There's a helicopter waiting for us at the edge of the track. And as we draw closer, I can see an insignia painted on the side of it: an enormous kernel of popcorn.

Chapter 35

"Get in here, amigo," calls Señor Popcorn.

He sits in the chopper's small passenger compartment with a big grin on his face. "Get the girl in too."

The popcorn man tosses a few kernels into his mouth, leans forward, and helps me pull Amy up into the chopper as it begins to rise off the track. More of Tiger's bodyguards come pouring out of the building and charge the helicopter; some fire their pistols at the pilot, others at the bird itself. But we're up too fast, and within seconds, we're out of range.

"How are you, Niña bonita," he asks Amy. She stayed with Señor Popcorn after Assad and Veronica's wedding … until she thought it was safe to return to Chinatown and her family. Big mistake.

"I'm a little better now," Amy sighs and tries to cuddle up to me. "Thank you for getting us out of there, Dr. Mann."

I put my arm around her, but I'm very stiff, still wanting to belong to my beautiful dead wife … if she'll have me.

"Nice work helping us set this up," Señor Popcorn tells Amy.

I'm dumbfounded. All the time she's taking me jogging, not talking to me, acting like some kind of robot, she's really working with Señor Popcorn to save my life.

She blushes and flips her wrist back, as much as to say, it's nothing. I give her a squeeze, and she sighs.

"We have to save Alicia, amigos," Señor Popcorn says.

"I hear she's cheating on me," I answer.

"Do you love her?"

"Of course."

"Then have faith, Carlos. An Austrian prince has traded her to the gypsies; that's all. But her love for you is strong. Mother Joy tried to convince her that you and Amy were getting married. Alicia's friend Chula was forced to support the story. But Alicia is still your wife. She still loves you. You'll see."

Amy snuggles up even closer. She likes the idea of being this close to me. She smiles. I kiss her forehead. "Sorry, doll. I'm taken."

"Chula also told me of Alicia's infidelity," I tell the popcorn man.

"Tiger's holding Chula's Mamá and Papá in a ghost trap, threatening to lose them in the middle of the Gobi desert if she doesn't cooperate."

"How do you know all this?" I ask Señor Popcorn.

He smiles. "Inside information, amigo."

"Amy knows all the secrets of Tiger's lair, and besides, another one of your friends has been at the Austrian court."

"The *ghost* Austrian court, you mean," says a familiar voice. And then the natty spirit of Carlyle August shimmers into the chopper. Unlike the rest of us, he isn't being jostled by the continuing ascent of the helicopter. He hovers in the middle of the open space, arms crossed, in perfect balance as the rest of us bounce around.

"The golden age of Vienna reborn," he sighs, "perhaps even more spectacular than the French Belle Époque, and definitely more fun than Victorian England. Plus, they have the advantage of bringing in ghosts from every century, anyone who's looking for a really good time."

"You saw Alicia?" I ask Carlyle.

"I'm afraid so."

"Is she seriously in love with this prince?"

220

"Of course not," Carlyle continues. "But Alicia has undergone some painful psychotherapy with Dr. Freud. It's muddled her head. Then, Mother shows up at one of those Hapsburg parties and tells her that you and Amy are getting married. It's a lie, of course, but Chula is forced to confirm the story. Then there's that moment of weakness when you let Amy kiss you. They show your wife a picture of the kiss."

"Oh shit."

"Yes," Carlyle says. "So, she's depressed, confused, and suddenly open to the advances of this very charismatic young prince. Now he's finally managed to give her to the gypsies, and they've stuck her in a horrific ghost chamber."

I stand up and want to pace, but another jolt of the chopper drops me back into my seat and right into the arms of Amy Joy. She squeezes me and won't let go. For a moment it feels very comforting.

"I have a jet waiting for us in San Francisco," Señor Popcorn says. "Assad and Veronica will meet us at the airport. They will join Amy and fly on to my estate in Cancun where they can all attend my wedding."

"And stay there until Tiger calms down?" I ask.

He nods. "That chica will never be truly calm, amigo. But perhaps she will decide to spend a more time with her business and less time on revenge … not necessarily good for humanity, but it will certainly help the rest of us."

Carlyle says, "So, you folks jet on to Vienna, reclaim Alicia, rejoin your friends in Cancun, and deal with Tiger sometime in the future."

"That's exactly my plan," the popcorn man says.

"I'd love to go back there with you and help set her free," Carlyle adds, "but I've been away from the Purgatory Bookstore and Ghosts Anonymous a little too long. There's pressing spiritual business for me to attend to."

"Gotta save a few souls whether they want to be saved or not?"

Carlyle grimaces, as though I've described the work ahead of him just perfectly. Personally, I feel relieved; the last thing I need is having Carlyle around to help rescue Alicia. He's still way too fond of her for my tastes.

"You've done a fine job, amigo," Señor Popcorn says as he pats Carlyle on the shoulder. "And fortunately, I have been able to find the perfect person to take your place. He'll help us through the rest of this sad affair."

"Who's that?" I ask.

Señor Popcorn smiles. "You find out soon enough, my friend. He is waiting onboard our flight to Vienna."

NICK IUPPA & JOHN PESQUEIRA

Chapter 36

The ghost of a very hot Latina waves to us from the entry ramp of Señor Popcorn's private jet. And since she's made herself visible to all, the grounds crews from several nearby planes can't help but gawk at her smart sun-colored suit with the short, short skirt and the high, high heels. She hurries down the ramp and then breaks into a run, charging toward me, waving her arms, and calling my name: "Carlitos! Carlitos!"

When she reaches me, she jumps up, throws her arms around me, and gives me an enormous hug. It's Sylvia Morales.

"We have to save Alicia," she says.

"You're right there."

Señor Popcorn catches up to us, takes us each by the arm, and almost drags us back to the jet. We have already seen Amy Joy safely into the company of Assad and Veronica, and they're all off to Cancun.

Carlyle August has also flown away, back to the Purgatory Bookstore to run his Ghost Network meetings and probably dream of old Vienna and Alicia. If he weren't so damn well behaved, I'd worry about the guy. Someday, I may worry anyway. In fact, in the few steps it takes to get onto the jet, my mind starts spooling through the possibilities of an Alicia/Carlyle tryst. My body is tingling all over with jealousy and stress when Señor Popcorn's next comment snaps me back to reality.

"There's someone very special that I want you to meet," he says.

A tall, slender ghost stands as we enter the cabin. He has a high forehead, long sharp nose, and red muttonchops that fluff out from the sides of his cheeks. In spite of their odd appearance, the man himself is most impressive in his well-tailored black suit.

"His Imperial Majesty Don Maximiliano the First," Señor Popcorn announces, "by the grace of God and will of the people, Emperor of Mexico."

Maximilian turns to me.

"Dr. Mancowski," he says as he gives me a handshake that's extremely firm for a ghost.

"Your Imperial Majesty," I respond. "I've read about you in the history books."

"I hope they were kind."

"Certainly kinder than your enemies."

He flinches and then nods.

"They say that you were a liberal, a reformer, a supporter of the rights of all the Mexican people, and that you died because you refused to abandon the Mexicans who supported you."

"Unfortunately, they were wealthy Mexican monarchists who wanted the return of royalty and the status quo," he answers. "But I do think I could have done a great deal of good in spite of them."

Sylvia puts her hands on her hips and turns toward him.

"You're so full of shit," she says, and she can barely contain her anger. "You were a foreign interloper who caused the Mexican Revolution."

"That's not right, Niña," Señor Popcorn says quite sternly. "I'm surprised you weren't a better student of the history of your country."

Sylvia blushes and begins to twirl her hair around her finger. "I had a serious boyfriend at the time."

"So, then, don't condemn a hero because you would rather make-out than do your homework.

"Maximilian had genuine concern for the poor people of our country. The military struggle that led to his execution 1867 was not *the* Mexican Revolution. That began in 1910."

"I don't care," Sylvia says. "An Austrian still had no business trying to be the Emperor of Mexico."

In my heart I have to agree with her. But, I say none of this to anyone. I know we will need Maximilian's help to save Alicia.

The pilot's voice booms out over the intercom telling us all to take our seats for the flight to Vienna.

"So, what do you know of this gypsy carnival that has captured the beautiful Alicia?" Maximilian asks as we become airborne.

"I understand that the ghost of Crown Prince Rudolph traded her to the gypsies for a great deal of drugs, and now her captors display her in an attraction that's called a ghost chamber."

Max winces. "Ghost chambers, I remember them from my boyhood in Vienna. Very sad places where the public comes to hear the ghosts lament over all they have lost.

"And just where is this gypsy carnival located?"

Señor Popcorn speaks up from across the aisle. "Carlyle tracked it to a vacant lot on the outskirts of Vienna. He had to be quite careful, or he might have been captured himself."

"Some things never change," Maximilian sighs. "It's the very same place where I witnessed the ghost chambers in my youth, over a hundred years ago."

"Do you think the very same gypsies could be running this carnival?" I ask.

"Who knows," Maximilian answers. "Gypsies are ageless."

"But they're not ghosts?"

"Fortunately not," Maximilian answers. "Otherwise, our job might be a great deal more difficult."

Chapter 37

It's already nighttime when Señor Popcorn's rented Mercedes pulls up to edge of the field where the gypsy carnival hums and whistles on the outskirts of Vienna.

It looks like the kind of sleazy little carnivals that sometimes came through our village of San Lucero, Mexico. There are rickety rides that rumble around the edges of the place and something like a *midway*, a string of stages with cloth posters advertising different attractions: the alligator man, a dancing bear, the world's ugliest, fattest woman. Toward the end of the midway little booths offer games and prizes for anyone who can throw a ring around a peg or knock over a small pyramid of bottles. I've seen similar attractions in the little carnivals of Mexico. What I have not seen before are individual gypsy wagons offering fortune telling, palm reading, intimate sessions with gypsy beauties, and terrifying encounters with the spirit world.

The wagon with a big sign that says **GHOST CHAMBER** is at the very back of the field, near a small stream with overhanging willow trees. There is a steady flow of interested men, women, and children making their way in that direction.

Señor Popcorn and I fall into line and follow the others. As we get closer I see that the wagon is even larger than I imagined: about the size of one of those *covered wagons* from those old western movies, but with faded yellow and orange paint and a dingy canvas tarp pulled down over the side that faces the audience. A guard stands at each corner of the wagon, big men in dark coats holding rifles across their bodies.

It's clear no one from the audience will be allowed near the wagon.

In front of the seating area and a pretty good distance from the wagon and its guards, a small booth painted the same dingy orange and yellow blocks direct entrance. Inside, a buxom old woman with shadowy ghosts sewed into the fabric of her jacket asks for two Euros from each person who wants to see the show.

"My treat," says Señor Popcorn as he pats me on the back, and I shrug in agreement. I had no money with me when I escaped from Tiger's dungeon, and although Señor Popcorn did give me a nice change of clothes to wear, I'm still broke. I look around and notice that Maximilian and Sylvia Morales are nowhere to be seen. Hopefully they're off making some kind of ghost arrangements to save Alicia.

We head all the way up to the first row of seats and settle in. This is twenty-first century Vienna, and the customers look like typical modern working class folks. There are a few children in the audience, a couple of kids who can't take their eyes from the glowing screens of their iPhones. Goth teens with plenty of tattoos and piercings seem to be out in force. A haunted chamber is just their thing. But there are also patrons in their mid thirties, young couples, and a few small groups of older men and women.

On the far side of the front row seating area I spot several people who seem really out of place. A young, frighteningly pretty woman in a ragged dress, dark curly hair, and great round earrings sits on the aisle across from us. With her is a young man in a top hat and a long dark coat who seems to have stepped right out of the 1890s. He looks so damn familiar: little nose, fair skin, and a royal way of moving and talking to the woman.

"Rudy!" I suddenly growl.

"What's that, amigo?" Señor Popcorn asks.

"That guy sitting over there in the top hat," I say. "Isn't that Crown Prince Rudolph, the guy who was kissing Alicia in those pictures?"

"I never saw the pictures, my friend. But the guy does look a little out of place, like someone going to a costume party."

I can't take my eyes off of him. He's chatting with the scary young woman and with the couple beside her: a girl with blond hair, and a small fat man who's already reeling in his chair.

"That guy's drunk," I say.

"He is," Señor Popcorn answers. "Anyway, no need for a confrontation now. Watch and wait, Carlos. Let's see what happens. The show's about to start."

A shaky spotlight falls on the side of the wagon, and a tall, thin gypsy man steps slowly into the glair. As he does, the tarp rises to reveal a thick, milky-glassed window with an almost sickening green cast to it. The window only allows a very limited view of what's inside the wagon. Shapes move in there, but they're distorted and pretty damn frightening.

Moans come from behind the smoky glass: the sighs of men, women, and children. "Please help us," a little girl calls.

"We're prisoners in here," says a young boy.

The crowd begins to stir nervously. Rudy though, if that's who he is, just leans forward in his seat and smiles at the reaction of the crowd. The dark haired woman next to him beams.

She's checking out the crowd and seems to be counting heads as though she's one of the owners who will profit from the size of the audience.

"Alicia," calls the gypsy man. "Step forward, Señora."

I realize that he's speaking German and English (and even a little Spanish) as though he knows that the audience includes guests from America.

A shapely figure moves forward inside the wagon ... toward the smoky glass. Her shape is distorted, and yet I recognize Alicia.

"Let me out," she shouts immediately, angrily, and I want to get to my feet and rush toward her. Señor Popcorn grabs my arm.

"Wait," he whispers, and it takes every ounce of self-control I have to stay in my seat.

"I must go home, Señor gypsy," she sighs, "I miss my husband, I miss Carlitos."

The gypsy laughs. "I think we can all agree that you've seen the last of Carlitos, Señora."

The crowd titters, not exactly sure if they are on the side of the gypsy or not.

"But I must go to him. I've been away for so long."

"Is he alive, sweetheart?"

"Yes, of course."

"Well, you're dead. End of story."

Now the crowd *does* laugh. But Alicia sobs. It breaks my heart to hear it.

The gypsy man steps closer to the glass. "And what would you do if I did let you out, Alicia?"

"First I would kill you!" my wife hisses, and the other ghosts in the chamber seem to share her feelings because they add wails of anger and growls and threats to her words.

"I just can't let that happen," says the gypsy. "Guess you'll all have to stay in there forever."

"Noooo," cry at least a dozen voices from inside the chamber.

"Okay then, tell me Alicia," the man says with a suggestive smile, "if you promise not to kill me, and I agree to let you out of there, what will you do for me?"

"What would you like me to do, Señor?" Alicia's voice is sexy too now, and the audience can guess just how beautiful she is.

The gypsy laughs. "It's a family carnival, Señora. I'm afraid I can't answer in mixed company, but if you want to meet me behind the wagon a little later this evening ..."

"Instead of killing you, Señor ..." Alicia begins flirtatiously but then her voice goes stone cold, "I will just tear your eyes out, rip off your face, and set your hair on fire." And as she says these words the window on the side of the wagon glows bright red with her anger. Orange bursts of fury pulse across the screen. An image of the gypsy man's face appears on the smoky glass and then it's torn open, eyes fall from their sockets, skin rips away to reveal a bloody skull, hair suddenly bursts into flames.

It's really a hell of an effect, I think, as I watch the Goth kids who must have come here just for this moment. They squeal with delight, smile broadly, and even cheer.

"And that's why you're *not* getting out, Alicia," says the gypsy. "You can stay in there till the end of eternity for all I care. Now go back to your sorry little corner of the wagon and think how lucky you are to have a place to stay at all. You could be in hell right now, you know."

Alicia lets out a terrible sigh and backs away from the glass. As she does, the audience gives her a round of applause.

"Anna Maria Pessler," the gypsy man calls as the cheers fade. Another very feminine shape makes its way toward the murky widow.

"Mein herr?"

"Tell me, Frau Pessler, what do you think of Alicia?"

"She is a very beautiful woman, sir."

"Ah, so she is. But what do you think of her temper?"

"It's dangerous."

"I agree, and do you think she should be punished for threatening me?"

"She is a ghost, sir; she has already been punished enough."

"But she scares me ... and she scares my audience, isn't that right, people?" The audience mumbles in agreement.

"She has made your shows so much better," Anna Maria says. "Her anger is so powerful that you can actually *see* it; you can see her thoughts and the evil plans she has for you."

"Another reason to keep her prisoner," the gypsy says. "So that our show can get better and better and our audiences can truly enjoy themselves."

"Yes, sir," Anna Maria says. "But I have no such powers."

"You do hate me though, don't you?"

"I hate myself as much as anyone, sir. I'm in here because of my own weaknesses."

"You're a drug addict?"

"***Rapture***, sir."

"I've never heard of it."

"A ghost drug, mein herr."

"Would you share some with me if I let you out?"

"I might, sir. The drug does give you beautiful visions." And as Anna Maria says these words, the window of the ghost chamber explodes in bright oranges and blues, swirling together almost dancing, and then breaking apart into a kaleidoscope of color.

"I might consider it," says the gypsy.

"But I'm safer here, sir," Anna Maria answers. "I'll escape the powers of the drug if I stay here. This is good for me."

"See, folks," the gypsy tells his audience. "We're doing the Lord's work here ... curing the addicted."

There's a taste of applause, not much.

"Thank you, sir," Anna Maria says and fades back into the depths of the chamber.

One after another, the gypsy man calls the prisoners of the ghost chamber forward so that he can talk to them. One or two are able to affect the murky window with their emotions. An eight-year- old girl fills the glass with a tragic display of blue as she tells how much she misses her mother. A young couple sings a love song that sends a gentle pastel stream rippling across the window.

In the end, the gypsy sends each ghost back into the chamber with some cruel remark. Until all are done and there is silence.

"Any of you ghosts have anything more to say?" calls the gypsy man.

"I will spit in your face and slit your throat!" Alicia shouts back from the depths of the chamber.

The audience gasps.

"Just another trick she's working on," the gypsy says with a laugh. "Come back tomorrow night, and you may even be able to watch as Alicia imagines slitting my throat and seeing the blood squirt out."

"These are more than just imaginings, you monster," Alicia shouts, and again the whole window glows red as my wife's beautiful face suddenly rises up to fill the entire surface. Her expression is almost bloodthirsty.

The audience is shocked at first, but then they jump to their feet and applaud wildly ... not realizing perhaps that these are real ghosts, not special effects or some expensive light show.

The tarp falls over the window of the wagon, the spotlight goes out and the gypsy man disappears. Still the ghostly wails continue from inside the wagon.

"Better hurry away, friends," the gypsy calls from behind the spotlight. "The spirits are restless. I wouldn't want any of them to hurt you. But do come back tomorrow to the Ghost

Chamber of Madam Miriah's Gypsy Carnival. Only two more days before we move on."

#

There's a stirring at the back of the seating area. Most of the patrons have gone, but a few are still making their way down the path and away from the ghost chamber. Now the very solid form of Maximilian marches toward the wagon leading a small band of policemen. The cops, like Miriah, the gypsy man, and all of their guards, are living. No one seems to realize that Maximilian is not.

"Arrest these criminals," says Max.

"What for?" asks the gypsy man as he steps forward. The guards who were stationed around the wagon now fall in behind him.

"Do you have a license to operate here?" asks a rather small cop with a tidy moustache.

Apparently he's in charge.

"We do," says the dark haired woman. She steps forward, reaches up her sleeve, and pulls out a document. Max takes it, gives it a quick look, and passes it on to Officer Moustache.

The cop shrugs, "Papers are in order, sir."

"Well then, arrest them for kidnapping."

"Kidnapping who?" asks the gypsy man.

"We heard the voices inside your ghost chamber."

"Just prerecorded audio," says the dark haired woman.

"Is that right. And who the hell are you, anyway?" Max asks her.

"Miriah Septova, owner of this gypsy carnival."

I can't stand by and watch this any longer, I decide. I have to speak up.

"I saw the whole show," I call as I run up to the policeman. "My wife's inside this *chamber* or whatever the hell they're calling it. She's being held against her will."

"There's no one inside," Miriah answers.

"There are ghosts in there, madam," Max says.

Now Officer Moustache is looking on in total confusion.

"Arrest these people," Max orders him.

"On what charges?"

"Ghost-napping."

Voices are growing louder. Rudy and his friends are moving away from the confrontation, hoping to disappear when they are far enough away not to be noticed.

"All they have to do is open the damn wagon!" I yell.

"Do you have a search warrant?" Miriah asks as she motions for her guards to go back and position themselves in front of the doors to the wagon.

Max reaches into his pocket and takes out a search warrant that he has come up with somehow ... magically, I guess.

Officer Moustache takes the warrant, studies it for a moment, and then looks at Max suspiciously. Right now Max is the only ghost involved in this discussion, though no one is able to notice it, not even the gypsies. Rudy and his ghost pals have been able to sneak away. There are several live gypsies who may *look* a little ghostly, but they're not. Señor Popcorn and I, the police, and the guards are all real people ... with real guns.

Officer Moustache finally decides that the search warrant is legitimate. "Open the wagon," he orders.

The guards in front of the wagon door point their guns at the cops. In response the cops draw their weapons. I take the opportunity to walk up to the gypsy man who had been so cruel to Alicia and just accidently shoulder-slam him back against the wagon ... a dirty little blow on behalf of my wife.

The crowd is now moving back toward the wagon to see what's going on. They might be on our side, I think.

Meanwhile, Miriah gives a loud whistle and dozens of gypsy carnival workers drop whatever they're doing and begin running toward the wagon from everywhere.

Officer Moustache looks at Max, who looks at Señor Popcorn, who looks at me. I turn back to the former Emperor of Mexico.

"Blow them all to hell," Max says.

The gypsy guards cock their guns. The carnival workers close in on the police and have them outnumbered ten to one.

"Open the damn door!" Officer Moustache calls out.

One guard steps forward and aims his rifle right at the officer's head.

Suddenly, the canvas tarp on the side of the wagon flies up and the murky glass window begins to pulse a dark bloody red. The spirits inside the wagon begin wailing, crying, moaning, and cursing. The sounds take shape in the glass and begin growing with the rising volume of the cries. Harsh blood-red waves roll out from the sides of the window. They crash together and seem to shatter into bright red and yellow sharp-edged fragments. They do it again and again, building with each crash like a gathering storm.

I suddenly see Rudy reappear on the edge of the field. He's looking on in amazement. The crowd doesn't see him. Their eyes are fixed on the monster show going on in the window of the ghost chamber. They fall back in fear. The cops and the guards all drop their guns. The gypsy man frowns. So does Miriah. Maximilian and Señor Popcorn both look terrified.

The window of the ghost chamber is now heaving in and out, back and forth, with crashing waves of blood-red anger, the visible form of the ever-growing screams and calls from the ghosts inside.

Alicia's voice rises above all the others: "LET US OUT, DAMN YOU!" she calls, and suddenly the window explodes outward, sending shards of jagged glass spiraling over the heads of the crowd. One knife-sharp fragment spins out from the window and slices directly across the gypsy man's throat: Alicia's revenge. Another almost decapitates Miriah, but somehow she manages to dodge it.

Now the crowd is running in all directions. The police scatter too, as do the gypsies.

Maximilian suddenly launches himself across the field and horse-collars Rudy. The ghost of Sylvia Morales appears beside the Crown Prince and helps Max drag him back to us.

"I think it's time we had another long talk with your father," Max says sternly. Rudy nods his head, but he's not really listening. He's gaping open mouthed at the seductive form of Sylvia. She bats her eyes at him, and I can tell that he'll do whatever she asks ... which will be whatever Max wants.

I turn to the wagon and see spirits flying out through the broken window and into the night. A woman, who must be Anna Maria Pessler, flits around Rudy angrily; then she zips off for her safe haven in Vienna. All the captive ghosts eventually sail out from the ghost chamber and disappear into the distance.

At last a very worn Alicia climbs through the window and lowers herself to the ground in front of the wagon. I run up to her immediately and throw my arms around her. She clutches me to her and buries her face in my shoulder. I feel her tears flowing so freely that I know that my coat will be drenched in a matter of seconds. I don't care. I have my wife back in my arms, and I will never let her away from me again.

237

Chapter 38

"And who is this?" Sigmund Freud asks as Alicia leads me into his office the next morning.

"This is Carlitos, my husband," Alicia answers proudly. "He is Dr. Carlos Mann, also known as Mancowski."

"Doctor," Freud says as he holds out his hand to me. We shake. "But you can't stay," he tells me. "Doctor/patient privileges."

I nod, but Alicia crosses her arms.

"I did not come here for privileges, Señor Freud."

The psychiatrist responds calmly. "I think it would be best if we simply have our regular session, Alicia. Please, lay down on the couch. Your husband can return in an hour."

"I am very sorry, but we are only here to say goodbye."

Freud sighs, picks up his cigar, and lights it. "After Anna Maria filled me in on your display of temper last night," he says, "I filed a report on your progress."

"Did you say terrible things about me?" Alicia asks.

"Not at all. You were able to take advantage of that emotion-sensitive window that the gypsies have, and use your temper for what it was intended."

"Which is?"

"Self-preservation."

"Just how the hell did that thing work?" I ask Dr. Freud.

"Who knows the kind of things gypsies are capable of. My best guess is magic?"

I laugh. "Not very scientific, Doctor."

Freud offers a wry smile. "Sometimes magic is just plain magic, Dr. Mancowski. In any event, I've told the judges that your wife is doing very well."

"Then *well* must be enough, Señor."

"Apparently you now have that choice," he answers.

Alicia's eyes widen. "I do?"

"You're not cured, you understand. But you've recovered enough to satisfy the judges."

"Then I can go straight to heaven?"

"I didn't say that. They tell me you'll still have to spend more time here on earth … as a ghost."

"Dios mío, that is the happiest news of my life!" Alicia says as she claps her hands and twirls around like a little girl. "Is this not wonderful, mi amor?"

I smile. "It's great."

"So then we must get married again, Carlitos."

"What? We must what?"

"Sí, I will not hear any more of this *'till death do us part.'* You will not be available for any Joy girl who wants you. You will be mine. Forever! Husband and wife! Man and ghost! ¡Para siempre!"

"The dead can't marry the living," Freud sighs.

"You just watch us, Señor."

"Maybe he's right," I say.

The look I get from my wife could bore through a diamond.

"Of course, he is not right, Carlitos. He knows of cigars, and couches, and my memories of the little girl I hate because she hurt my Papá and tried to kill my Mamá."

Alicia freezes in place. Her eyes grow wide as she realizes what she's just said. Her hand moves to her lips and covers them. She stands like a statue.

Then she shakes her head quickly as if to clear away the thoughts. And she's back.

"I do not want to live in those memories, Señor Freud. I have my husband once again. And we can be man and ghost together."

Freud smiles sadly. "The rules are even stricter for ghosts than they are for the living. You can't ignore them."

"I will not ignore them, Señor."

Freud sighs in relief. But Alicia grits her teeth, and I suddenly see the tough little girl I grew up with. "I will *defy* them. I will throw them back in the faces of those who tell me I cannot marry my husband just because he is *alive*. That is prejudice. It is illegal. Right, Carlitos?"

Hell, I can't make sense out of any of this. All I can do is smile and admire her.

"And who will you get to perform the marriage ceremony?" Freud asks.

"The ghost of a disgraced priest would be perfect," she says.

"I thought they all went straight to hell," I say.

"All right, then, the ghost of a disgraced priest who was also a *hero* and so must still haunt the earth. There have to be a few of those around."

"Maybe," Freud says. "But I'd think you should continue your treatment. You're on the verge of a real breakthrough."

"I want my husband, not your breakthroughs, Señor. I want to be a wife, not an angel."

"Alicia," Freud says as he moves toward her and takes her by the hands. "You're a beautiful, strong, intelligent woman. I'd like to encourage you to face your demons and resolve your conflicts. But I have been told that you are well enough to leave my care, and I want to respect your wishes."

Alicia smiles triumphantly. "Then respect them, Señor! And tell whatever judges there are that I want to be left alone. Carlitos and I are together; that is enough."

She takes me by the arm, smacks a hard kiss onto my cheek, and leads me from the office. As I turn and nod to the

Father of Psychoanalysis, I see that he's shaking his head and smiling in amusement.

"Stay well, Dr. Mancowski," he says. "You may be both the luckiest and the unluckiest man I have ever met."

I have to agree.

Chapter 39

We're having the wedding.

Señor Popcorn and Alicia want to hold it back in Cancun as part of his upcoming nuptials, but I barely survived the last big wedding there. I want something simpler. So, this wedding will take place in a small private chapel at Schönbrunn. Maximilian sets it up and promises to keep out all the curious ghosts who want to attend.

Señor Popcorn will be my best man, Sylvia the maid of honor. As for the priest … we don't know yet, but Max promises someone really great.

Max also offers to have the ghost of Rudy's mother help Alicia choose her gown. Mom is the famous Sissi (Elizabeth, Empress of Austria, Queen of Hungary, Bohemia and Croatia, etc.). She's also one of the most beautiful women who ever lived. A crazy anarchist assassinated her in 1898. Check her out on Wikipedia.

Sissi and Alicia meet at Sissi's room in Schönbrunn. I'm staying at a downtown hotel. I'm not present at their meeting, but Alicia tells me everything.

Sissi's ghost is delighted to have Alicia for a friend, and she really likes Sylvia too.

That evening, Alicia asks me if she can go out with Sissi and Sylvia and visit some old haunts that the Empress has talked about. My mind immediately goes on a wild ride through images of libertine places that are not fit for my wife:

steamy clubs where bizarre sex practices are required of the membership.

Damn it! I don't want Alicia going out with Sissi.

"But she's the Empress, and she's dead," Alicia says. "And you and I are about to marry. This will be my bachelorette party, my farewell to freedom."

"Do I get a bachelor party, then?" I ask.

Alicia ponders the idea. "With strippers?" I add.

"I think no." She crosses her arms and pouts like a little girl. It melts my heart. Besides, how much trouble can she get into. After all, she, Sissi, and Sylvia are all dead.

"Go ahead," I tell her. "Haunt your hearts out."

"But no strippers for you, mi amor."

"Of course not."

"Then what will you do?"

"Spend a quiet evening talking to Señor Popcorn."

"Yes, you talk with El Señor, and I'll go into town."

"But remember that you are my wife."

"Always." And then she flits from the room leaving me alone to fight the obsessive thoughts that start pouring into my mind.

#

It's four o'clock in the morning when Sissi finally brings Sylvia and Alicia back to my hotel. I wake for a moment and exchange a few words with Sissi. I don't hear the full story of last night's revelries until the middle of the afternoon when I'm finally able to corner Sylvia and force her to tell me everything that happened. After that, I'm more pissed than ever. Here's what she says:

Sissi leads her new gal pals into the heart of Vienna, to a forgotten old bar near the opera house.

Happy music bubbles from behind the doors of one private room. Sissi approaches, gives a rather rhythmic knock and then glides right through the wall and on in. There are a number of ghosts inside: handsome men, young and old. Several of their lady friends are in various stages of undress. Wonderful ghost-Austrian ale, beer, and spring wine are flowing.

Sitting at the piano with a wench who's down to her bra and panties is a short kid with a funny pointed nose. His fingers fly over the keyboard creating music that flows like a fast- moving stream.

"Your Majesty," the kid says as he sees Sissi and her girls enter the room. He doesn't stop playing as he waves to the Empress, nor does the piece get any simpler.

"We've come to hear you play ... and watch you *at* play," Sissi says with a wicked grin that would shock her imperial courtiers.

The little guy stands, slams a questioning chord into the piano, smiles angelically and asks, "Would you like to hear me play ... something *nice*?" and he tinkles out a little nursery melody, "or something *naughty*?" and he twirls out a high-pitched trill with one hand as he yanks down his girlfriend's top with the other.

Everyone gasps, and then the kid turns devilish. "Or maybe you'd prefer something to help you *shit*?" His music now builds greater and greater tension until the climax when he blasts out an enormous screaming fart.

Everyone groans, and the kid cackles like a madman. "Gross as always, Mr. Mozart," Sissi laughs.

"It's what I do," the kid answers with a grin. Then he turns and eyes Alicia and Sylvia.

"You've brought a couple of goddesses for us to enjoy. Thank you very much, Your Highness."

Alicia immediately stiffens. "We are very good girls, Señor. I am about to marry to my husband in two days."

Mozart sits back down at the piano and begins playing a little waltz. "Why would you marry him if you're *already* married to him? Give *me* a chance instead."

"No, Señor, not I," Alicia says. "But maybe Sylvia." Her friend blushes bright red.

"Come on, Wolfey," his half naked girlfriend calls, "You and me can make our own fun."

"Sorry, beautiful," Mozart says, "but it's time for some new blood. Don't you agree, Freddie?"

A tall, handsome young ghost rises from the back of the room and approaches the Empress.

"Your Royal Highness."

"Call me Sissi."

The suggestion makes Freddie nervous. "All right, Sissi. I'll play the piano so Mozart could play with your lady friends."

"And just *how* will we be played with?" Alicia demands.

"You know, you're just too damn defensive, <u>fräulein</u>," Mozart says. "I'd rather get to know your companion," and he grabs Sylvia by the arm and drags her to a table in very the back of the room.

"A little Austrian wine?" he asks.

"Sounds good."

"A little Austrian sausage?"

"Ummmm."

Alicia is shocked to see Mozart unbutton Sylvia's gown and deftly remove the whole complicated outfit right there in front of everyone. The beautiful ghost cooperates; she doesn't seem to mind. In fact she sips wine and giggles through it all. Once she's down to a tightly laced corset, she encourages the kid to fondle her every way he can and offers plenty of sighs of encouragement to go with it.

Meanwhile, Freddie is creating gorgeous melodies in the piano. Sissi slides in beside him.

He frowns at her. "I'd like you more if your family hadn't oppressed the Polish."

Sissi sighs, "They've oppressed me too."

"I understand," responds Freddie, and he kisses her on the cheek, then the lips, the eyes, and never once slows the intricate little tune he's playing.

Alicia finds herself alone. Her planned evening-out has turned boring. Her friends have found lovers. She's nowhere.

Alicia sighs. *What fun is this?* And then suddenly, a new young ghost strides proudly into the room.

This guy is tall, with a regal face and long, blond hair. His eyes are deep and penetrating. He speaks with an accent that reminds my wife of a vampire movie.

"Ah, so the Queen of Hungary has decided to grace us with her presence," the new guy says as he takes in the whole room, "and she's brought some beauties with her too."

At this point Mozart is ravishing Sylvia's entire body with kisses, and Sissi and Freddie are staring into each other's eyes as he plays romantic melodies.

"And what about you, beauty?" the regal guy asks Alicia. "You seem so alone."

"Yes I am, and we are celebrating my wedding."

The young man swings a chair up beside my wife, straddles it, and then pours her a glass of ghost wine. "They're ignoring the bride."

"Yes."

"How sad."

"I think so."

"And what's your name, beauty?" "Alicia."

"Mine's Franz."

"Very pleased to meet you, Señor Franz."

"So, tell me Alicia, honestly, what's your opinion of Mozart's music?"

"I'm afraid I don't know it."

"Hah! Do you hear that, Mozart?" Franz calls. "This girl's never heard of you."

Mozart takes his tongue out of Sylvia's mouth long enough to let out a high pitched laugh, and then he's back at her again.

"Do you know Chopin?" Franz asks.

"Who?"

"How about Beethoven or Brahms?"

"Brahms' Lullaby, Beethoven's Fifth," my wife answers.

"Excellent! See, Mozart, I told you your fame would never last."

"Asshole," the kid answers, and then he gets up on the table and moons the entire room.

"I don't like him." Alicia says.

"None of us do," Franz answers. "But it's hard to deny his genius."

"I guess so."

"You do like music though, don't you, Beauty?"

"Rock and roll, salsa, reggae."

"Me too. John Lennon. Another genius."

Alicia nods. Franz studies her. He reaches up and runs his fingers down the side of her face and across her upper lip. Alicia smiles.

"We need something with more gusto, don't you think?"

Alicia nods.

"Chopin, get off the keyboard. Take the Empress into the side room and do something to her in the name of Poland."

The Empress giggles, and Freddie immediately pulls her aside. "Now, let a real virtuoso have a go at it."

Franz sits down at the piano bench and motions for Alicia to join him.

"Do you like this?" and he pounds out a few chords from a Beatles' classic. Alicia smiles.

Then, suddenly he makes the melody frilly.

247

"Mozartian!" he says.

"I like it."

"No you don't, Beauty. Listen." And suddenly the tune becomes deep, melancholy and very romantic. "How's this, Freddie?"

Chopin turns back to the piano, and stands there admiring the performance. Sissi has her hand on his shoulder, and her cheek pressed against his. The Polish master nods his approval.

"But if you want real fire, Alicia," Franz says, "it has to be Hungarian!" and with that his fingers dive at the piano and soon fill the room with a quick-paced *Hungarian Rhapsody*.

The tempo increases.

Mozart jumps up and draws Sylvia, Freddie, and Sissi together into a circle. They dance enthusiastically around and around.

Alicia is quite taken with the spirit of the dance. She climbs up onto a table and does her best fiesta performance to all the Hungarian madness.

The tempo builds further, and the dancing becomes riotous: more wine, more beer, more young men and women ghosts come charging into the room. The place is packed to the walls with revelers, and the pace never slows again.

For four solid hours, there is dancing and music and drinking and kissing and groping, while Franz bangs out mazurkas and polkas and Hungarian dances without end.

Finally, Mozart pushes Franz away and undertakes some spirited variations on the Mexican Hat Dance, while Alicia finds herself up on a table again stomping frantically to the ever-building tempo that the kid lays down.

#

As I said, it is four o'clock in the morning when Sissi, Sylvia, and Alicia make their way back to my hotel. They are all tipsy from ghost wine and no small amount of partying. I become frantic when I see how really messed up they are, but I try not to panic.

Sylvia and my wife can do nothing but giggle and glide away to haunt the quieter corners of the hotel. Only Sissi regains her regal bearing and gives me a moment.

"Your wife's a wild one," she says. "Are you sure you're up to marrying her again?"

I close my eyes and slump into one of the chairs. After all I've been through, that's not a question I want to answer.

"What'd she do?" I ask.

Sissi lowers her head, looks up at me through those long lashes and says nothing.

"What?" I demand.

She gives me a world-weary sigh, and starts to leave.

"WHAT?"

"Well," the beautiful Empress answers, "she just about castrated Franz Liszt when he tried to make love to her after a rousing version of his *2nd Hungarian Rhapsody*."

"But she didn't ..."

"Of course not; she has already defied Sigmund Freud and all the powers of heaven and earth to be with *YOU* ... you dummcopf!"

And then Sissi studies me for a very long moment.

"Better take care of her, Carlitos. You have a tigress on your hands."

I nod silently and smile, wondering if Sissi has any idea how much I know about dealing with tigers.

Chapter 40

I stand beside Señor Popcorn at the front of the little chapel in Schönbrunn. It's my wedding day, and we're waiting for Alicia's appearance. We still haven't seen the priest who'll perform the ceremony, though Maximilian assures me he'll be a wonderful surprise. Meanwhile, far more people are crowded into the chapel than I thought would be here: the ghost of Dr. Freud for one, Crown Prince Rudolph has been allowed to join us. There's also Sissi and her husband the Emperor Franz Joseph, the rag-tag ghosts of Franz Liszt, Chopin and a bevy of young ladies who must be the wenches Sylvia said were in the bar on their night of revelry. They've cleaned up beautifully, I guess, and now they're each wearing ornate Viennese gowns in bright, happy colors.

I think I may see the ghosts of John Lennon and George Harrison standing in the back of the chapel, but I can't be sure. Liszt told them how much Alicia liked their music, and they said they might attend.

The Purgatory ghosts are here too. Carlyle August and the others have made the journey to cheer us on. Royce Brilliant is clapping. Freeman calls out, "Mazel tov," and I'm sure I see Jenny Beck eyeing Chopin and then turning to her friends and whispering, *"Bitchin!"*

In the choir loft, ghosts of kids from the Vienna Boys Choir break into song. It's a beautiful processional from *The Marriage of Figaro*, and I think I recognize Mozart's ghost conducting the chorus. At least the little guy up there matches Sylvia's description (and several album covers I've seen with his picture on them).

After a moment, the wedding march rings out, and Sylvia comes down the center aisle of the chapel. Three young couples follow her. They're all ghosts. I've never seen them before and figure they must be former members of the Austrian court.

The music swells. Alicia enters on the arm of Maximilian himself, and everyone gasps at her beauty. She wears a spectacular off-the-shoulder gown with strings of pearls, layers of white silk and a long magnificent train. It's the very dress Sissi wore for her coronation as Queen of Hungary.

Alicia reaches the front of the chapel, and Max guides her into my arms. There are tears in her eyes. "Tears of joy," she whispers. Maybe mixed with a touch of regret over her doubts about my love and her fascination with Rudy.

"Dearly beloved," we hear the priest say behind us, and we turn to find a face I've seen a thousand times, a face you too would recognize if you grew up in Mexico. It's Father Hidalgo, not only *father* as in "priest," but also *father* as in "the Father of his Country," the Father of Mexico.

I turn to Maximilian and give him a big thumbs-up. How the hell did he ever arrange this? It's like calling for a surveyor and having George Washington show up on your front lawn. It's exactly like asking for a priest to marry you and getting the Father of Mexico to say your wedding mass.

Twenty minutes later, things are going great. Alicia and I are saying the vows, finally realizing how lucky we are to be joined together, man and ghost. It's a miracle.

"If any of you have reasons why this man and this woman should not be joined in marriage," Father Hidalgo says, "speak now or forever hold your peace."

At that moment a dark-robed figure stands slowly up in the middle of the congregation. He looks like a monk who somehow slipped in for the ceremonies, but as he lowers his hood, his face seems deathlike.

"I'm afraid I have an objection, padre," he says so solemnly that it scares me. "This is sacrilege." Then, at the corner of the front pew, another hooded padre rises as well. "Sacrilege," he says.

In the very back of the chapel a bearded man stands and says, "I too object." Then around the chapel one hooded figure after another rises to his feet and offers the same accusation. "Sacrilege."

"Sacrilege." "Sacrilege."

Now, out from behind the altar, yet another hooded figure steps forward. This man is enormous and his hood barely hides a face as gray and angry as death itself.

"THIS IS AN ABOMINATION OF THE SACREMENT OF MATRIMONY! THIS IS SACRELEGE!"

Father Hidalgo eyes me quickly and points to the side door. But it's too late. Other dark figures rush forward. They grab Alicia and me, pull us apart, and hold us fast.

I turn to Max, and he shrugs.

"No one expects the Spanish Inquisition," he sighs.

Rudy charges the front of the chapel. But there are dark-robed figures to stop him in his tracks.

"THE DEAD SHALL NOT MARRY THE LIVING!" the ugly guy at the altar says. I'm thinking that this must be the ghost of one of the Grand Inquisitors, maybe even El Bernardo, one of the most merciless of them all.

"Let's burn the witch in the Dread Zone," one of the hooded monks hisses, and I get the feeling the whole idea turns him on.

"Burn her husband at the stake as well," calls another.

As they drag Alicia away from me, one of the monks hisses at her. "In the Dread Zone you can really *feel* the pain!"

Then he roars with laughter, and at that moment, my wife works one hand free, reaches into her sash, pulls something from it, and tosses it toward me.

I jerk my arm away from my captors just long enough catch it. It's a ring, my new wedding ring. Massive, gold, encrusted with Aztec images. I wrestle away from the guards long enough to slip it onto my finger. Then I jerk my hand upward, and flash the ring into the eyes of our captors.

They release their hold and shrink away immediately. The ring catches a glint from the stained glass windows, and our enemies turn and run from the chapel. The Grand Inquisitor, El Bernardo if that's who it is, slinks out from in front of the altar and vanishes into the vestibule.

Everyone looks on in amazement.

Alicia throws her arms around me. She's trembling.

"Christ, what is this thing?" I ask.

"Ghost magic," she murmurs. "Aztec ghost magic."

"In a ring?"

"Sí, mi amor. To drive evil away."

"And what could be more evil than the Inquisition," Father Hidalgo says. It's a statement not a question.

I pull Alicia to me. The wedding guests are buzzing with wonder and curiosity. The sound grows louder until Father Hidalgo steps forward.

"A ghost-magic ring," he says to everyone with a smile. "We're all ghosts here. We've all seen magic. No big surprises."

The guests heave a collective sigh of relief and after a moment become quiet again.

"Come together now, children," the padre says to us. "The Inquisition didn't get me either, you know. They put me on trial, but never found me guilty. Sooner or later they'll be back. But I think we're safe for now.

"So ..." and he looks down at his book of prayers, "where were we?"

Alicia is still trembling from the struggle. Me too. But the Padre smiles at us again. "Let's take our time," he says. "In fact, to help everyone calm down a little," he winks at Alicia, "Carlos, why don't you kiss the bride right now, and then we'll proceed."

Let me tell you, the kiss is amazing. It goes on and on, until Alicia and I are both over our stress and smiling against each other's lips. I'm hoping everyone in the chapel is kissing too. I know they're cheering. And they should be. They're seeing a man and wife enjoying the most wonderful moment of their lives and afterlives, becoming man and wife again ... man and ghost ... forever.

Chapter 41

It's 3 AM on our first night as re-married man and ghost. Alicia's rewards me for swearing to ignore our earlier marriage vows that say, "Till death do us part." She gives me amazing, never-ending, and exhausting love.

Now, I wake, sit up in bed, and see her lying beside me staring at the ceiling. "Ghosts never sleep, Carlitos," she says.

"I'm sorry."

"Don't be. It gives us time to think."

"About what?" I ask as I turn to her and study those ghost eyes that glow so brightly in the darkness.

"Now we can go back to Cancun and celebrate Señor Popcorn's wedding in great gladness," she says. "And after that you will take a nice safe job as a gentleman farmer."

I sigh. No matter how many times I say 'no' to Alicia, she always tries again. We've had this conversation before. I've already refused to work for the popcorn man and stay in Mexico. Yes, our first effort to return to Leland almost got me killed and ended with my dismissal from the faculty. But I know I have to go back and somehow reclaim my position and my reputation.

I walk around the bed, sit down beside my wife, and take her hands. I tell her that whole story, about Lupe Bravo, about Dean Applebee, about my paper, *Revelations on the Rights of the Poor*, the plagiarism charges, about the hearing that the Psychology Department held behind closed doors, without my even knowing about it. And then I tell her about my final disgrace.

Tiger Jcy only added insult to injury, although she did seem to know an awful lot about the incident, as though she somehow had a hand in it.

When I'm done my wife smiles. "Is that all?" she asks.

I shrug. "Isn't that plenty?"

"Yes, but I can fix that easily."

I smile and kiss those sweet, but oh so naïve lips. "You're a little crazy, you know?"

"Not crazy," she answers. "It will be very simple, for a ghost, mi amor. I will go back to Los Altos, to the University of Leland."

"Leland University," I correct. "But what can you do back there?"

"I can make everything right."

"No way."

"Way, Carlitos."

I study her for a moment wondering if she's right. It seems too good to be true.

"You have a plan?"

"A very simple one."

"Tell me about it?"

Alicia turns to me and gives me her tough little girl look. "No, I will not. It must be a secret that I keep so no one can spoil it … not even you."

"I'll go with you then."

"Let a ghost do ghostly work, mi amor. Do not try to interfere."

I sit there looking at this vision, afraid for myself and for her. Maybe I'm just getting desperate, but I'm starting to think that maybe Alicia *can* go back to Leland and set things right. Sounds impossible I know. But then, so is the fact that I've just become married to a ghost. Hell, Alicia can probably do anything she sets her mind to.

"Will you let me do this thing alone?" she asks again.

On her own, Alicia can be like a bull in a china shop.

"Not sure."

"Say 'yes,' Carlitos, or I will never say '*yes*' to you again."

"Yes," I say immediately setting aside all macho logic, because it's been overridden by more powerful macho instincts.

"Then I say 'yes' to you too, right now," Alicia answers as she grabs me, giggles, and pulls me down on top of her.

I do the best thing I can think of at the moment. I start kissing her all over again.

VI
Alicia

Chapter 42

I am so angry with this Lupe Bravo that I'm ready to pick her up and throw her out of the Leland Library window. I follow her through the library stacks, which is where we are. I am invisible, but ready to corner her, show her my most terrifying death face, and then scare her into telling the truth about Carlitos and the article he wrote.

I place myself at the end of the long aisle near the back of the poetry books. I feel my ghost blood boiling up in me, sending ugliness to every part of my body.

Lupe turns the corner. She smiles stupidly, comes up to the stacks of her husband's work and pulls one book out of the shelf. She opens it, and I'm ready to jump into sight. But before I can do it, another ghost, uglier, more horrible than I could ever be, throws himself at her and screams like the devil.

Lupe drops the book and clutches her skinny little bosoms. She lets out her own wild scream that seems to terrify the ghost, and he raises the level of his cries making them even louder and scarier.

His face goes crazy, ghost-slime squirts from his body, and now his screams become questions.

"HOW DARE YOU PUT WORDS INTO MY DEAD MOUTH?

"HOW DARE YOU ALTER MY THOUGHTS AND MY POETRY?"

Lupe falls back against the bookshelves; her hand is raised in front of her face; her eyes are wide.

"Pedro?"

260

"Yes, Lupe. You have shamed my memory. You have shamed our whole family."

I cannot believe this. Señor Pedro Bravo, the great poet, has come to face his wife and charge her with crimes against everyone. Why did he not do this sooner? He could have saved my husband so much sadness. I want to ask him many things, but I think I'd better not slow him down.

"What would you have me do, Pedro?" Lupe asks.

"Right this wrong."

"But how?"

"Go to the university, and take back your words. Have them restore my poetry."

"But you agreed with Señor Mann's ideas."

"Have you even *read* my poems, woman?"

"All right. You *used to* agree with his ideas."

"Only when I was a child." The ghost grows larger and now stands over his wife with an evil look on his death face. "But I did not write those ideas. You have made *me* the plagiarist."

Lupe crosses her arms and faces up to the ghost of her husband. Like so many brave Mexican women, she does not seem to fear her husband or even his *ghost*.

"And, if I refuse?"

Pedro Bravo swells up to even greater size, his eyes are wild, his hands turn to claws and reach out for her. "I'll scare you to *death*!"

"But it will be so embarrassing."

Pedro's ghost can't believe his dead ears. A death wale reverberates through the stacks. "Embarrassment or death?"

"You just try it!" Lupe challenges.

And now I am glad I am here. As Pedro's ghost tries to terrify his wife, I slowly appear behind her. My anger is feeding an ugliness that is more than I could have wished for. My body is bones and slimy dead flesh; my face is monstrous, rotting teeth, rotting eyeballs, the entire rotting package. I drop my skeleton hand on Lupe's shoulder and squeeze. Lupe looks up at her husband, and I feel her body become so stiff.

"W—who's behind me?"

Pedro smiles. He's looking at me and likes what he sees.

"I am Alicia Mann, the ghost wife of the man you have wronged," I moan spookily. I feel Lupe's body begin to shake. She sobs like a scared little girl.

"W—what do you want, Señora Mann?"

My ghost hand squeezes into her shoulder. My fingernails prick her skin and draw blood.

"Justice," I say as I really start to enjoy myself. "Either you give me *justice*, or you will feel my *revenges*."

Lupe turns slowly and looks at me. I swell up in front of her, pop out my dead eyes, which look up at her in a spinning view as they roll across the floor. I chatter my ghost teeth, and scream with all my power.

"REVENGES!"

Lupe falls back. Her lips form words, but they are not spoken. Terror shines in her eyes.

She's trembling.

"I—I—I'll do anything you say."

"RECANT," Pedro says.

I say it too, though I am not even sure what it means.

Lupe closes her eyes, squeezing a fountain of tears down her face. She nods her head over and over.

"I will."

Pedro and I look at each other and smile horribly. I think he is having fun too. "So be it," he adds, and we disappear together.

Lupe is still shaking. She falls into a chair in the corner of the stacks and sits there without moving for a very long time. I think she may be asleep. But, finally, she picks up the poetry book and slowly carries it back to the stacks. And as she walks, she begins to talk to herself.

"Did that really happen?" she says out loud as she brushes the tears from her cheeks. "Did I really see all that or just imagine it?"

She pushes the book back into the shelf.

"Maybe I was frightened by a noise, passed out, and dreamed the whole thing." She turns to leave.

"Ghosts in the Leland Library?" she asks herself. "I don't believe it ... don't believe it at all."

She begins walking out from between the stacks.

"Nonsense," she says. And WHAM! The place is filled with hideous ghosts: Pedro Bravo, Carlyle August, Jenny Beck, all the other ghosts from the Purgatory Bookstore, and me ... at our worst.

Madre de Dios, do we look scary.

"RECANT!" We all shout in unison, and Lupe takes off running from the stacks, down the great stairway and out into the night.

"Yes, yes, yes!" she screams as she keeps running. "I'll do it. I'll do it!"

Chapter 43

I am now haunting the office of Dr. John Christianson, President of the College of Arts and Letters at Leland University. The volume of Pedro Bravo's poetry, the one that plagiarized Carlitos's article, sits on the edge of the desk. Lupe Bravo is also here, and we are waiting for Dean Oliver Applebee.

Lupe is uncomfortable. She shifts in her seat and straightens her ugly black dress. It is so covered with pictures of Macaws that I am getting dizzy. She tries to smile, but Christianson makes a nasty face at her.

And just then Applebee rushes in through the door and falls into the chair next to Lupe. "You know why you're here, don't you?" the President of the College asks.

"Something about Carlos Mann," Dr. Applebee answers, and I can see his eyes going first to Lupe and then to the book on the desk

I'm smiling, just because I like to hear people say my husband's name, though Señor Applebee's tone has no respect for Carlitos.

"Mrs. Bravo is asking that we revisit the charges of plagiarism against our esteemed colleague."

I like his big words, and I smile.

"We've already had our hearing," Applebee says. "The university wouldn't be stupid enough to go through it all over again … would we?"

"If what she says is true, we could set things right and not go through any more hearings. We just reinstate Dr. Mann and offer a reasonable settlement."

Dr. Applebee looks shocked. "What did Lupe tell you?"

"That you and she knew that Carlos didn't copy anything from her husband's book. That a group in Chinatown, under the direction of some person she keeps calling Tiger, inserted very authentic looking pages into Pedro's original volume to make it look like Dr. Mann had copied it."

"You can't really believe *that*?" Dean Applebee says.

President Christianson doesn't even stop to answer that question. He just keeps talking. "Lupe tells me that Dr. Mann was framed and that *you* knew about it. She says that you and she met with a group in Chinatown headed by this 'Tiger' person. Lupe wanted to destroy Dr. Mann's reputation, and so she agreed to testify that he copied from her husband's work."

Now Lupe and Applebee are *both* shifting nervously in their seats, and I would be shifting in mine if I had one. These words make me very angry and I want to do something evil to these two. But I know it would hurt my husband's chances. So I control my temper by using Anger Management skills. Thank you, Dr. Freud.

President Christianson continues.

"Lupe claims that you were in on the conspiracy, Dr. Applebee, and if it's true, you've committed a serious crime."

Applebee looks like a man whose hand has been caught in a jar full of cookies. "She's nuts," he says.

"Then you were *not* part of a conspiracy to discredit Dr. Mann?"

"Of course not."

"Mrs. Bravo is making it all up?"

Applebee glances nervously at Lupe and sighs. "She must be. I don't know anything about a conspiracy."

"Why would she want to retract her statement?"

Applebee shrugs. "Maybe Mann is paying her to help him get his job back."

I am now screaming mad. I cannot believe the way this man can lie. I want to spit in his face. Would he even feel ghost-spit, I wonder, but I already know the answer. If I want him to, and I make it slimy enough ... he will.

"Did Carlos Mann pay you to help him get his job back, Mrs. Bravo?" Lupe is throwing daggers at Applebee with her eyes.

"Dr. Mancowski has never contacted me," she says. "I hate him as much as Applebee does."

"Oh, I see." Dr. Christianson smiles. "And why do you hate him, Lupe?"

"Because he is an upstart who gets all the attention ... and he pretends to be Mexican when he's really Polish."

"Oh my," Christianson says, and his look gets serious. "Is that why *you* hate him, Dr. Applebee?"

"I don't hate him. He's a fine professor."

Like the President of Arts and Letters, I am suddenly filled, not with anger but with the silliness of these two foolish people. They are lying so much about each other and themselves that I would like to giggle. But ghost-laughter can sometimes be heard. So I do not.

"Let's try another angle," Dr. Christianson says. "Lupe says that the book was manufactured in China through a process that allowed the makers to insert pages that look exactly like those in the original book. Dr. Applebee, you say that the book is authentic and that Mrs. Bravo is being paid by Dr. Mann to retract her testimony against him."

"Maybe she's just starting to feel sorry for him," Applebee says. "Anyway, the book's authentic. Mann's a fraud."

My anger is back again, replacing just a minute of giggliness. I'm ready to appear in my most horrible form and scare this Dr. Applebee so badly that he will have a heart attack and die right in front of us all. In fact, I am just about to do that when President Christianson touches a button on his phone and says, "Send him in please."

I feel suddenly better. I'm sure that the ghost of Pedro Bravo will walk through the door ready to tell everyone that Carlitos is innocent. But it is not Señor Bravo's ghost. It's a tall, handsome young man who is alive. He looks like Carlyle August and carries a laptop computer under his arm.

"This is Dr. Andrew August," President Christianson says. "He did not attend our previous session. But I understand that he has ways of checking the age and composition of the paper on which this document was written. Isn't that right, Dr. August?"

"Yes. My company is developing new computer systems and technologies, and the chemists in our lab came up with a way to date materials, to within a year or two."

"So, if the pages of the book with the section attributed to Dr. Mann were printed at a time far later than the rest of the book ..."

"Then the authenticity of the expanded volume is definitely in question."

"And, based on this bullshit you're going to let Mann back onto the faculty?" Applebee asks.

"I'd just like to hear the story one more time. If you don't mind."

"I do mind," Applebee responds defensively.

"I was being rhetorical. I don't give a damn whether you mind or not. I'm much more interested in the opinion of another expert, Dr. Steele of the Leland Physics Department."

President Christianson again touches a button on his phone and a small cheerful man, whose name must be Dr. Steele of the Physics Department, comes in through the door.

"Dr. Steele was on sabbatical when Dr. Mann's hearing took place, so he really has no knowledge of the event. Isn't that right, Dr. Steele?"

The cheerful doctor smiles. "Pretty much … only hearsay."

So, now begins a slow, careful, and very interesting presentation on Señor August's laptop, which has everyone amazed except me, because I don't understand it at all. Dr. Applebee's understanding also seems to be different from the others I think, because, as the presentation goes on, he becomes very small in his chair, slouching down deeper and deeper until he almost shrinks away to nothing.

Dr. Steele is nodding and smiling. Señor August is presenting and brilliant, and in the end President Christianson says, "I think that about wraps it up. So, what do you think, Dr. Steele?"

The scientist never stops smiling. "It seems pretty clear that Dr. August has demonstrated that the pages of the book containing Dr. Mann's essay were created much later than the rest of the book, far after the poet's death."

"So, the section that Dr. Mann is accused of plagiarizing was never part of the original book?"

"Right."

President Christianson turns to Dr. Applebee. "Let me ask you again, did you have any knowledge that there was a conspiracy to frame Dr. Mann?"

"Of course, not. This is all news to me."

"Liar!" Lupe screams. She jumps from her chair, and begins beating Dr. Applebee with her purse.

Young Dr. August steps between the two of them and takes several good blows from Lupe too, before she sees who she is hitting and stops.

Christianson rises to his feet. "I think we can let that little outburst end our meeting."

Everyone nods in agreement, even I.

"Thanks very much for your time and advice, Drs. Steele and August. You may leave now." Both men gather their things and walk quickly out the door.

"Thank you also for your testimony, Mrs. Bravo. I appreciate the fact that you've finally decided to step forward and help clear the name of Dr. Mann."

"May I go now, Señor?" she asks.

"Yes, but leave the book."

Lupe nods and hurries away.

So now it is just President Christianson, Dr. Applebee, and I. And my grinning is from ear to ear.

"So," Dr. Christianson says, "What do you suggest we do, Oliver?"

Applebee flinches at the use of his first name but then says, "You don't really believe all this bullshit, do you?"

"Every word of it."

Dr. Applebee clears his throat and glances around the room. There doesn't appear to be anything that he can pick up and throw at Dr. Christianson (as I would do if I were in his clothes). So, he simply murmurs: "Reinstate Dr. Mann, I guess."

"What was that?" Christianson asks.

Applebee clears his throat again and runs his hand through his ugly gray hair.

"I said, 'Reinstate Dr. Mann.'"

"I think that's only appropriate," Dr. Christianson says. "And what do you propose as a settlement?"

"Return him to his former salary?"

"With a sizeable raise?"

"If you say so."

"And should we pay for his pain and suffering?"

"I'm not sure that's necessary."

"It is."

"And punitive damages?"

Applebee makes a nasty face when he hears this new question.

"… If Dr. Mann requires punitive damages." President Christianson continues.

"I'd leave that up to the negotiation between the university and Dr. Mann." Applebee answers.

"Good idea."

President Christianson is twirling a pen in his hand now, chewing on the end of it, and sometimes pretending that it is a cigarette.

"So, tell me, Dr. Applebee," he asks, "*Who* do you think should be Dean of the Psychology Department here at Leland?"

"Me, of course."

"No."

Applebee jerks backward at the single word. He pauses for a long time, and I think he is going to cry. But he surprises me.

"Dr. Charlotte Burke, then?"

"I like that idea," President Christianson says as he pretends to take another puff of his pen- cigarette. "And what should we do with you?"

"Demote me?" Applebee whispers.

"Nice try."

"It's only right."

"No, it's not."

"Termination, then, with a year of severance?"

"Another inappropriate suggestion."

"Six months of severance?"

"TWO WEEKS!" President Christianson slams his hand down hard on the desk and Dr. Applebee jumps as high in the air as I do. Even ghosts can be startled.

"I promise to try and talk Dr. Mann out of pressing charges against you," Christianson says. "Maybe the settlement we offer him will be good enough to save you from going to prison. I'm not sure Dr. Mann will go for it, are you?"

Applebee is shaking from nerves and bad news. "Carlos Mann is actually a very nice guy," he answers.

"I think so ... softhearted even."

Applebee smiles as though he wants to be Christianson's buddy by insulting about my husband.

"He's even a little bit of a pussy, I think."

Christianson laughs. "You'd better hope so."

Chapter 44

Carlitos has made a shrine to my sexiness. I'm standing in the middle of it, surrounded by my best magazine ads, nude pictures of me that he took on the happiest night of my life. High heels, underwear, negligees, everything is laid out like the window of a Victoria's Secret store.

I have come back to our little apartment in Los Altos, walked right through the wall and into the place that Carlitos has managed to pay for all these months.

It is musty, I think; I open the windows; I air out the bathroom, and then I open the doors to the closets. My closet has become this sexy shrine.

Tears fill my eyes. How many women have their husbands worship them in this way.

Oh, Carlitos.

I go to the telephone and pick up the receiver. The phone still works; Carlos has kept paying the phone bills too. I call him directly, on his cell phone, in Cancun.

What greets me on the other end of the line is wild Latin music. A fiesta! "Mann here," Carlitos says in his business voice.

"Woman here," I answer. "What's going on?"

He laughs. "Señor Popcorn's engagement party."

"I'm missing it?"

"Sorry. But the wedding is still a week away. Can you make it for that?"

"Oh yes, I would like to be there," I answer. "And I have such great news for you, Carlitos."

"About the job?" he asks.

"You know?"

"Dr. Christianson called me."

I stamp my foot. I wanted to tell him.

"You worked another miracle, mi amor," he says. "They've offered me a big pay increase and one hundred thousand dollars in damages."

"You were damaged much more than that, Carlitos," I say.

"It's more than enough, though. Thank you for making it happen."

"Many of us worked on it together," I answer, "even Pedro Bravo. He is a fan of yours, you know, even though he hates your thoughts."

"My ideology?"

"He said something like that."

"You met his ghost?"

"His ghost convinced Lupe to change her testimony about you. I just helped a little. So did all the purgatories."

"Carlyle August and the others?"

"Sí, even his living brother Andrew."

"I think you're wonderful."

"And from where I am standing, you also think I'm very sexy."

"Where are you standing?"

"In the closet in our little apartment."

"Oh, shit!" I can hear that his voice is embarrassed.

"I love it, Carlitos, it's so sweet, and the next time we are in here together, right here in this closet, I will screw out all of your brains."

"Or even screw my brains out."

"That too."

"I'd like that."

Now, I hear laughter, women's laughter. My negative ghost-senses turn on, and I can guess who is at the fiesta with my husband.

"Who are you with?" I ask.

"Assad," Carlitos answers. "He and Veronica have just had a little boy."

"How nice, what are they going to name him?"

Carlitos moves the phone away from his lips and calls to his friend. "Assad! Tell Alicia what you're going to name your new baby."

Assad gets on the phone.

"Hola, Alicia," he says. "We will call our new baby Carlos."

"Dios mío, fabuloso," I giggle. "There will be a new Carlitos running around, but this one will not have a drop of Mexican blood in his little body."

"Or Polish," Assad says. "But he'll survive. Can't wait to see you, beautiful."

"I think you are beautiful too, Assad."

"Adios, Amiga."

"Adios, Assad, and give my love to Veronica." I say this though I don't really love her. And now I hear a woman's laughter though the phone again.

"Isn't that great news?" Carlitos asks as he comes back on the line. "Sí, mi amor ... only ..."

"Only what?"

"Who is there?"

"I told you. Assad."

"AND?" I try to control my growing anger.

"Oh, just Amy Joy."

I will not say the words that I am suddenly thinking. Instead I put on my most supporting voice and tell my husband that I love him, I miss him, and that I will be there as soon as I can be ... definitely for the wedding.

I do not mention Amy Joy, or the fact that I have just decided that I must go to Chinatown tonight. I have to see this Tiger person, and I must defeat her. Then Amy can move back to Chinatown where she belongs …

AND SHE CAN LEAVE MY HUSBAND ALONE.

Chapter 45

I have never walked down so many dark passageways in my life. Yes, there were all those deadly tunnels that Señora Yolanda and I walked through on our way to see La Bruja. But these dark passages under Chinatown seem even longer. My friend Mr. Foo showed them to me the last time we saved Carlitos from Tiger Joy and her army.

Mr. Foo is a very patient ghost, I think. He carries a lantern, which we do not really need to see in the darkness. We are ghosts, after all. But we have the lantern, and now, as we approach the end of a long and terrible tunnel, we hear the crack of a whip and the sound of a strong man crying out in pain.

"Tiger's enjoying herself," Foo says to me with a smile, and I start to think that maybe he sometimes comes here to watch. I ask him if this awful thing can be true.

"When Tiger is punishing bad guys," he says, "I take pleasure in watching."

This knowledge makes me uncomfortable, and now I wonder how I should ask (as Carlitos would say) the next logical question Maybe I should just ask it.

"You are hot for her, Señor?"

"I've been dead for three hundred years, Alicia," he tells me. "But I must confess that she turns me on."

Disgusting old man, I think as Mr. Foo now dims the lantern, and we enter Tiger's room-full-of-chains. I can still remember Carlitos being in here, chained to the wall as Father's bad guys prepared to murder him.

A tall, handsome, young Asian man is held captive in the center of the room. Spreading devices are attached to the ceiling and floor, and they hold his arms and legs far apart. He's naked, and I'm ashamed of myself for admiring his very sexy muscles with the sweat shining on them, his broad shoulders and arms. His chest is ripping; his abdomen looks like my grandmother's washing board.

Tiger wears no top, and her big store-bought breasts entrance the young man even though he is in pain. Mr. Foo is entranced as well. But not me, I've got my own breasts to look at if I want to, and no plastic doctors have built them up for me.

Tiger does wear a black skirt that's very, very short and tight, and her shoes are strapped up around her ankles. They lift her high off the floor; but she is able to walk comfortably in them ... far better than I ever could.

There is a leather band around Tiger's neck and, when she turns away from the young man with the sexy muscles, I can see that the band says "mistress."

"You didn't have to kill her, Albert," Tiger growls as she looks back at the guy in the chains. "I didn't mean to."

Tiger moves up to him. She has a long whip in her hand, and she drags it behind her. "Nurses are damn hard to come by, you know."

Albert closes his eyes when she is right in front of him. "Please," he begs.

He is so cute, with a rough pile of black hair on his head and those rippling muscles that are pulled so tight by his chains. Still, his look is hopeless. He knows Tiger will soon beat him even more.

Tiger curls the whip in her hand, lets it drop again, and then, with a flick of her wrist, she lets it fly. It cracks across

Albert's chest and opens a bloody slash. Then she hits him again and again … in between almost every word she says.

"It took us ten …" (Snap!)

"Long …" (Slash!)

"Fucking …

"Years …

"To get Abigail …

"Where …

"We …

"Wanted her to be!"

Blood now pours from the deep wounds all over Albert's handsome body.

Albert's head is bowed. I hope he's no longer conscious so he cannot feel the pain, but I cannot be sure.

"AND YOU KILLED HER!" Tiger screams at him. "Asshole!"

Tiger charges Albert again. She lashes out with terrible cruelty, slashes the whip across his arms and shoulders. And then she moves behind him, and beats harder and harder on his back until poor Albert must be dead.

Tiger is covered in sweat. Her large breasts glisten as they heave. She prowls around in front of him again. Albert's eyes are barely open. His face is covered with pain, but he still manages to be very handsome, I think.

Tiger drops the whip. She smiles, moves to him, touches his blood-soaked chest. He groans at this new torture.

"Ummm," she purrs, as she leans forward and tastes his blood. She cocks her head, and smiles.

"Now I think it's time to feed my pet, don't you?"

"Your pet?" Albert's voice is filled with great fear.

"Sid Vicious."

"NO!" Albert cries as his eyes now fill with panic. But it doesn't matter The door to the room opens and the big cat comes charging in. He rushes up to the young man and pounces on him at once.

Tiger Joy turns and walks back to the corner of the room. She leans against the far wall where she can watch. She smiles.

"Jesus!" I duck back into the tunnel. I cannot bear to look at this.

Foo, on the other hand, wants to see more and more. I did not know that he liked watching this kind of murder. But why else would he haunt these underground tunnels for so many hundreds of years?

The sounds are disgusting, animal, and violent. Albert screams like a bull being slaughtered, but not for long. The sounds soon are those of flesh being torn apart, of growling and slobbering and other even more sickening sounds whose names I do not know.

At last I hear Sid Vicious padding up to the doorway and leaving, I think. Now all I can hear are the moans and sighs of Tiger Joy, who sounds like she was having sex with herself while she watched the murder. But soon, even her sexy moans become silent.

My eyes have been closed tight, but now I open them.

Albert has been eaten alive. He no longer looks like a human being. He is a hunk of ravaged meat hanging from the chains. Meaty bones that have been torn from his body are scattered everywhere. Even my ghost stomach wants to throw up. But I do not. I close my eyes again and feel ghost sweat spilling over me.

I open my eyes again and look around. Mr. Foo has disappeared.

Uh oh, I say to myself.

"Mr. Foo ... where are you?"

Nothing happens. No one answers. I step invisibly back into the torture room to find him, and immediately—

I am captured.

"Ghost trap!" I hear a wicked voice cry out.

#

I have been in these traps before, caught by the same evil Joy Lum Clan that has me now.

The space inside my trap is small and frightening. I can't see anything, and I know that if I am not saved, I will be held in this trap forever.

"Shit!"

"So we have her," Tiger says, "don't we, Uncle Lum?"

"Caught like a cricket in a cage," that ancient, ghost-voice answers.

"Yay!" Tiger cheers. She kisses something. I hope it is only her ghost-uncle's cheek.

"Don't start with me, girl," Uncle Lum says.

"Sorry," Tiger answers. "But you know you've always been one of my favorites."

"Stifle," he commands, and Tiger goes silent. Then, after a minute, I hear her ask the question that I have already asked in my own mind. "So, what shall we do with Alicia?"

I call out through the walls of my trap, "You will set me free, you evil puta."

Tiger laughs cruelly. She kicks the trap and sends me flying across the room. I'm upside down when I hear her high heels march up to me, and then one of them slams down onto the trap. But this trap is very strong and it does not crack.

I hear Tiger's ankle twist. I hear her curses. Then she picks it up again, and brings it back to her Uncle.

"The bitch attacked me!"

"It looked like *you* were attacking the ghost trap … very ineffectively."

Tiger growls at him, "Anyway, what to do with Alicia."

"The obvious answer," Uncle Lum says, "is to hold her here until the good doctor comes to rescue her."

I smile. I would like that very much. But Tiger does not. "I'm fed up with both of them."

"Me too, actually" Lum says. "Besides, Amy seems to have Dr. Mann very well in hand."

Now I am angry as well as frightened. What does that mean? Amy has her hands all over Carlitos? I hate that thought.

Mr. Lum's voice now smiles. "You know, we do have a group of investors, who are willing to pay a large sum of money for Mrs. Mann ... especially now that she's packaged up so nicely."

Tiger purrs. "Ummm, easy delivery, quick payment, big paycheck. Sounds good. Who are these ... *investors?*"

"Guess," the evil voice of the old spirit asks.

Dios mio, I don't know myself. They could be the agents of Maclovio Renta, the ghost of the dead Luis, or even some nasty Austrians. Whoever these investors are, I know they will want to harm me very much.

Mr. Lum chuckles. Tiger giggles.

"Come on, Uncle," she says. "Tell me who they are. I was never good at guessing games."

"You probably wouldn't get it right anyway," Lum answers, and then he snorts like a pig.

"These days, no one even remembers *the Spanish Inquisition.*"

281

VII
Carlos

Chapter 46

"SACRILEGE," an invisible voice calls across the wind. "THE DEAD SHALL NOT MARRY THE LIVING." I look into the distance and see my beautiful wife.

She stands on a monstrous pyre built from jumbles of tree limbs, shattered furniture, crumpled dolls, worn out carts, mounds of books, rags, and papers. She's tied to an enormous stake that juts up from the very middle of it all.

The wind swirls her long hair over her face blinding her for a moment, and then the wind dies, mercifully, and I can just make out Alicia's eyes, so filled with desperation.

Her lips tremble as though she wants to scream but just doesn't know how to anymore. Her robes billow in the wind, and as they do, they jerk her back and forth.

All around Alicia, hooded inquisitors and their agents work to add more wood to the pyre.

They drive across a dark chasm on horse-drawn carts, unload their boxes, toys, furniture; smashing them on huge boulders that circle the pyre and then tossing the shards high onto the mound around Alicia's feet.

The inquisitors are going to ignite it all very soon. And then I'm sure they'll watch and cheer like obscene little boys as my wife burns out of existence at the stake.

GOD ALMIGHTY!

The sky is angry. It crackles with lightning as Padre Hidalgo and I crest the top of a rise and view that windswept plain where Alicia's death pyre is growing.

Sand dunes ripple all around it; there's no vegetation anywhere. To the right are the High Sierras of California, to the left Alicia's pyre, and between the two stretches a deep chasm that's only spanned by a narrow bridge.

"They built the pyre in the Dread Zone," the Padre says as he gestures with his staff. "She can't escape, and when the flames have consumed her, she'll never return to existence. They've sentenced her to oblivion!"

As we hike into this forgotten corner of Death Valley, the Aztec ring (the one Alicia gave me as a wedding gift) still glows on my finger. It hasn't stopped since it first called to me three days ago.

Padre Hidalgo came running that morning as though the ring had summoned him from miles away.

Things had been so damn beautiful in Cancun; I was surrounded by all that love and happiness. Suddenly the Padre is in my room, warning me that Alicia is in terrible danger.

"They have her," he says.

"Who has her? Tiger? The Joy Lum Clan?" "Someone far worse."

I shake my head wondering who or what could be worse than those barbaric flesh traffickers, and now, as I see Alicia about to be burned at the stake, I know.

The Spanish Inquisition.

We come nearer and see hooded figures that have to move quickly or the Dread Zone will take them too. Once back across the bridge, the Spaniards turn to study my wife. A few of them smile sadistically; others seem overcome by her beauty, which even their wicked treatment can't diminish. The wind stops for a moment. We can barely hear Alicia's voice. She's praying the Hail Mary in Spanish ... and between the words, she sobs.

A crow calls, and a fat greasy old monk gets down from a wagon that has just crossed into the Dread Zone. He picks his nose with filthy fingers, then reaches under the wagon and pulls out a torch that's almost as big as he is. He pulls some flint from his pocket, and—with a few quick strokes—he lights the torch. Then he lifts it above his head, bellows like some drunkard, and stumbles along with it toward the pyre.

The wind tortures Alicia's hair, swirling her robes up around her thighs. The Spaniards jab each other, point to her, and laugh like jackals. They just can't wait to see her burn to death, and I'd give anything to be able to strangle each and every one of them personally.

"Does this turn you on, you vultures?" I shout at them.

They stop, twist around, and look to me. Alicia sees me too, and, weak as she is, she lets out a cry that's suddenly full of hope.

"CARLITOS!"

I start to move toward her, but Padre Hidalgo reaches for my shoulder and stops me. "Everyone has to face up to the monsters within our their souls," he mumbles as he steps in front of me.

"In the name of all that's holy," he calls to the evil monks, "end this blasphemous cruelty. You're all dead now. Don't you ever wonder *why* your fellow inquisitors are not here with you?"

The monks outside the Dread Zone push back their hoods, wipe their filthy brows, and look up at him. Those on the wrong side scurry across the bridge so they can listen to him in safety.

"Are you foolish enough to think your brothers have gone on to some eternal reward?" Hidalgo asks. "They're all in HELL! I've seen them; I've seen their suffering. They would call to you from beyond the grave if they could. They'd say, 'Spare this beautiful young woman. Her husband is here; let her go to him!'"

The Spaniards are silent, even thoughtful. They stand frozen in place. And then we again begin to hear Alicia's sobs. Her shoulders droop, her head hangs weakly. The Dread Zone is destroying her before the flames can even claim her.

The unholy monks look at her and at each other. They mumble among themselves, and then they snicker. The tallest of them glowers up at us. It's the same monster that confronted us in the chapel at Schönbrunn on our wedding day. It's El Bernardo, the Grand Inquisitor.

"The dead shall not marry the living; it's sacrilege," he curses. "She's a witch and must be destroyed!"

The Aztec ring around my finger glows and burns painfully, and then it pulls my arm heavenward.

"FREE HER!" I shout at them.

The Spaniards turn to their leader. There's a moment of silence, confusion, even hope maybe, and then he starts to laugh. The others catch on, and they too break out in obscene laughter. The wind joins them. It roars up and swirls the sand above the dunes. It blasts into Alicia tearing her ghost flesh and plastering her hair against her face.

The fat fire-bearing monk is on the move again. He lifts the torch above his head and charges up to the pyre. He touches his flame to the ragged kindling at the edge of the pyre, and it erupts into flame.

I look up at my hand still raised above me, at my ring still burning into my finger. Right below it, my watch tells me that it's exactly three o'clock in the afternoon, the perfect time for martyrdom.

"God save her!" I pray, lowering my head. "Please, God, save my wife or she'll burn *far beyond* death."

Chapter 47

The Aztec ring on my finger begins to glow even brighter. The Spaniards see it and shield their eyes. Padre Hidalgo catches my arm, and the glow of the ring floods into his body.

"Fools, monsters!" he calls the evil monks, "why won't you listen to me? SAVE THIS YOUNG WOMAN! There's still time."

El Bernardo turns to Hidalgo and, in a voice that sounds like it's straight out of hell, he shouts, "SILENCE, HERETIC! OR WE'LL BURN YOU TOO!"

Padre Hidalgo shakes his head. "These are truly evil men," he whispers as he turns away from the monks to face the mountains.

"Are we going to stand for this?" he shouts. "They have done such evil; can we allow them do even more?"

The mountains answer. They begin to rumble. And suddenly a great fissure *rips* across the valley from the edge of the High Sierra to the chasm at the edge of the Dread Zone.

Flames are still moving quickly toward Alicia's feet and, as Padre Hidalgo prepares to continue his rant, I decide I've heard enough speechmaking.

I charge toward my wife, screaming as I come, and the monks immediately come together and form a barrier at the bridge that separates us.

From behind me I can hear Hidalgo calling to someone, something, somewhere. But I don't know who or what it is. His words are something like:

"Rise up, all of you who have suffered at the hands of these monsters! THE TIME IS NOW!"

I don't give a good god damn who or what is rising up. I continue my charge across an endless distance as I watch the flames reach for my wife and catch fire to the hem of her robe.

The inquisitors are facing away from Alicia, looking at me. But at the moment that her robe catches fire, their mouths drop open, they scream in panic, and rush for cover ... clearing the way for me to charge across the bridge.

Can *I* be that terrifying? I wonder. Don't think so, but something must be. Still, I can't take the time to look behind me. All my energy is pouring into my legs as I rush faster than I ever thought I could.

And now I'm at the pyre!

I bound through the searing heat and crumbling shards of wood. I reach Alicia, slice the ties that hold her to the stake, rip the flaming robe from her, lift her naked body into my arms, and carry her away. She's holding onto my neck as tightly as she can. Her tears flood over my face and shoulders.

As we leap from the pyre and regain our footing, I set Alicia down, pull off my shirt, and drape it over her. She looks at me gratefully for a moment, moves to kiss me, and then freezes as she too sees what Padre Hidalgo has summoned up. I turn to follow her gaze and can't believe my eyes.

From out of the fissure in the earth comes crawling, tumbling, buzzing and flying, a bloodthirsty swarm of victims of the inquisition: the rabble, the kings, the poets and scientists, Aztec and Jew, French and Italian, women young and old, men of every age, any and all who have suffered at the hands of these monsters.

The inquisitors and their agents turn to the left looking for a way to escape, but the flying, screaming ghosts offer none. They outflank the monks on that side.

El Bernardo leads a swift charge to the right, but a band of ragged, flesh-rotted women launch themselves into the air with a series of blood-churning sheiks. They soar high above the Spaniards, circling them and then diving down directly at El Bernardo and his followers. They cackle and spit in the faces of the monks driving the Grand Inquisitor and his gang back across the bridge and into the Dread Zone.

El Bernardo draws a sword and slashes wildly at the air, but it's no use against these phantoms. One especially fearsome young woman must be half ghost and half banshee. She takes El Bernardo by his throat, raises him above the pyre, and slams him headfirst into the raging flames.

Soon all the monks are forced onto the pyre. They cry desperately for mercy and forgiveness, but the victims around them offer no escape. The inquisitors and their aides soon boil and melt in the flames. They pop and sizzle until there's nothing left of them but their charred remains and those of the pyre, which itself soon crumbles into nothingness.

I've taken Alicia across the bridge and out of the Dread Zone. She's still holding tightly to me, still shuddering from the ordeal the inquisitors have put her through. Finally, she sighs.

"Take me from this, Carlitos. I have seen enough horror for more than twenty lifetimes." I kiss her on the forehead as though she were a little girl.

"You want someplace happy?" I ask.

She nods, tears still burning down her face. I wipe them away, kiss her again, and smile. "I think I can manage that."

Chapter 48

Señor Popcorn looks like *the most interesting man in the world*, the guy described in all those beer commercials of 2012. Eva Córdoba looks like she's out of a beer commercial herself, the one where a bunch of guys stumble through an ice cave and into a bar loaded with cowboys and smokin' hot women like Eva ... even though today she's wearing a virginal-white wedding dress.

The couple stands facing Padre Hidalgo on the beach at Cancun. The sunlight shows right though the ghost-of-a-priest and sparkles into the eyes of the bride. I'm close enough to smell the heavenly scent of her perfume and wonder how the popcorn man can be so composed. I'd have carried her off into the jungle long ago.

I'm the best man. Alicia's the matron of honor. All along the beach, the ghosts and the living mingle as though there's no difference between us. Austrian princes stand beside hot-blooded chicas from Señor Popcorn's mansion. Six of El Patron's most gorgeous models and handsome hombres make up the rest of the wedding party.

Lilia Garcia (Eva's best friend) is a bridesmaid. So are Sylvia Morales and Chula Contrerras. Chula's parents are still in one of Tiger Joy's ghost traps, I'm sure. Finding and rescuing them is high on my to-do list ... but not today. Today is all about love and marriage and one hell of a party.

Eva's parents watch the ceremony from further up the shoreline. Enrique smiles, happy to see his daughter married, and probably equally happy that the union will put Señor

Popcorn's drug cartel out of business. Enrique has already received a commendation from the Mexican government for helping to make it happen.

Señor Popcorn's lieutenant, Miguel, sits in a wheelchair. His wife Marie Elena is beside him, holding his hand; she's teary-eyed with the wedding and the fact that her husband has somehow managed to escape death yet again. The best doctors in Mexico have put him back together and saved his life after the bloodbath at Tizimin.

At the very edge of the ceremony stand Assad, Veronica and Amy. Veronica holds little Carlos. The kid sleeps contentedly and never makes a sound. What a guy.

"I now pronounce you husband and wife," Padre Hidalgo says. "You may kiss the bride." Señor Popcorn leans over and places a chaste kiss on the lips of Eva Córdoba de Cervantes, or—as she will be known forevermore—Señora Popcorn.

Eva pouts. Padre Hidalgo chuckles. "Come on, Fernando. You can do better than that. Kiss her like a real *Mexicano.*"

Señor Popcorn sweeps Eva into his arms, bends her back, and kisses her with all the romantic flourish of a Latin movie star. When he releases her, Eva staggers to regain her balance, takes a deep breath and then attacks her new husband with kisses that have him backtracking like one of my opponents in the prize ring.

I catch him from behind and push him forward forcing him to accept all of Eva's adoration.

The crowd cheers, some throw their hats into the air. Then DJ Jazzy-Jose drops the needle on a mariachi grove that we turn into a recessional as Alicia, I, and the rest of the wedding party dance up the beach and into the huge tent that's set up near the infinity pool.

Inside the tent we meet more friends, local dignitaries, members of the Mexican government, representatives of the US Department of Agriculture, and other American officials.

What a show.

"Now, stand over here," the photographer says as he pulls me up beside Señor de Cervantes, "now, go over there." Soon I'm feeling like a manikin in a store window, being moved here and there to be part of one display after another. I don't mind, especially since I see Alicia eyeing me with love and admiration through all of it. Still, I'm damn glad when we're finally able to take our seats at the head table.

There's a benediction, followed by toasts and other speeches. Then the food is served: *corn* in every variety imaginable. Most notably corn tortillas, which form the basis of some of the most spectacular Mexican food ever made: the fruits of the sea, carnitas and roast beef served with rice and beans, pico de gallo, sliced avocados, champagne, California wine, and a delicious golden beer that Señor Popcorn has begun brewing on his new estate.

As we continue to dine, a mariachi band strolls through the crowd taking requests and playing all the old Mexican favorites. There's a very touching moment when the group stops beside the wheelchair of Miguel and strikes up the strains of the old classic, Marie Elena.

Everyone tears up immediately as we realize how close his wife (his own Marie Elena) came to losing him, yet again.

I'm surprised when I see Marty Marinara in the crowd. He's the FBI agent who helped us finally nail Mother and Father Joy. He's now sitting at a table with Assad, Veronica, little Carlos, and Amy. He and Amy are engaged in friendly conversation, but when he sees me looking at him, he motions for me to come over. I excuse myself from the bridal table and make my way in his direction. As I do, I walk behind Alicia who's eyeing both Marty and Amy suspiciously.

"Be careful, Carlitos," she says. "That man brings danger wherever he goes ... and that Joy girl ..."

"Relax," I say. "You and I are married; Amy's not an issue. And as far as Marty's concerned, he saved you the last time you were caught in a ghost trap, remember?"

"*You* saved me Carlitos, maybe with his help. But Señorita Tiger is still prowling." Alicia has a point, I realize, as I walk over to Marty. Tiger *is* still out there, isn't she?

Marty stands, shakes my hand and immediately gestures to the rest of my friends. Assad too stands, and we shake. Veronica gets to her feet, gives me a hug and kisses me sweetly on the cheek. Baby Carlos gurgles contentedly, and Amy immediately glances back to Alicia who is staring at her accusingly.

"Hi, Dr. Mann," Amy says as she stands, reaches out, and shakes my hand very formally. "Congratulations on your wedding." She says it so loudly that even my wife can hear. I actually feel the relief emanating from Alicia as this happens. My back is to her, so I wink at Amy.

"Thanks." I whisper.

"De nada," she answers with just the hint of a smirk.

"You're Chinese, and you're talking to me in Spanish?"

"De nada," she repeats. "It's like the only Spanish I know."

As soon as we take our seats, Marty speak up.

"So, I guess you've heard the good news?"

"That we finally whipped the Inquisition?"

"That too, but how about the fire?"

Another surprise. "I didn't hear anything about a fire."

"Yeah, spontaneous combustion if you can believe it. The whole Joy Lum compound erupted in flames two days ago ...

went up like a tinderbox. All of the living quarters and offices were destroyed, killed a lot of slave traders and thugs too."

"What about Tiger?"

"As she fled, we captured her and a half dozen of her boys. We even rounded up most of the sisters."

Amy is taking all of this in and not saying a word. Veronica and Assad are trying to not pay attention, I think. They're far too caught up in their own little world.

"What was the exact hour the fire started?" I ask as a crazy idea pops into my head.

Marinara closes his eyes and tries to remember. "It was in the police report," he says,

"Friday ... three PM, definitely."

"That's the exact time that the Inquisitor set his torch to Alicia's funeral pyre."

Marinara gives me a crooked smile and shakes his head.

"Cross-dimensional rip, you think?"

"Cross-what?"

"Heard the term in that *Ghostbusters* movie. Seems to fit; you know ... a connection."

"Don't laugh. There *could* be a connection between the two events."

Marinara shrugs, "Guess so. Lucky for Amy that she was down here in Cancun and not in Chinatown."

"Oh yeah," Amy cheers, and then her happy expression falls. She suddenly looks frightened ... as though she's seen a ghost. That's because she has.

"Mrs. Mann ..." Amy says.

I turn to see Alicia making her way up to the table. My wife doesn't say anything, just smiles and absorbs the friendly greetings of Assad, Veronica, and Marty Marinara. Amy smiles too. Alicia nods to her, acknowledging her congratulations on our wedding. Amy finally seems to relax. So, I decide to speak up.

"Alicia, Marty tells me that the feds have captured Tiger Joy."

"They're holding her under heavy security at the Women's Correctional Facility in Chowchilla," Marty adds.

"They will charge her with murder, no?" Alicia asks. "And then give her the penalty of death?"

"I'm not sure they have enough evidence to convict Tiger of murder," Marty answers. "But human trafficking has some very severe penalties anyway … probably life imprisonment."

"Good," Alicia says. "As it should be."

As the conversation continues, Amy begins to sway in her seat like she's about to faint. She clutches my arm and even ignores the harsh look from Alicia when she does it.

"Chowchilla," Amy murmurs. "What about it?" Marinara asks.

Amy looks like she's going to be sick. "Something I heard in one of those meetings," she says.

"What meetings?" Marinara asks.

"I was Tiger's secretary. I had to take all the notes at the meetings. Somewhere in there I wrote down something … about Chowchilla."

She closes her eyes as if summoning up the very words that she wrote. And then she begins. "About a year ago I took down a discussion that said Tiger would be captured one day and taken to Chowchilla, but she'd strengthen her position while she was there."

Marinara glances nervously at me and then back to Amy as she continues.

"She intends to use her leadership abilities to organize the inmates, and make her prison cell the hub of a new Joy Lum Empire."

Marty sighs audibly. He might have expected something like this, but wasn't prepared to hear that it was part of a detailed plan

"Tiger will be able to lead a luxurious life behind bars. She'll have the handsomest men and women brought to her as submissives, and she'll trade them for favors on the outside. The organization for all this is already in place, I think."

Amy's eyes dart from one of us to the other: Assad, Veronica, me, Alicia, and finally she stares at Marty Marinara.

"Go on," he whispers. He's shaking is head continuously now.

"After fifteen weeks, there'll be a break-in that substitutes Tiger's double for my real sister. Tiger will be back in Chinatown where she'll gain even greater power. With access to so many potential slaves through the prison system, she'll be able to establish a new order with twice the profits and ten times the depravity."

"Jez-us!" I say. Amy turns to me, her eyes almost apologetic as she continues.

"The union with Maclovio Renta will be reestablished too. Tiger's international slave trade will spread to Mexico where beautiful Latinas will be added to her holdings. Soon the Joy Lum Empire will expand around the world and will have headquarters on every continent."

Amy stops abruptly. She closes her eyes as if searching for more information and then sighs. "That's all I can remember."

"Couldn't stand much more," I say.

"Not exact quotes from the meeting," Amy adds, "but close."

"When did you hear all this?" Marinara asks.

"A few months ago. It's part of her contingency plan, I think. But when you said that she was taken to Chowchilla, I figured that the plan was already being carried out."

"Maybe it's not a contingency," Marty says. "Maybe this is what she and that spooky uncle of hers have been going for all along."

"A Joy Lum Empire."

Alicia squeezes my hand more tightly. "This is so frightening, mi amor," she sighs.

I look at Marinara. "If it's true, then the battle hasn't even begun."

We all sit there dumbstruck. No one says a word. Then Marinara suddenly reaches into his inside coat pocket and pulls out a small package wrapped in a red silk cloth.

"Almost forgot," he says as he pushes the package across the table.

Alicia takes the package and unwraps it to reveal a small wooden box with dragons carved all over it.

Alicia's eyes widen. "A ghost trap! How did you get this, Señor?"

"Agents took it from Tiger when they captured her. I wanted to show it to you and Amy and ask what you think it is."

"The ghosts of Chula's parents," Amy says. "I remember opening it at our dinner at McArthur Park ... letting out only Chula."

Before I can start tripping on those evil memories, I raise my hand and wave to our ghost- friend Friedman. The former safecracker is sitting across the room at a table reserved for Carlyle August and the other Purgatory Ghosts. The old man nods to me, and waddles over.

"Can you open this?" I ask, as I take the trap from Alicia and hand it to him.

Friedman's skillful fingers lift the box. He raises his glasses onto his forehead so that he can look at it more closely.

"I know how to do this," he says. "Alicia, come with me to the hacienda. I'll have to borrow one of your towering high heels."

"They're not such towers," my wife says.

"Of course, not, beautiful." Friedman smirks. Then he taps the side of the box. "But they're perfect for cracking these things open."

Alicia stands, and she and Friedman make their way out of the tent. On the way she asks Chula to join them.

I follow the trio with my eyes and then turn back to Amy. The old fear is back as strong as ever.

"Christ, what a mess!" I say.

"The bitch wins again, doesn't she?" Amy asks.

"No way in hell."

"Execute her!" That's Veronica, who hasn't said a word up to this point. We didn't even know that she was listening.

"Can't do that, much as we'd like to," Marinara says. "There will have to be a trial first. She may even be let out on bail. Then the whole legal process will finally begin ... slowly. The best solution is for us to just watch her closely, tap her phone calls. Focus surveillance cameras on her when she's in prison. Let her make the first move."

I shake my head. I'm suddenly very tired of all this governmental bullshit. No matter how well we think we know what Tiger's planning, she's so damn nuts that she might do anything. In the end there's only one real answer I can think of.

"I'm gonna kill her myself," I whisper to Amy.

"Yes, Carlos," she answers with surprising enthusiasm. She grabs my arm and leans in close to me.

"I mean it." I say.

"I know," she answers. "Good."

THE END.

BONUS CHAPTERS

Alicia Bewitched

The Alicia Trilogy – Book Three

Carlos sets out to murder Tiger Joy in her prison cell. Unfortunately the gorgeous queen of human traffickers captures him and ships him off to the Yucatan where the evil witch, La Bruja, uses all her powers to try to weaken and destroy him.

Meanwhile, Alicia calls on friends both living and dead to help save her husband, and in the process she learns many terrible secrets that were born in the days of the great Mayan Empire ... secrets that could save or even destroy both Carlos and Alicia.

Read on for a preview of the further adventures of Carlos and Alicia

Chapter 1

Carlitos is missing.

I run from room to room in our little apartment wringing my hands on the apron I wear around my waist. It says, "Kiss the Cook," which is something I want Carlitos to do. But when I call my husband for kisses and supper, a supper that I have made with great love and spices ... he is not here.

He was supposed to be home by six-thirty ... or at least call me.

I thought for a moment that he *was* here, but, really, I did not hear him come in. I was chopping up fat chicken pieces and throwing them into the mole sauce. I was singing loudly as I cut the cilantro and onions and jalapeño peppers. I danced around the kitchen while I set the table using my best Mexican plates and silverware. I poured a big margarita that I made myself by squeezing limes and mixing everything else.

During all that noisy work, my husband did not appear. He did *not* return from his appointment by six-thirty as he said he would. And now it is nearly nine.

Maybe he stopped to get me a bouquet of roses for the table, I think. But would that delay him for more than two hours?

"Don't worry. Carlitos will be home soon," I say out loud as I stir the sauce for the very last time ... I hope.

It is an hour later. "Carlitos!" I call into the courtyard through the window above the kitchen sink. No one answers. So, for the next two hours I pace and stir and pace some more. I cannot eat the dinner of course. I am a ghost. Ghosts do not eat. We *wait* mostly. So that is what I do. I wait ... and it gets later and later.

#

I have never been obsessed with time the way my husband is. He has clocks in every room of the house, and not just regular clocks. These, he tells me, are *atomic* clocks that are in tune with the great world clock that is somewhere in England. Every single one of these clocks tells me the exact same thing ... that Carlitos is now almost six hours late for supper.

I hate clocks; I hate telling time. Ghosts should have no sense of it. And yet tonight I do, and all these clocks remind me again and again that my husband should have been here a very long time ago.

I walk up to my husband's desk. I look at the telephone that is sitting in the corner. Even the phone has a clock built into it. And then I wonder, "why am I so stupid? Why do I not just call him?" And so I pick up the phone and push the button that dials him directly, knowing that his special ring will tell him that I am calling.

The phone rings and rings. I do not like this. Carlitos always has his cell phone with him, always answers on the second ring when he knows that I am calling ... but not tonight. Tonight I get his answering message:

"Mann here. IF this is important ... THEN leave a message."

That is some kind of logical joke, I guess, some silly *syllogism*, a word Carlitos uses all the time that I do not understand at all. But tonight I am so mixed up I am using the word too. I do not know why. What is important is that

Carlitos is not answering, and there is nothing logical about that.

"Please call me Carlitos and tell me when you'll be home," I say to the voice mail as sweetly as my fear will allow. Then I hang up and decide to do something to fill the terrible time while I continue to wait.

I go into the kitchen and throw out the margaritas that have now grown watery from sitting in their shaved ice. And I start all over again, squeezing limes and adding the other ingredients. I tell myself that by the time I am through, my husband will walk through the front door with a big bouquet of flowers and an even bigger kiss for me.

I take my time. I wash all the margarita glasses, stir the mixture together and wish that I had some ghost-margaritas that I could drink myself. But I do not. And now it is past midnight, and my husband is STILL not home.

I go back to the phone and call again. I close my eyes and feel tears. My hands shake as I hold the phone to my ear. My lips twitch between hopeful smiles and sadness. And then, on the fifth ring, there is an answer. It is Carlitos, but his voice is tragic, and heartbreaking.

"Alicia," he sobs.

Yes. He is sobbing, and that makes me gasp.

"Carlitos, what is it?"

He sighs, struggles to say something and then, finally whispers, "God cannot forgive me."

I flinch.

"What? Of course, God can forgive you. That's his job."

There is silence. No warmth coming to me from my beloved, only great sorrowful sighs. "But I think I killed her, Alicia," he says at last. "She was so innocent, and I think … I'm almost sure I killed her."

I listen in terrified silence. This is not a man who is coming home to share kisses and margaritas. This is a man who is

303

suffering so much that he may never come home again. I have to say something, find out where he is, what is happening.

"Carlitos," I begin …

And then the phone goes dead.

I slam down the receiver, spin around, march into the kitchen and reach for something to throw against the wall. But my hands are trembling too much. I pick up the margarita glass but I cannot hold it. It seems to jump away from me and shatters on the floor spilling its contents everywhere. There is no relief in breaking glasses if you cannot throw them at something. I cross my arms, say something that is both praying and swearing, and then I go back to the phone, pick up the receiver, and push the call button again. Carlitos answers on the first ring.

"Alicia."

I hear even greater pain in his voice now, if that is possible. And then there is a screech as though some wild animal is lunging at him.

I hear the phone smash very hard and loud against the floor, and then it goes completely dead.

"Carlitos!" I call into the silence.

"Carlitos!" I scream across the empty apartment. But there is no answer, no way to reach my husband, or even to know where he is.

Chapter 2

It's now the darkest part of night, a perfect time for ghosts. But I am shaking with fear. Something terrible has happened to Carlitos. I go out into the night pacing, racking my angry brain for ideas on where to find my husband.

I am sure you understand that Carlitos really *is* my husband even though I am dead and he is not. I will not let you remind me of the words, "Till death do us part!" I do not want to hear them. The ghost of Padre Hidalgo married us again ... *after* I died ... while Carlitos was still alive.

Padre Hidalgo is the Father of Mexico. I never paid much attention in history class, but every Mexican schoolgirl knows that fact.

I wish I knew how to contact Padre Hidalgo right now and ask him about my Carlitos, but I am sure the old priest is haunting some holy places in Mexico. I cannot contact him, and so I go to the only spot I can think of where ghosts gather to talk all night and share information: The Purgatory Bookstore in downtown Los Altos, California ... where we live.

I zoom through the streets and am at the store in minutes. I pass through the locked door, up the stairway, and into the attic where I can hear ghosts talking. They turn to me when I show myself. I expect them to smile, but they look as terrified as I am. Do they know what I know?

How could they?

"Alicia, sweetheart," sighs Royce Brilliant. He's the ghost of a gay biker. He sits there with spiky hair and silky biker's shorts and shirt. Beside him is the Goth shadow of Jenny Beck, who died in a skateboarding accident. For once she does not have a blank stare in her eyes. Her look is tragic. She sits there twisting her stringy hair, saying the word "hopeless!" over and over.

Carlyle August is the leader of the group. He stands and comes up to me. He looks like the ghost of Cary Grant, the star whose old movies I loved watching on television when I was a little girl. Of course, now that I am all grown up, I am only in love with Carlitos.

But Carlyle really loves me, I think. So I try to be nice to him. Who knows when I may have to take advantage of that love? Maybe right now, because my ghost-body suddenly flames with anger.

There, right in the middle of this meeting of ghosts, sits a living person, and worst of all, she is my enemy, my rival.

"What is *she* doing here?" I ask Carlyle turning my most hateful eyes on him.

"Please darling, don't upset yourself," he says. "She's just begun to tell us something very important."

"I don't want to hear it."

"You need to."

"If it is from her lips ... then NO!"

"It's about Carlos," my rival says, and even my angry stare cannot make her go away. "He's in terrible trouble."

My anger abandons me. "I know," I whisper sadly as I slump into a chair amid the other ghosts and this living person.

She is Amy Joy, a sad victim of human trafficking, which is a Chinatown business run by her sister, the terrible, evil, wicked, and nasty Tiger Joy. Even though Tiger is younger than I am, she is the boss of a great worldwide empire of buyers and sellers of young women who are trained to be wives and slaves to men.

"Where is my Carlitos?" I ask.

"I don't know," Amy answers. "But I know that he vowed to kill Tiger, and he went after her last night."

I stare at her. Carlitos did not mention killing anyone when he left this morning. He just said that he had important business.

"I don't believe you, Miss," I say.

"Perhaps then, you'll believe *me*," a disembodied voice suddenly interrupts.

We all look around knowing that this is a technique often used by ghosts who want to catch everyone's attention. And so it is. A wispy, old Chinese gentleman suddenly flickers up at the table.

"Mr. Foo," I say giving my best smile to the man who has helped me save Carlitos over and over again.

"Alicia, my dear. I am so sorry," he says. He shakes his head and takes a seat among us.

"Tell me, please," I beg him. "What happened to Carlitos?"

"I was there," he answers. "I saw it all."

Again he shakes his head and closes his eyes as through it is difficult to talk about the things he witnessed.

"Spill it, man," Carlyle says as he steps forward and puts an anxious hand on my shoulders. "Can't you see that the lady's suffering?"

"Yes, of course," Mr. Foo answers. "But it is all so tragic and terrifying." He pauses again, nervously.

"TELL IT!"

I did not know that Carlyle's ghost was capable of rage. But I see it burning in his eyes. Mr. Foo see is as well. So he lowers his head, thinks for a moment and then begins his story.

About the Authors

Nick Iuppa *began his career as an apprentice writer with famed Bugs Bunny/Road Runner animator Chuck Jones and children's author Dr. Seuss. He later became a staff writer for the* Wonderful World of Disney. *As VP Creative Director for Paramount Pictures, Nick did experimental work in interactive television and story-based simulations. He is the author of seven novels,* Management by Guilt *(Fawcett Books 1984—a Fortune Book Club selection) and eight technical books on interactive media. He lives in Northern California with his wife, Ginny. For more about Nick, visit www.nickiuppa.com.*

John Pesqueira's *studies at the University of Arizona, Columbia, and Stanford prepared him for an impressive career in media design and development. His passion for the visual arts and popular culture continue to inform his creative efforts and still inspire his writing and photography. John grew up in the Sonoran desert and his love of the history, legends, and people of the American Southwest and Mexico remain a major focus of his work. John lives with his wife in Northern California.*

Contact Us

We love hearing from our readers and learning what they like or don't like about our stories. We'd be very grateful if you would send us a quick e-mail and tell us what you think of *Alicia's Sin*. We promise we'll answer personally and directly.

Please contact us at the link below to tell us what you think and let us thank you for reading our books.

Contact Nick & John at
dosmilagrospress@Gmail.com